TO JANE

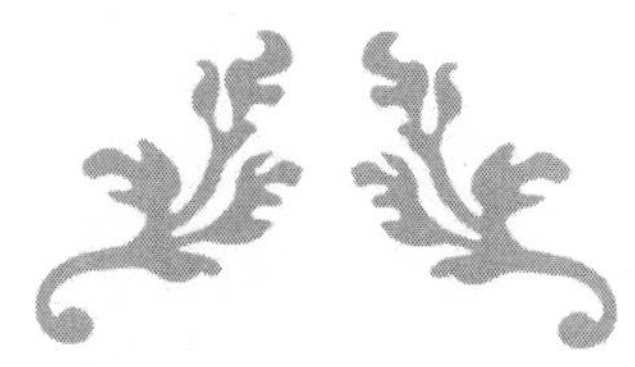

SECRETS

Shifting Sands

By Emma Palova

Emma Palova

Published by Edition Emma Publishing
A division of Emma Blogs, LLC
Lowell, MI 49331

Cover design "The Face of Gossip" used with permission from The Belding Museum at Belrockton.

This is a work of fiction. Names, characters, businesses, places, events, and incidents are either the product of the author's imagination or used in a fictitious manner. Any resemblance to actual persons, living or dead, or actual events is purely coincidental.

Join Emma's email list for special offers.

www.emmapalova.com

I also would like to thank everyone in advance for writing reviews.

For posting a review go to Amazon Author Central customer reviews:

https://authorcentral.amazon.com/gp/community

Goodreads

https://www.goodreads.com/review/guidelines

Also by Emma Palova

Screenplay

Riddleyville Clowns, registered with The Writers Guild of America, West, Inc.
7000 West Third Street
Los Angeles, CA 90048-4329

Dedication

This second book in the Shifting Sands Short Stories series belongs to my fans, friends and family around the globe. I thank everyone for supporting me on my publishing journey from a newspaper reporter to an author. The series can also serve as encouragement to aspiring writers, and a tribute to unglorified heroes.

When I am this deep into my characters, I suffer with them, until their suffering is transformed, and they emerge anew – Emma Palova.

Review
"Shifting Sands: Secrets"

In reading these short stories within the "Shifting Sa nds: Secrets" book 2 collection, I found I enjoyed the fact that locations in many of the stories reminded m e of my hometown. Some town names were very fami liar to me, giving the stories a more personal feel.

Many of the characters within the stories were despe rate for a fulfilled life; one that seemed to elude them . In trying to fill a void, there were at times some cho ices made which created the secrets that were kept. S ome secrets were assumed by acquaintances, friends or co-workers, while other secrets were kept under w raps for many years.

In Silk Nora, the "Silk City Girls," spent their days w

*eaving silk from stockings. It was a pleasant read as
a friendship developed between Nora and Doris, the
matron of the dormitory in which Nora lived. Set in t
he 1920s, the factory work was a good way for a sin
gle woman to make a living. Once she met Harry and
fell in love, her life seemed complete, until Harry lea
ves to be a war correspondent in London and her bes
t friend becomes seriously ill.*

*This collection has such a variety of stories and char
acters that there will be ample opportunity for reade
rs to enjoy many of the tales written. Even though thi
s type of writing is not my strongest area of interest, t
here are such heartwarming sections and intriguing
people depicted that I was glad I read it. I think you
will be also.*

Carol Briggs, PERSON OF THE YEAR 2019
May 19

Table of Contents

Contents

Acknowledgments

I would like to thank the following people and organizations who have helped me move along the Shifting Sands Short Stories series with the sequel "Secrets:" Editor Carol Briggs, the Belding Museum at Belrockton for inspiration and for the cover and Scottville author Joan H. Young for technical advice. A big thank you to LowellArts for hosting my book signings at the gallery on Main Street in Lowell. Special thanks to the hometown newspaper, The Lowell Ledger for featuring my work and press releases.

Introduction

I wrote the core of Shifting Sands: Secrets during the National Novel Writing Month in November of 2018. It is the second book in the short stories' series. The first few stories are an overflow from the first book published in 2017.

The last stories I wrote in the spring of 2019 during the Camp NaNo project. This laid the foundation for a third book in the series.

Thematically the subjects of the stories cover the epic human struggle for happiness. Some stories like the Chief and Secrets in Ink are based on my journalistic experience from covering small towns.
Typishly Magazine wrote:
"The story Chief has a nice premise: The town had two memories; one forgiving and one unforgiven.
The ambitious characters of chief Will in the Chief and Father Samuel in White Nights rock the scene in their vivid portrayal of the doomed.
The main historical fiction story Silk Nora digs deep into the turn-of-the- century Belding and beyond into the roaring 1920s with the inventions and advancements such the Ford Model T automobile and the telephone.
In the action-packed 40 Hunks, driver Jose transports Mexican men across the border to work in the Michigan orchards under a shady governmental agreement. Underlying are themes of sexuality and loneliness.
Aging and time create the main premise in Waiting for Snow and in Six Palms by the Tiki. In Six Palms by the Tiki, a doctor renders a scary diagnosis. I explored the theme of mature love.
Other stories like When Layla met Corey and Oceans Away touch on longing for love in spite of distance.
Devil's Elixir questions a doctor's expertise and misuse of opioids.
Catholicism and sins shape the following stories: White Nights, Being Faustina and Six Palms by the Tiki.

Also, the category of addiction to drugs plagues the characters in Cupcake Wine and Raspberry Rage.
The Booksafe Code digs into the history of an old village.
The main insights include the transformation of characters such as in Waiting for Snow and in The Writer, the Nun and the Gardener not always to the positive outcome. Some end tragically due to the characters' inability to cope.
People often ask me what inspires me, and how do I come up with the ideas for the stories? The answer varies from day to day, even from morning to night.
Most of the characters are simple men and women, who do not always find a way out of different situations and challenges; their perception shifts like the grains of sand in an hour glass. Some get stranded in the narrow part, others pass through.
But good also prevails over evil as in Waiting for Snow, as the two friends explore different dimensions of time.
About the cover and the main story Silk Nora. The genre is historical fiction.
I have visited the Belding Museum at Belrockton on countless times. It was built as a dormitory for silk city girls in 1906 when Belding was known as the silk capital of the world built up by the Belding brothers. While visiting the museum in the fall of 2017 with a friend, we found the photo "Face of Gossip" in the bathroom. Not only did it inspire the cover of the book, but also the name of the book "Secrets." I firmly believe that gossip lies at the bottom of any secret. It is also one of the major sins, along with lies.

I picked the character from the oval picture on the wall in one of the dormitory rooms, and changed her name on the marriage certificate to Nora.
Then, I went back to the historical piece to consider its possibilities by adding another a friend, Mathilda to Nora. From then on, I was able to spin the story, just like the "Silk City Girls" spun silk threads at the Richardson Mills. The only remaining former silk mill building standing to this day.
I became fascinated by the process of creating under pressure; in other words when you have no other choice that to pound out 1,880 words a day.
Most aspiring writers never complete their writing projects because of the lack of accountability or the pressure of daily writing. I can second this from my experience from writing for daily newspapers. Once, you have no other choice than to write, you write. It's like punching a clock at the factory or a store. I know what that's like, but it works.
To quote Jodi Picoult:
"You might not write well every day, but you can always edit a bad page. You can't edit a blank page."
Silk Nora ended to be 12,000 words long, which is considered a long short story.
Today, I am glad I kept a diary of everyday writing, not just the word count.
Sometimes, I woke up in the morning and I had no idea what I would write about.
I wrote Silk Nora for seven days with a final note:
"Goodbye to characters: Nora, Mathilda, Harry, John and Doris. See you in print."

Chief

It was the biggest night of the year under the moon of falling leaves. The town of Riddleyville has been getting ready for the annual Ladies' Night Out since last year.

Everyone has forgotten the fiasco when the city manager dressed up in an ugly sweater with black cats and pumpkins and black pants that had a hole in them. He came running out of the city hall to greet the mayor, and the pants fell off of him.

However, being a man of no shame, Ricky just pulled them up and shook the mayor's hand smiling.

"You're dressed up Ricky, what's going on?" asked the mayor.

"It's girls' night out, and it's almost Halloween," Ricky put on his regular grimace of an enslaved man. "I wanted to dress for the occasion."

Ricky was stubby with black hair and an occasional mustache that he from time to time either shaved off or grew it into a goatee.

"You're not a girl or a lady Ricky," said the mayor walking into the well-lit building. "We need to talk about a few things."

No one has ever found out what the two had talked about in the big corner office that night.

The town had two memories; one forgiving and the other unforgiven.

Ricky for the most part fell under the first category.

He did remember not to dress up this time, since it was a chick flick night. Ricky watched from his window the action on Main Street. He had a lot of paperwork to finish, and the mayor too usually came in to chat.

Women of all ages were running in the street enjoying the warmth of late autumn. Some were dressed up in their prom dresses from a long time ago; yellow, red, purple and blue. Ricky wondered how the heck they fit back in them. He himself couldn't fit into anything remotely resembling his high school years. His pants were small, and his belly was overflowing like the proverbial muffin.

Ricky fought it for years, then he gave in.

This was his dream job that he had longed for years. He was in charge without a lot of responsibilities. Everything he could, he delegated. And he delegated well.

Ricky bought himself a leather chair so he could sit in the corner and relax. He liked cushy things, and cushy people like himself. He was good at hiding. He learned that in politics as an intern for the state rep.

Ricky was proud of his nickname the "Spin Master." He could put a spin on anything.

“There are two sides to the story,” was his standard answer. “Which side do you want to hear?”

Ricky was as slick with journalists as he was with the city council, and the good willed residents of Riddleyville.

In a small town like Riddleyville, everybody knew everyone else’s business. The residents didn’t lock their cars and parked overnight in the municipal parking lots. The local police force tolerated some violations that were of no particular importance.

But not only did the town folk know each other’s business, they also did not lock their houses. They left messages taped to the front doors of homes and businesses. This post-modern communication style worked better than the Internet or the smart phones.

It was quite intricate in its simplicity. You had to know certain things, like that particular person's interests and friends.

Everyone knew about Ricky's love for hunting.

It was a boring Monday morning when the mayor decided to have a major talk with Ricky. He sank into the corner leather chair, while Ricky was perched behind his big desk.

“You should close the door,” said the mayor all of a sudden decisively.

Ricky was alerted and stopped his comic act as he closed the door. He pulled up his pants and started chewing on the nearest pencil.

The mayor in his late 60s lacked any personality. Sometimes he wondered why he even ran for the office. He had no agenda, nor did he own a business in town. He certainly didn't need the headache from late night meetings packed with angry people.

And now this mess just before the holidays. In earlier years, he would light up a cigarette to fight off the anxiety. He couldn't even do that anymore. Nervously, he tapped his fingers against his thigh. He noticed he needed new pants.

Ricky in the meantime was staring blankly into the Monday rain on Main Street. His strategy was as always to wait until the other side spills out all the information putting him at the advantage. But this time it was taking longer than usual. Ricky was afraid of eating the whole pencil. Plus, he had a long day ahead of him with a meeting in the evening.

"I got a letter," said the mayor pulling out a folded sheet of paper.

Ricky looked directly at the mayor fidgeting.

"Did you want to read it to me, Carl?" asked Ricky, "or you just want to tell me?"

The mayor too knew how slick Ricky was from previous dealings with him. He decided to be careful this time.

"It's about the chief," he said softly.

Of course, Ricky should have known right from the get go that it was about the police chief. The other day when he was getting a haircut at Salon 111, he overheard a conversation from the neighboring stylist's chair.

That was another bad habit in his portfolio: eavesdropping coupled with gossip, according to the town talk.

"The chief was trying to change something in a file and he got caught," said the cute redhead hairstylist leaning over the head of the lady in the chair fluffing her blonde hair.

"What was he trying to change?" the blonde raised her eyebrows looking at herself and at the redhead in the mirror.

Both of them started into the mirror, as if the answer was inside that piece of glass.

Ricky rubbed his forehead, as he tried to chase away that scene from the salon from his mind. He knew it was going to be a long day and a long week in Riddleyville when the salons and the bars start buzzing with tidbits from the city hall.

"What about him?" Ricky looked up at the mayor. "He called in sick or what? I know it's Monday and he worked the Ladies' Night Out and the weekend. I don't have a problem with him calling in."

As always Ricky was trying to steer the conversation in his preferred direction.

"Somebody else can fill in for him tonight at the meeting," he said. "I'll take care of it."

The mayor looked up puzzled at the manager, and back at the letter. His hands were shaking.

"It's something about him behaving inappropriately while on a call," said the mayor.

Reluctant to admit it, Ricky had heard the one too about the chief at the local redneck Café on the dam by the mills.

"He's a groper," said one of the workers in blue gulping down his coffee.

"Really?" the other man in blue refused to believe it. Orval, the owner of the Café just brought out two big lunch plates for the guys.
"Yup, he grabs women before he arrests them," said Orval jovially. "Enjoy your food guys. I gotta run back and call the plumber, because the toilet is not flushing."
That seriously spoiled Ricky's breakfast. A piece of omelet just got stuck in his mouth. He looked over the dam, its silver surface, and he knew there would be trouble.
That was a few weeks ago when everything seemed so harmonious and in place like a perfect puzzle. Ricky held several pieces of that puzzle. First, he was the one in charge, he controlled the city council. He always steered them in his direction, no matter what it was.
"Ah, you want a new piece of equipment, I gotta check the budget," he said lifting his head from a stack of papers, "There is no money in the budget."
"You want money to fix the potholes?" nodding his head. "There is no money in the budget. What do you want me to do?"
And he heard it all before that the city of Riddleyville pays the second highest taxes in the county and how come there is no money in the budget?
Not all things in this world have explanations.
The chief was the second highest paid official in the city, right after Ricky. And the police department took up the biggest chunk of the budget for obvious safety reasons. You have to feel safe every night, not

just on Halloween night or Girls' Night Out when the police head out after drunken girls.

The first thing Ricky did when he was hired in was to increase his salary. He made sure in a contract that he would be compensated well.

He had to look after himself first. And then looking after the public safety meant compensating the chief well. So, he gave Will, the chief, a fat salary too.

"Don't come to work today, Will," Ricky said on the phone.

"What do you mean? There is a meeting tonight," Will was defensive on the other line. He couldn't quite understand what the manager was up to this time.

"Look, you worked the girls' night out and the weekend," said Ricky. "You don't need to come in."

Will already lost all his hair while on the force. He felt the sweat on his scalp, and then dripping down his neck and back.

"You know I have to be at the meeting," Will said.

"And you know that I will excuse you," said Ricky resolutely.

The council room was full of angry people. The word had gotten around town. As Ricky walked into the room, he smoothed the lapel of his expensive jacket. His wife got it for him when he interviewed for the manager position. It cost $1,000 at the downtown store. Ricky had to have it adjusted because of his small figure.

He was thinking about the upcoming hunting season. As long as he could remember, he always hunted with his stepfather Jack. Ricky was adopted; his own dad was a drunk. The rural school district always had a day off on the opening day of the hunting season in mid-November. Men headed out into the woods, while the hunters' wives congregated in social clubs like the "Dead Salmon Society."

Ricky forced himself back into the present.

"Before I take any questions, I have an announcement to make," he said turning to the upset residents. He looked straight up and picked the redhead hairstylist from Salon 111 out of the crowd to stare into her eyes

"The police chief resigned this morning to pursue other opportunities," he said. "His personal file is protected under the law. I will not discuss it any further."

"But I will," a local businessman stood up.

"He took advantage of my daughter when on a call behaving inappropriately, the chief made propositions to her."

The whole town knew that the chief together with the sergeant extorted drunken women behind the wheel during local events. Ricky or the chief usually increased the budget to pay the force for overtime.

Typically, the exchange took place in the police cars. The willing ladies never got charged with a DUI in exchange for sex.

"Well, he is gone now, so don't worry about it," snapped back Ricky at the business person.

"You covered up for him, you should resign too," the redhead from the salon stood up and faced Ricky.

"I swear I knew nothing about the chief's dealings," Ricky was red and sweating.

"Mayor, he should resign, he knew all along," said the businessman. "The whole town knows it."
Now, it was the mayor's turn to be scared; after all he could be recalled by a petition.
"No, he stays, the chief goes," said the mayor resolutely. "We can't lose two good men. It could be hearsay. This town is full of gossip."
"You should vote on this," challenged the businessman.
"It's administrative personal action, we do not have to have a public vote," said Ricky using his political savvy.
The police chief was put on administrative leave before any further action.
Back at the office the mayor was holding a letter from the sex victim demanding the chief's resignation threatening to blow the whistle to the public if the chief doesn't get fired.
"You know, he has to go, Ricky," said the mayor running his hand through his hair. "It's either him or you, or both. You were covering up for him."
Ricky leaned into the chair and breathed heavily, as he read the letter.
"We'll make it look as a resignation," said Ricky. "I expect it immediately."
The week of the election, Will showed up at the city hall. Instead of a uniform or a suit, he was wearing sweatpants, a jean jacket and a black beanie hat.
"I came to say goodbye, Ricky," he said to the manager who walked out of his corner office to talk to Will in the lobby.

"You knew about this all along and never said anything," Will said. "I thought we were in this together. You broke the rules of silence."
"Will, you're not welcome here anymore," he said. "You have resigned to pursue business opportunities. Good luck to you."
The stubby manager turned around and walked down the long hallway without looking back at the former chief.
The local paper "Riddleyville News" put out a headline in big bold letters "Police Chief resigns to pursue business opportunities."
Only the good folks of Riddleyville knew what had really happened.

Being Faustina

Faustina entered the church cautiously. She always did. But, today more than ever, she watched around her for souls who haven't passed to the other side. In layman's terms those were ghosts.
She made sure to sit in the second pew on the left side of the nave facing the shrine made of photographs of the dead. As she knelt, Faustina realized she forgot to sign the Book of the Dead placed by the entrance. It was a big leather-bound book with hundreds of signatures.
The Book of the Dead was annually on display during the month of November; wide open for more signatures. It was chilly in the church, and Faustina

shivered. She did not know if it was from the cold or from her eternal sorrow.

On this day only, she still wore black: a black dress with a black slip under and black undies and a bra, black pantyhose, black shoes, black shawl, black coat and a black hat. Faustina purchased the complete black attire 14 years ago when she found out Gabe was going to die.

By then, she was ready. Together they went through the roller coaster of high hopes of healing and lows of despair. The highs became just as exasperating as the lows. In the final days of Gabe's, her beloved husband's life, the doctor team gave him one month to live a life free of pain numbed by morphine and oxycontin opioids.

When Gabe finally ceased to be in pain, he was so high that at times he didn't recognize Faustina, the love of his life. They were high school sweethearts who met at a Valentine's dance.

Faustina would always remember those days of young love. Even now, sitting in front of Gabe's big photograph framed in black, she felt Gabe's soft kiss in her hair moving slowly to her cheek and lips. Faustina had to touch that spot on her head, where he kissed her so many years ago. It was kind of warm unlike the rest of her half-frozen body.

The priest entered with the altar boys and girls followed by the kids from the school. Faustina always followed the kids closely, because they never had any children with Gabe. It's not that they didn't want them, they just didn't come before Gabe got seriously sick. She remembered the endless conversations about whose fault was it that they couldn't have kids. She listened to the shuffle of the shoes as the kids filed into the pews with their teachers. Every year on this day, Faustina tried to convince herself that it wasn't her fault; after all they both underwent treatment for infertility.

The endless trips to various clinics and hundreds of dollars spent on drugs resulted in nothing. After years, they both gave up and lived a full life. When Gabe was diagnosed with cancer, Faustina blamed the infertility doctors.

The answer was always the same: "There is a slight probability that the drugs and the treatment may have triggered some of the mutations."

Faustina snapped back into reality to watch the handsome priest by the altar. She never married again. Now, close to 50, Faustina was her own woman with a shining career as the executive director of the city gallery. Under her leadership, the gallery exploded with exhibits from far and near. People and artists flocked to the gallery in search of the same thing Faustina was after: serenity.

Faustina found peace among the works of artists from oil paintings of pastoral scenes to environmentally conscious pieces depicting urban rooftops of high rises.

But she also found peace in this little church far out in the country, where no one would recognize her. Once on their Sunday trip, Gabe and Faustina discovered this small Irish church in an Irish community in the middle of nowhere. From then on, they attended the Sunday mass here amidst the cornfields and farmers far from the bustling crowds in the city. It was their sacred spot.

When Gabe was in different hospitals, Faustina drove to the church to pray for his healing. She found reprieve from daily burdens right here. In the summer time, the breeze created waves in the fields while in winter, the frost covered the remaining stalks of corn and grasses.

"Where are the souls that didn't make it to heaven?" asked the priest. "Are they in purgatory? I don't want to say the alternative in here."

Faustina sometimes wandered if Gabe made it to heaven or hell? He was no angel by any means. Gabe loved cards, hazard, gamble, and everything that goes with it:

booze and loose women.

At first, they played together, but as the game started consuming him, eating him up, Faustina stopped going to the casinos. She was tired after the long sleepless nights in the loud halls filled with smoke and empty souls.

If the priest was looking for a place for souls, who haven't made it to heaven, a casino would be one of them. As she watched Gabe lose his soul to the game, Faustina understood why the children never came. They would have never seen him around.

She closed her eyes, as the children's choir sang "I Know that my Redeemer Lives."

"He lives my hungry soul to feed. He lives, my kind, wise, heavenly friend."

That first year when she put up the photograph of Gabe in the shrine by the altar, Faustina couldn't see for tears. She still cried as she looked at his face with inquisitive eyes, dark hair and a dark mustache. Gabe looked nothing like the gambler he became.

He would come home in the morning all disheveled as she was readying for work at the gallery.

"Come, let's make love," Gabe breathed into her face. Gabe smelled of alcohol, cigarettes and scents of other women.

"Leave me alone," Faustina yelled as she pushed him away. "I have to go to work."

"You call that work with those crazy artists and playwrights?" he grabbed her by the shoulders and tried to push her on the bed. "I want you now."

Sometimes he succeeded as Faustina gave into lust with Gabe.

Faustina realized that all Saturdays and Sundays were the same; drunken Gabe trying to make love to her, while Faustina was either pushing him away or giving in.

But there were times when she could convince Gabe to go with her to see a play by one of the local playwright's premier at the old theatre. At times of normal love, Gabe touched and kissed her even in front of her gallery colleagues and friends from the theatre.

"Hey, Faustina, I thought you were having trouble with that guy," a colleague joked. "This doesn't look like trouble, you love birds."

Looks were just as deceiving as official declarations of everlasting love.

“I will love you forever,” Gabe used to say out loud at the theatre plays to embarrass Faustina.

“Do you have to show off here, Gabe?” Faustina asked.

“Of course, we’re in a theatre after all, right?” he touched her breasts and kissed her neck.

In the church, Faustina felt cold sweat going down her spine as she listened to the somber hymns and looked up at the yellowing photograph. She thought to herself, the paper must have been really cheap that it’s already yellow.

The kids were dressed in school black and white uniforms. They were off a note a bit. The pianist wasn’t all that great either.

“Stop criticizing me and others,” Gabe used to yell at her.

“I am not criticizing, I am just stating the obvious that your shirt is dirty and you have wine spots on it,” she argued with Gabe.

Faustina needed to fix her nylons that were constantly curling down her hips and thighs. She decided to wait for the prayer petitions as everyone stood up. For the first time this year, Faustina submitted a petition for Gabe.

But the priest almost forgot the petitions. Luckily enough the servants reminded him.

Standing up, Faustina pulled her nylons up. She already spotted a hole in them and a run.

“We pray for Gabe’s soul to go to heaven soon,” the priest finally said.

Faustina looked up and responded:

“Lord, hear our prayer.”

"Can the soul of a gambler and a salesman go to heaven?" Faustina asked herself.

She recalled that late afternoon, when Gabe came home sober and pale. He walked directly up to her in the kitchen. Faustina hasn't changed yet into her sweatpants. She was wearing a yellow dress with floral print and high heels. They just finished putting up a new exhibit at the gallery "The World I See from Within." It was a mixed exhibit of photography and paintings. The expectations were high and the jurors were tough.
"Are you coming with me to the opening reception at the gallery?" she asked taking of her shoe carefully balancing on one leg.
A deaf silence surrounded her. She could only hear the fridge humming. Still all engaged with her shoes, Faustina didn't look up.
"I am sick," Gabe uttered. "Very sick."
"You're drunk? It's too early." Faustina straightened up to look at him. "Go and wash yourself in cold water. We're going to the opening reception."
Gabe's face turned white.
"What's wrong?" she panicked.
The panic of that late afternoon remained in her for years. Even now, Faustina felt like something was trying to crawl out of her skin. She stood up and waited her turn to receive the bread and wine from the priest. Carefully, she tipped the chalice and wetted her lips in wine.

On her way from the communion past the shrine, she took another long look at Gabe's yellowing photograph. He wasn't smiling because he rarely smiled.

"I am very sick, Faustina," kept ringing in her ears.

"How sick?" she heard herself whisper.

Months into the sickness, Gabe grew weaker and weaker. Faustina stopped counting days. Instead, she started counting minutes. She still took him to the casino, and he enjoyed the game in the cigarette smoke puffs.

"I love you and I love cards," he said. "My disease is not going to change my love for you."

Later, he couldn't go outside the house as much. So, they played cards together and Faustina even invited friends from the gallery, that Gabe hated. One of his last wishes was to drive out into the country to the church that they both loved. Gabe didn't want to pray, he just wanted to be there amidst the cornfields.

When they arrived, there was an all-day adoration inside. Hand in hand, they walked inside and sat side by side.

"I am sorry if I did you wrong," he whispered.

"You didn't, Gabe." Faustina said. "You were yourself all this time."

It was their last trip to the country. While others were getting better, Gabe was getting worse, until he was gone.

Faustina waited for the priest to leave first. Then she put the same flowers that they had for their wedding and for Gabe's funeral by the photograph.

Fragile "forget-me-nots" twinkled into the darkness as the lights went out.

Secrets in Ink

In the year of James Cameron's "Titanic", the newspapers were still buying ink by the barrel, printing the rags off the hot presses, and the coffee was brewing by the gallons in the oversized coffee pots in newspaper backrooms.

Publishers, mostly men, hid their flasks in the right bottom drawer of their desks, and unlike the staff wouldn't disclose the name of their favorite watering hole. Depending on the size of the newspaper operation, some had cubicles instead of offices, others had open layouts. Some hometown newspapers had branch offices strategically located around counties, not to get scooped by the bigger papers.

In the "dog eats dog" business, to be scooped by the competition the bottom line was fewer advertising dollars.

On the cusp of the Internet, most newspapers had credibility, that would be lost later in the binary digit maze and social media of the new millennium. Whether large operations or hometown newspapers, they all had one thing in common; they could be bribed by the advertisers.

Behind every 50-point bold headline was a tragedy: small or big, but always newsworthy in line with the slogan:

"All the news that's fit to print."

In the decadence of the late 1990s, scandals abounded: nationwide and hometown.

Each story had to pass the test: Will it upset the advertisers?

The other motto, followed by 100 percent of the newspaper industry and later picked up by the multimedia news streaming business, was:

"If it bleeds it leads."

The infinite media mistakes have always materialized for the public to see and to scrutinize, long before the Internet trolls started to dig in on Twitter and Facebook.

"I read the newspaper word for word," was a common response.

Then the spin that all the media put on the stories to keep the hungry advertisers and the public happy kept growing and growing. The label "fake news" originates in the spin, the media put on the news to create sensation and to increase ratings.

"The story has changed," was the usual justification.

The story could change all the way from a local theater being sold to a group to the fact that the theater was never for sale in the first place. But a representative lied in front of the city council.

But not all secrets can be hidden behind the bold screaming ink. However, some of them hide forever.

"You're guilty by omission," attorney and correspondent Bill used to say about the paper spinning the stories, while smirking under his lawyer's nose.

And there were other correspondents including John Q, Public.

Everyone in the business of the written word knew that the real news and stories lie in what is not told. It cannot be found by reading in between the lines either. In between the lines are wide-open white spaces.

That white space turned gray when it touched a politician's agenda or the taxpayers' money. The two became a powerful fusion: an obstacle in the transparency of newspapers and government.

Treading the muddy waters of politics were always the editors caught in between the advertising dollars and their wannabe passion for truth and justice.

"We can't run that story," yelled editor PJ. "We don't have enough corroboration of the facts. It's just hearsay."

There was no such thing as hearsay in newspapers. Once, the story hit the newspaper offices, it was beyond the gossip on the streets. By that time, the gossip had been magnified and blown up into proportions larger than an elephant. And the newspaper in the neighboring town, blasted the story with a bold screaming headline.

Lately, there has been some closely non-identified scuttlebutt around town.

"Let's put an end to this," said PJ. "Go and find out. I don't care how. Just go."

In most hometown newspapers, as well as in small dailies, the publishers took on the role of editors as well. In the worst-case scenario, they acted as reporters in the forbidden one-man show. Wearing the two hats in front of the scrutinizing public was a lot like fishing for a big fish in a small pond.

"Don't make me look bad," PJ yelled at the rookie reporter, whose name he couldn't remember. "Get the story and come back as soon as you can. I want to know by the end of this day what's going on out there."

PJ pulled out a big bag of chips and munched on them until he reached the bottom of the bag. He had another one ready for tomorrow. If he ran out, he would send out the newspaper handyman for more.

PJ was known around town for never following through on anything, let alone on a story. He was easily swayed on the other side of his true journalistic hunch. That's why he let the underpaid rookies do the hard-investigative reporting job.

He smashed the phone for the tenth time on any particular day.

"There they go again asking me why the story wasn't in the paper," PJ was flushed red with anger. "Because nobody wants to talk about it, that's why."

Yeah, no kidding. Prior to the millennium and the "Me too" era, the matter of sexuality or homosexuality was a taboo. Nobody talked about it, let alone put it in print. There was no ink left for that. PJ wasn't ready to put out his skin for the inuendo around town about two homos getting into trouble over taxes.

"What did the street have to say?" he yelled at the helpless reporter. "I don't even know your name yet."

"It's Luke. Let me introduce myself," the rookie said. "I am Luke Pinkas."

"Nice to meet you, Luke," said PJ without really caring.

"You hired me, remember?" the rookie challenged PJ.

Yeah, he might have hired this rookie along with the other long-forgotten rookies. Most of them didn't last anyway during the good times. The job paid less than cashiering at the local grocery store.

Luke sat across from PJ with his reporter's notebook filled with scribbles.

"Can you read that?" PJ mellowed out when he recalled his running up and down the streets in search of stories.

"Not, a whole lot," he said. "Nobody wants to go on the record."

The town talk had it that one of the business partners in the chiropractor's office wasn't paying taxes. There were at least six chiropractor offices in town and the surrounding areas. More over who knew if the town's gibberish didn't have it mixed up with the vet's or medical offices.

"Do we have the right profession?" laughed PJ eating his lunch. "Are they human or animal doctors? Yummy, this is really good."

"Either way, they have to pay taxes," said Luke. "It doesn't matter whether they treat humans or animals."

"Hey, don't get smart with me," laughed PJ. "You haven't been here long enough."

Since, it was after the production deadline, PJ put off the story for another week. All of a sudden, he turned to Luke:

"I should probably introduce you around town, actually around two towns," PJ said. "You will have two towns to cover."

It was Luke's first newspaper job. He could hardly wait to get his byline in print.

The thrill of the first byline and the first story was almost the same as the thrill of getting laid for the first time.

Luke could remember having both things for the first time quite well. The first laying happened while he was still in high school, and since then he had been waiting for the print job to happen.

On the eve of his first story, when he covered a city hall meeting, Luke was nervous. PJ had introduced him to the city manager, Ruby K. The blonde was chatty.

"You're the new kid on the block," she smiled. "Welcome to the club. We will have fun."

Luke had no doubt that Ruby was right about having fun. Ruby gave him a steady handshake.

"We're really progressive around here," said PJ. "We have a lot of women in top positions. Look at our publisher; she really wants a story about those two."

Luke realized that the pressure on PJ this time was coming from within, from the boss herself, not just from the streets.

Together, they walked the small hometown, not far from a big university city. The competition with the big city's daily was driving PJ nuts.

"Sometimes, I wish they would just go to hell," PJ said. "Our boss is paranoid about being scooped. She's nice as long as we are the first ones to break the story. If not, she turns into a witch and goes on a witch hunt."

Luke loved his hometown newspaper office; he was there by himself since the salesperson either never showed up or stayed for an hour. In two weeks, the salesperson got fired. He was never replaced; Luke was relieved to have the office to himself.

"It's always good to keep your distance from the main camp," PJ advised him. "All you have to do is write a story a day and take a good photo."

Luke remembered that and never had any intentions of changing it.

That year, the sleepy hollow with the population of 2,000 and its adjacent sister town with 1,500 heads buried themselves for the winter deep.

PJ wasn't happy with Luke's first story.

"That was already reported at the county level," he said throwing the paper across his desk.

"You didn't tell me that," said Luke.

PJ was munching on his sandwich with his feet on the desk.

"That's okay," he said with his mouthful. "I didn't expect a Sherlock Holmes here. Let's just keep the boss happy."

Keeping the lady boss happy meant getting after the town "scuttlebutt." Each new day added more to the story. Lady boss called a meeting on Tuesday prior to the paper's deadline.

"I need to introduce you two," said PJ, who had ordered pizza for the meeting. "This is Mrs. Abbey," he said. “Mrs. Abbey, meet the new Sherlock Holmes, aka Luke.”

The first company-wide meeting in months also indicated the seriousness of the situation. Mrs. Abbey took charge in the small conference room without any windows.

Luke was feeling claustrophobic already. He watched the lady boss explain why the story about the two homos needs to be handled carefully.

“First of all, we’re going to pretend that we don’t know,” she said her hands resting on the table.

“That we don’t know what?” asked PJ eating his slice of pepperoni pizza.

There was a silence in the conference room. The lady boss looked at her editor wondering why she had ever hired this man, who had his mouthful all the time. Why didn’t she just hire a woman? She could always promote the copy editor in PJ’s place.

“That they’re homos,” said the top-ranking salesperson for the entire newspaper group. “They do advertise with us though.”

PJ looked surprised. So, this salesperson Toby knew all along and wouldn’t tell him. PJ wondered if the lady boss was trying to get rid of him again.

“Would you Toby please share with us who these two gentlemen are,” said the lady boss. “So, our editor can pursue the story that has been out on the streets for more than a month.”

Toby walked up front and directly faced PJ.

“I’ve been telling you all along,” he said. “They’re the chiropractors located on the west side of town. One of them got into trouble for not paying taxes.”

Now, the lady boss, in her fifties, got up too with all her weight and looked at her employees over the top of her eyeglasses, and then at PJ.
“If the Gazette scoops us, you’re in trouble PJ,” she said. “The Star will always be first. We’re going to report it; we don’t have to tell the world they are homos.”
PJ took Luke aside after the meeting.
“Look we’re going to cover this when one of them goes to court,” said PJ. “Toby thinks I am an idiot and so does the lady boss. Never fear, we will show them.”

The court hearing was set for Friday before Thanksgiving at the district court.
“That’s going to be a hell of a Black Friday,” said PJ. “For you, Luke. I’ll be near a phone if you need help.”
Luke had heard of stories of christening by fire, but this exceeded his expectations.
“I’ve never covered a court story before,” Luke said. “I’ve been to jury duty if that counts.”
“That’s good enough. There’s always the first time,” said PJ. “The reporting business isn’t as glorious as you thought, ha? You will always come across issues such as the ‘homos’, you’d rather not talk about. It doesn’t mean they don’t exist.”

Sitting in the courtroom, Luke was nervous imagining windows, where they did not exist. He felt the old claustrophobia magnified. But there was no escape from this courtroom.

The chiropractor already took his seat without a defense attorney. It was the first time;Luke had heard the chiropractor's name spoken out loud by the judge.

"I don't like to see you Mr. Brown without representation," said the judge known for her bias toward men. "You do realize that what you have done is pretty serious."

The judge was also a stand-up comedian, performing her acts for the local charities. She favored women, no matter what they had done.

Luke remembered vaguely reading about this woman who looked almost like a man. She had a harsh voice and harsh facial features. However, judge Rita Scott did not shy away from wearing dresses. Her favorite one was a sleeveless red knit dress. It showed off well her biceps. Luke could recall a photo of her in the regional magazine.

"District judge delivers great comedy for a great cause," the headline said.

The article successfully compared her to Seinfeld without revealing her sexual preferences.

"I studied your case, you haven't been paying taxes for seven years, Mr. Brown," she said.

"It is not in the constitution that I have to pay taxes, and I can be my own attorney," Brown charged back.

Was Luke's mind fooling him, or was that Brown's partner seated in the back?

Luke had trouble focusing on the case, as the prosecutor cited the charges against Mr. Brown.

"How do you plead?"

"Not, guilty," said Brown strongly. "I repeat; it is not in the constitution that I have to pay taxes. Therefore, I am not guilty of tax evasion."

Brown stood up to defend himself and found his partner Paul sitting in the audience.

Judge Rita flashed another hard look at the chiropractor claiming his innocence.

"Mr. Brown, tax evasion is a serious crime against your fellow citizens who are paying taxes," she said.

The prosecutor called Paul to the witness stand to Brown's sheer disbelief.

"That fricking rat," Brown thought to himself. "How dare he; it was all between us. Nobody else knew. It was our own deal that had non-disclosure clause."

The non-disclosure cause was the sexual relationship between the two partners. Neither one of them was going to say anything about their flair for each other.

Paul took the stand without hesitation or looking at Brown. The prosecutor approached the witness stand:

"Mr. Gabb, you knew about the tax evasion?" he asked.

"I did," Paul said.

"Why, didn't you report it?" asked the prosecutor.

"I was scared to death," Paul looked at his partner. "He was threatening me."

"Do you realize you could go to prison for conspiracy?" the prosecutor said.

"I do," said Paul.

"You can both end up in prison together," said the prosecutor. "What was the defendant threatening you with?"

Paul knew this was going to happen. It was the trade-off for not going to prison with his partner. In a split second, the ordeal of the previous year flashed in front of Paul's eyes; his crying wife threatening to leave him with the kids. That's why, Paul told his wife about the tax evasion ordeal, who in turn called the IRS.

"He was going to tell my wife about our relationship," said Paul steadily.

Brown jumped to his feet.

"You fricking liar," he yelled. "We did not have a relationship other than our partnership."

Judge Rita slammed the mallet.

"Quiet in the court," she said.

"Were you using coercion tactics on Mr. Gabb?" asked the prosecutor piercing her eyes through Brown.

"I definitely was not blackmailing that asshole," screamed Brown.

"Yes, he was," said Paul resolutely. "He was threatening to tell my wife about us."

"You have the right to remain silent, Mr. Brown," said the prosecutor.

"Since, you do not have representation, Mr. Brown," said Judge Rita, "I find you guilty of both tax evasion and extortion of your partner."

"You have absolutely no proof of the second charge," said Brown taking strong stance. "I was not blackmailing Paul. It's his word against my word. Prove to me that I was using force to keep him silent."

But, the deal with Paul was struck before the hearing behind closed doors.

"He should go to prison with me, then," Brown was yelling at the top of his lungs.
"Get him out of here," judge Rita said.
"You're guilty as charged," she said. "The court will come to order."
Luke stood up to watch the judge leave the courtroom. As soon as he got out into the hallway, he managed to corner Paul who tried to run outside.
"Mr. Gabb, I am a reporter for the Star, was Mr. Brown blackmailing you, and what was your relationship with him?" Luke quickly asked.
"No, comment," said Paul and ran out.
Luke turned to the prosecutor, who was standing in the hallway available for comment.
"I am a reporter for the Star," said Luke nervously. "Did Mr. Gabb admit to being blackmailed by Mr. Brown?"
The prosecutor unbuttoned his jacket and looked at Luke closely.
"Yes, he did in exchange for not being charged," said the prosecutor coldly. "That is not an unusual bargain. Mr. Brown should have hired himself an attorney.
Luke stared at the cold-hearted prosecutor smiling to himself as he looked back up at Paul.
"You know about our correspondents?" Luke breathed heavily.
"I make it my business to read the local papers," the prosecutor said slyly. "I have deep respect for people who buy ink by the barrel. You represent them. Thanks for showing up, keep up the good work."

Back at the newspaper office, PJ had just finished reading Luke's article about the chiropractors' case. It will be the lead story in tomorrow's papers. He finished his sandwich and walked over to the lady boss. PJ handed her printout of the story.
"What do you think?" he asked her after she was done reading.
"I think you made a good hire, PJ," she said. "You get to keep your job, at least for a while. Luke navigated the story well far away from the crux of the matter."
Only the Star staff knew about the sexual relationship between the two partners, while the town just guessed it; for the rest of the world it remained a secret.
The next day, all the papers of the group, screamed the news in 50-point bold headline ahead of the neighboring Gazette into the world.
"Local chiropractor blasted for tax evasion."

Silk Nora

Nora arrived in Belding by train at the Pere Marquette Station on a hot summer day in July of 1916 from the East Coast to work at one of the four silk mills.
At the turn of the century, Belding known as the Silk City of the World, was booming with the silk industry. The silk mills founded by the Belding Brothers attracted hundreds of young girls who worked in its silk mills. In was the avantgarde era of the flapper dresses and hats. The girls worked in the mills for eight to ten hours a day.

The nature of the business required The Belding Brothers Co. to employ a large number of women from the most intelligent and desirable class. The company originally built and maintained three high-class boarding houses, “The Ashfield,” “The Belrockton” and “The White Swan,” with ample accommodations for 125 women each.

The dormitories were all handsome pieces of architecture and were fitted with all the modern conveniences of their day. Steam heat, hot and cold water, baths, electric lights, free libraries, and comfortably furnished in order to afford the young women employed by Belding Brothers & Co. as good a home as could be found only among the more prosperous citizens of the country.

The Belding Brothers’ experience had taught them that highly intelligent, contended, well-paid employees would produce goods of superior quality and would inspire the success of the establishment.

The dormitories were presided over by a matron and governed by rules and regulations similar to those of college dormitories of previous years.

Nora stayed at the Hotel Belding in the thriving downtown on Main Street because the dormitories closed as the town clock struck 10 p.m. The Main St. was paved with bricks and lined with two-story brick buildings after the fire in 1893.

Hotel Belding known as the “perfect palace of the hotel” had been a traveler’s mecca since 1888 fitted with cold and hot water and electric lamps. The furniture was all antique oak.

Nora looked outside on the Main Street. She took in the city rush and bustle lasting into the night.

In the morning she checked into the Belrockton dormitory. Nora received the bigger corner room at Belrockton. The dormitory for silk girls was built in 1906 in classical revival style with porches. She shared the room with Mathilda who came from Alpena.

Each room had a window, a closet, and an electric light. Electric lights were a new luxury in 1906. Each room was equipped with one light bulb hanging from the center of the ceiling turned on and off with a switch attached to the bulb. Wiring for a wall switch and fancy shades came much later.

Furniture was provided by the company and the girls were allowed to decorate their rooms with pictures, pillows and "mementos" from home. The corner rooms were very popular because of the light and ventilation. There was always a waiting list for occupancy.

Nora worked at the Richardson Mill located on the banks of the Flat River. Every morning she punched the clock at 6 a.m. and sat at her station by the window with hundreds of other girls. They made silk thread used to fashion stockings, long before nylon or rayon had arrived.

Long days spent inside the factory were offset by leisure time in the city parks located on the Flat River and on the boardwalk leading to the library.

Nora and Mathilda walked the city streets together enjoying their youth and independence. The women flouted conventional standards of behavior of housemakers and were on the cusp of the women's right to vote in 1920. The 1920s represented the jazz age, a time of liberation for the feminine form. Women's clothing became more comfortable and simplistic. The flapper proudly showed her liberation by bobbing her hair, rolling down her stockings, dancing the Charleston in her shorter gown and wearing the new look in hats.

Signs of progress were present everywhere from the interior six bathrooms at the Bel to a space designated for women in the saloons of the bustling city. At the time, the city of Belding had four hotels.

Known as the "Silk City Girls" the young women spent much of their time weaving silk on spools. Silk at the time was on high demand as the major feminine fabric due to the existing shortage of woolens and cottons.

Nora and Mathilda worked together long hours at the silk mill earning 47 cents an hour. The Belding Banner called the girls "Sweethearts in Silk" blasting propaganda about their happiness with headlines such as "The Silks with Happiness Woven into Them."

The girls sat at their stations on the floor of the factory in orderly rows. The downstairs of the Richardson Mill was used for making stockings.

Sentiment played a big role in the founding of the silk industry in Belding by the Belding brothers. After prospering in silk manufacturing in New England, they built a plant in Belding, where they made their start as door-to-door textile salesmen.

Mathilda traveled home to Alpena twice a year for the holidays, while Nora stayed year- round at the Bel. She had a beautiful view of the Flat River and the boardwalk from her room. Nora was an avid reader and she frequented the dormitory library.

Nora easily made friends with other girls, both at work and at the dorms. She soon cut her hair short, a sign of changing times.

Matron Doris Applebaum managed the Belrockton dormitory and the girls who lived in it. She came from England to take the job at the "Bel" when it opened in 1906. Doris kept her English accent and manners.

"Girls, I will make you into ladies," she said at the dinner table. "You already have the right foundation otherwise you wouldn't be here in the first place. You're a diamond in the rough. I will make you shine."

The silk girls respected this English lady from the county of Sussex on the English Channel seaside. Doris was single and constantly happy. She competed for the Belrockton job with other ladies from around the world and won.

She took a special liking of the well-mannered Nora.

"We're going to be friends," Doris said resolutely to Nora at their second meeting, since Nora arrived in Belding. "We have a lot in common. You come from New England, I come from the real England. I must say you have better food here."

They shared their longing for home, but learned to love the rural Midwest. The position of matron of the

Bel had a dual function; Doris also worked as a nurse at the local hospital for employees of Belding Brothers & Co. The corporation hospital was established for the convenience and welfare of their employees and their families. The charges were very modest, the equipment modern, and staff well-trained.

"I love the second-half of my job at the hospital, that's what I did in England," Matron Doris often said. "That's why I won the audition for the job, because I had the nurse experience as well."

Nora returned Doris' affection. Doris took her for her own daughter, and Doris was like mom for Nora.

"What do you want the chef to make for tomorrow's dinner," Doris asked during the evening supper.

The chef too an was import from New England, where he had met the Belding Brothers as they operated their silk enterprise in Northampton, MA. They asked the chef to come along with them as they established themselves in Belding in 1890. The Belding location was their largest single enterprise, operating four mills.

Mill no.1 was for silk thread exclusively, Mills no. 2 and 3 for fabrics and Mill no. 4 for manufacture of sewing and embroidery silks as well as a variety of crochet cotton.

In order to market their manufactured product, Belding Brothers & Co. established salesrooms in Chicago, New York, Philadelphia, St. Louis, Boston, Cincinnati, St. Paul, Baltimore, San Francisco, New Orleans, Montreal and Toronto. From these salesrooms traveling salesmen visited every city, town, and hamlet in the United States.

Nora soon began to settle in Belding as she participated in the social events such as the dances at the Hotel Belding on Friday and Saturday nights, and attended the opera inside the hotel.

She brought along some of her own "mementos" which was allowed at the Bel. Like most girls, Nora had her belongings shipped in. Porter Harry from Hotel Belding helped her move some boxes on the third floor of the dormitory. Harry also worked part-time for the Belding Banner. He was a man of words.

"You have it so nice and cozy here," he said. "You must love it. Are you coming to the dance tomorrow?"

They briefly met before when Harry was helping move in the other girls.

"I don't know yet," Nora said opening the drawers of the bureau. "I wonder if mom sent me also some of my favorite dresses. Was there anything else, Harry?"

Harry handed her a big package. Then he helped adjust the mirrors by the window.

"That will give you some nice light," he said.

"Do we have a telephone here?" Nora asked. "I need to thank my mother."

"Why, of course it is in the main lobby downstairs," said Harry.

Harry used to work for the Citizens Telephone Co. in Belding.

"I will perhaps see you at the dance tomorrow at the hotel?" asked Harry quickly unsure of himself.

Nora unpacked her petticoats, camisoles, bloomers, black stockings and an extra nightgown and went down to the main lobby. She could smell the dinner from the kitchen downstairs by the main dining room. Nora was waiting patiently to get connected.

"Mother, thank you very much for the dresses and the furniture," she said. "It arrived today on the afternoon train."

"How are you and how is your new home," mom as always wanted to know everything at once and immediately.

"I love it here, mother," Nora said. "I've already made friends, and there are only good people here."

"My dear, there are good people wherever you go," said mom. "But I did fear for you. It must have been a long journey, was it not."

"Yes, it was," said Nora.

"But, mainly how is the work, my dear?" asked mom. "Do they treat you well?"

"It's nice to have my own money, but I do spend a lot of time at the mill," said Nora. "I've made friends there and at the dormitory."

"Is it nice there? Is the Bel nice?" asked mom, who even knew that the dormitory was called the Bel.

"Oh, it's absolutely exquisite and Doris is fabulous," said Nora immediately feeling guilty about her friendship with Doris.

"Who is Doris, my dear?" asked mom.

"Doris is the matron at the dormitory and the main nurse at the hospital," Nora said.

Then, the phone went dead as it got disconnected.

That evening at the main dining room, a lively chatter warmed up the space between the white walls. Mathilda was back from her trip to Alpena. The two girls chatted about Mathilda's trip and family.
"Are we going to the dance tomorrow?" Nora asked.
"Of course, I missed the dances the most," said Mathilda.
The dinner was served on porcelain plates and consisted of fish and chips, ala British style. Doris made sure that Fridays were meatless. And of course, mindful of their diets, the girls wanted to fit into their dresses for Saturday night dance.
Doris was presiding over the dinner from her own table close to the kitchen.
"Are you going to the dance, Doris," asked Nora who walked over to chat.
The dining room was lit by crystal chandeliers and furnished with heavy dining tables and chairs. The ceiling was white made from pressed tin. Paintings of the surrounding countryside decorated the walls of the dining room, where the girls also socialized after dinner. They had a piano by the French door entrance. Anyone and everyone were welcome to play. Nora often played on it, but today she wanted to find out more about Doris.
"There's going to be a lot of fine men there," said Nora teasingly. "You might like it."
"I've never been to it, my dear," Doris said. "I am always too busy to go between the "Bel" and the hospital. But I am off this weekend, so I might come. Is it quite nice?"

"Oh, it's beautiful," Nora was all excited now with anticipation of tomorrow's dance.
Nora looked at Doris, who was still pretty, even at her middle-age. She had a pale complexion; a heritage from the cold English climate. She wore her long blonde hair in a bun, refusing to give in to the changing times.
"Aren't you going to cut your hair like I did, Doris?" Nora said. "You would look prettier than you already look.
"I am too old for short hair," Doris said. "I would feel naked without it."
"You can't be that old-fashioned, Doris," Nora persisted. "I can come with you to the hairdresser in town, if you're scared."
"I am not scared, Nora," said Doris. "I don't want my hair short. I've never had it short."
"But, when you have it all tucked in that nurse's cap, loose strands fall out," Nora noticed when she went to visit Doris at the hospital.
Nora couldn't figure out if Doris was looking for a man, or if she was fine being single at her age.
"You would look younger, Doris," Nora concluded carefully not wanting to upset Doris. "Let us know, if you're coming."
After dinner, Nora and Mathilda went for a walk on the boardwalk by the Flat River. It was still warm, even though fall was in the air. They walked carefree enjoying the evening on the river bank.
"Why do you think Doris never married?" asked Mathilda.

"Well, she told me she never had time for men with her two jobs," Nora said. "Maybe, something happened back in England."
True, Doris never talked that much about her past in England except that she worked as a nurse there.

They walked past Hotel Belding built in 1888 as "A Thing of Beauty and Joy Forever" according to the plaque. The magnificent structure was built of red and white sandstone with spacious porches and it offered views of the park. During her first night in Belding, Nora enjoyed all the amenities of the hotel for $2 per stay: hot and cold water, baths and toilets, the lovely writing room and parlors.
"I will remember it forever," Nora said to Mathilda. "I wrote in the writing parlor and read their newspaper."
The hotel with 43 rooms was always busy with guests coming from Chicago now also by the automobile. It was a temperance hotel without a bar on the premises.
"They have a great pastry chef and Mr. Hetherrington and Mr. Brecken run it so well," Nora repeated knowledgeably what she had found out from Doris.
She remembered Doris' words about respecting the town's elite.
"You know, dear, both gentlemen left their hotel jobs in Massachusetts for the management positions at the Hotel Belding," said Doris. "Just like I left my nurse job in England."
The new era of the 1920s was also an era for opportunism that came with the advent of the

automobile. But that wasn't the case for the Belding Brothers who had carefully designed the success of their world-wide silk enterprise from their humble origins in their Belding home to this hotel treasure.
Mr. Hetherrington and Mr. Brecken carefully guarded the hotel's reputation for catering to the public with their courteous treatment with a general greeting and an outstretched hand to the weary travelers. Strictest cleanliness was maintained in all parts of the house and nothing was spared to enhance the guests' comforts.
Mr. Hetherington was also the business manager for the Belding Land and Improvement Co.

Since, the girls had to work on Saturdays too, they went early to bed to get their beauty sleep for the upcoming dance at the hotel. They were restless behind their stations at the mill weaving the threads on the spools; in turn the looms spun out sheer silk for stockings, heavier silks for lining men's coats, nun's veiling and a host of other useful things.
Later, they would advance to the "Grecian Doublers" that carried 24 or 25 threads. Ed Belding was the boss with Carrie Williams as the floor manager. Some of their co-workers lived at the other two dorms: Ashfield and White Swan.
Whenever, the girls came back from work to the dormitory, they were grateful for the modern lavatory with automatic flush toilets and showers with hot water.
Then, came the big preparations for the Saturday night dance at the Hotel Belding. The girls laid their

skirts and white waists, camisoles and black stockings on the beds in front of them.

They both had quite a selection since they came from families that were well off.

"Where did you get this?" Mathilda held up a beautiful beaded evening dress by Elsa Schiaparelli.

"Mom just sent it to me," said Nora. "Isn't that beautiful?"

Nora also showed off her matching beaded cloche hat. The two women fell into their own independence with a passion.

Dressed up to the nines, they walked to Hotel Belding where everything was set up to start as soon as the town clock struck 8 p.m. Nora and Mathilda were in awe since they have never been in the ballroom reserved for special occasions.

This was a very special occasion because the Belding brothers, Hiram and Alvah were expected to attend the benefit ball for the Red Cross. In the meantime, the World War I had broken in Europe, and there was no end to it.

The Rose Ballroom was decked out in fall colors of orange, yellow, brown and green.

Doris decided to come after all, since it was a ball for the Red Cross. The stately matron was accompanied by the crew from the hospital.

They were all seated at the same round table for 12. Nora kept watching the door nervously, watching for Harry to show up. He was supposed to cover the event for the Belding Banner. Nora was shocked when Doris entered through the main door to the ballroom sporting a short bob hiding under the cloche hat.

"Doris, you look absolutely ravishing," said Nora as she stood up the greet the matron and the team.
"I couldn't resist, dear," she said jovially pushing her bob up. "How do you like it?"
"It's absolutely adorable," said Nora, "and your dress, it's lovely."
Doris had the dress made for New Year's Eve ball, but she didn't go because of an emergency at the hospital.
Seamstress Lulu with her Lulu's Fashions was located on Main Street next to the Millinery Shop. At the time, women were expected to wear hats. To go outside without a hat was considered not just unfashionable, but rude and a display of bad manners. Compared to dresses, hats were fairly expensive. Women spent between 20 cents and $7 on a hat. To have two hats look alike was unheard of. The milliner sewed each hat by hand and made it unique to the owner. Being a milliner, was one of the few occupations women were allowed to work along with the seamstress profession.
"Lulu does a fine job indeed," said Doris, "Meet my friends."
Doris introduced the hospital crew one by one, as they all sat around the table. The band was up front.
"Is your friend Harry coming?" she asked Nora.
"I would imagine so, he is covering the event for the Banner," said Nora.
The food was exquisite featuring glistening hoers-d-ours, whitefish in dill sauce, spiced baked ham and potatoes.

Since Hotel Belding was a temperance hotel, and on the cusp of prohibition, only cordials or mixers were officially served with plenty of orange and lemon slices.

Nora finally spotted Harry equipped with a Kodak autographic camera. He was talking to the band members. Nora got up and walked to Harry.

"Come and eat with us," Nora said. "I reserved a spot for you too. You know Doris from the "Bel." Come and meet my friends."

Harry was wearing a tweed Peaky Blinders callum suit, and somehow, he managed to sneak in a gin rickey with lime.

"I hear that the Belding brothers are coming," Harry said.

"Yes, why of course, we are expecting them," said Doris.

Belding brothers, disturbed by the unfolding of the war in Europe, organized the charity ball to benefit Red Cross.

The band was playing foxtrot now.

"You know the band members, Harry?" asked Nora.

"Of course, I went to school with John," he said. "I will introduce you later."

The party members under the crystal chandeliers immersed themselves in a world of their own. The long hours at the silk mills or at the newspaper dissipated into the night. It was only the moment at the hotel that lasted forever. There was no town clock or war in Europe or the Bel with its 125 female workers.

“Let’s dance, Nora,” Harry asked Nora for a dance as he set down the gin rickey. Both were skilled dancers. They danced the Charleston and other couples joined them on the dance floor.
The night under the golden stars was young and restless. The conversation at the table turned to the war in Europe, since Doris mentioned her home country of England. Doris didn’t have too much time to follow the news on the radio, but she did get letters from home.
United Kingdom introduced the conscription or the draft in 1916, while the U.S. declared war on Germany in April of 1917. The U.S. had been a supplier to the Allied Forces all along.
“I wonder if the brothers will speak about the war,” said Doris.
Although, far away, the war had been at the forefront of everyone’s minds since the U.S. declared war on Germany.
Alvah Belding took the speaker’s stand, as the band stopped the music. He thanked everyone for participating in the charity to benefit the Red Cross.
“Now, that the U.S. had joined the war in Europe, we have to contribute with physical and financial resources as much as we can,” he said. “We are fortunate enough to have our own hospital in Belding and I would like Doris to come up and tell us about its operations right here.”
Doris was a little surprised, but the hospital was her first love, that she brought to the new country from England.

"I am very grateful to be living in such a generous country, my homeland is torn by war, anything that I can do here will help," Doris said. "I too thank everyone for participating in this."

She returned to her table while the party resumed and everyone took to the floor to dance the Charleston.

Then, it was time for desserts set up as a luxury buffet station. The desserts featured pastry pigs or pigs in a blanket, tiramisu and fruits.

John holding a gin rickey walked up to the buffet and chatted with Harry.

"This is a marvelous event," he said. "I've never been in here. You know my other job keeps me busy."

John worked at the Hall Gibson Refrigeration Plant and played the trumpet in the "Belding Boys Band."

"Well, I would like to introduce you to my friend Mathilda," said Nora holding Harry's arm.

Mathilda still sported long hair, tied it up in a bun. She was somewhat shy in front of well-built John.

"How do you like my hometown of Belding?" he smiled at the young lady. "My entire family has lived in here for generations. I've never set my foot far from this town. You look like a city girl to me."

Mathilda's cheeks turned pink.

"I am not that city-minded as you might think," she said. "I have learned to dance to the music you play. I am really enjoying it."

"I'll ask a friend to play for me, and we can dance," John said eagerly, "that is if you want to."

Doris too was enjoying the night under the harvest moon with her friends from the hospital.

“Look at those two dancing,” she said lovingly. “They are my girls from the Bel.

“What do you mean by your girls? You seem like you’re leading a double life,” laughed the doctor from the hospital. “Our Doris has another love other than the hospital. I find that hard to believe.”

Doris was nervous with Doc’s presence. She didn’t expect him to come. But Doc was part of Belding’s elite along with Mr. Hetherrington and Mr. Brecken, managers of the hotel.

“We would be incapacitated without your British expertise, Doris,” Doc said. “I truly mean that. We value your Sussex background.”

Prior coming to Belding, Doris worked at a hospital in Worthing. However, she was an adventurer, and when she saw the ad for the matron at the Bel, she applied and auditioned.

“Why did you have to audition for this job?” asked Doc.

Doris never questioned any rules or regulations. She was used to a strict regime from England.

“I was just happy to get the job,” she said. “I was getting tired of England with all the war mongering. I feel safe here.”

Doris smoothed the skirt of the dress that she hadn’t worn yet. Lulu was a master seamstress with a magician’s touch. The beige color of the dress matched her blonde hair. A strange man from the other side of the ballroom came to the table and asked Doris for a dance. The “Belding Boys” band was playing ‘Strugglin’ Woman’s Blues.

The dance went late into the night. On dance Saturdays, Doris lifted the workday curfew at 10 p.m. Harry and John walked with the young women to the Bel on the boardwalk singing tunes from the band repertoire.

Sundays were dedicated to church, relaxation and handcrafts. The young women gathered inside the parlor to crochet or knit. Live chatter filled the parlor; the girls had a lot to talk about after the ball dance.
“Tell us all about it,” they nagged Nora and Mathilda. However, both were too tired and too happy with their new experience to talk about it.
“You will read about it in the Banner,” Nora said. “It comes out tomorrow. Harry was there to cover it. We all danced Charleston.”
Most of the girls were jealous that Nora was going out with a newspaper man. At the time newspapers were well respected. They didn’t know yet about Mathilda and John.
“You could at least tell us about who else was there and about the dresses,” the girls persisted.
Doris stepped into the parlor eager to join her girls.
“It was a splendid night and I love the band,” she said looking at Mathilda. “John is great on the trumpet. Everybody danced.”
“Oh, that is exciting, you must have danced,” cried one of the girls. “I wish I could have been there. I’ve never been to any dance. Don’t let us wait to read about it, please tell us, pretty please.”
Doris sat on the bench and spoke of the night under the Harvest Moon in the Rose Ballroom.

"But, where did you learn how to dance?" the girls were increasingly curious.

"Darlings, I learned how to dance in England," Doris smiled. "I took classes with Mr. and Mrs. Cooper."

"But, where did you learn to dance the Charleston? Surely not in England?" the girls laughed.

Doris loved the Sunday afternoons in the knitting parlor at the Bel with the silk city girls.

"And you cut your hair in a bob," the girls shrieked with joy. "Doris, you are so modern and you are such an inspiration."

"Well, my mom won't let me cut my hair," another girl chattered.

"Why not? These are changing times," said Doris dismissing the art of the Charleston. "Let's have some afternoon tea, high tea, British style."

All the silk girls at the dormitory loved Doris' high tea time in the tea room. They moved to the tea room to enjoy all the flavors. Doris had her tea porcelain set shipped from England. The fragile cups and saucers had floral print. The shipment included Ahmad Earl Grey tea with bergamot and the Darjeeling from London.

Doris modeled the high tea ritual at the Bel after the one she had once enjoyed at Claridge's, London. The three-tiered stand featured colorful macaroons, chocolate cake and fruit tarts on the top; freshly-baked scones, plain, apple and raisin, were always accompanied by strawberry jam with heavy Devonshire cream.

Chef Josiah at the Bel took special care in making the sandwiches for the Sunday afternoon high tea. He always placed the finger-sized sandwiches on the bottom of the stand. The chef didn't shy away from putting cucumber slices on the dill and smoked salmon sandwiches.

Doris was the true "Tearista" here with her knowledge of teas from around the world such as Jasmine Dragon Pearls, Tippy Golden Flowery Orange Pekoe, or Hathialli meaning 'Elephant Road.'

Doris baked the grand finale of the high tea-dessert-that changed from Sunday to Sunday. This week it was the lemon meringue cake, expressing Doris' nostalgia after the past summer.

The girls chattered not thinking about the work week ahead of them at the silk mills.

Doris and Josiah also enjoyed a glass of champagne with their tea.

Nora loved going out shopping on Main Street. She usually went to the E.R. Spencer general store where she could also mail her letters to mom and socialize with the town folk.

That afternoon, she ran into Harry who was on his rounds delivering the Belding Banner to the area merchants. He stopped in front of her to show her the main story on top of the fold of the Banner.

"Belding's elite benefits Red Cross to aid World War I."

A big photo showed Mr. Alvah Belding speaking about generosity and WWI.

"Look at this one, Nora," said Harry.

Nora looked at a photo of the two of them dancing in the Rose Ballroom.

"But you were the one who took all the photos," she was surprised and looked at Harry.

"John took this one, I asked him to," Harry said. "I wanted to have a memory of us."

"A memory, why?" she asked. "We're both here now. I got to get back to shopping."

Nora turned around disturbed about the mention of memories.

"I would like to ask you to come with me to the movies this Sunday," Harry said eagerly, yet afraid of the answer.

Nora looked at this guy sporting a Brixton hat and a tweed jacket holding onto a stack of newspapers.

"What's playing?" she asked hesitatingly as more people were coming into the store, where they stood around and chatted.

"Here, Mr. Spencer, today's newspaper," Harry said.

Mr. Spencer picked up the paper and looked at the photos.

"I see you and your friend here made the paper," he smiled. "Good job. The lady comes here often. You are a good writer, Harry."

Harry was happy with the town praise of his writing. He turned back to Nora with her basket.

"A Girl's Folly," Harry said. "I can meet you in front of the theater."

During the silent movie era, Belding had two theaters: The Star Theatre and the Empress Theater.

"Which one?" asked Nora.

“The Empress Theater at 4:30 p.m., if you can,” said Harry.

“But, Harry, I will miss Doris’ high tea ceremony,” Nora said. “She will be offended. She puts all the treats and teas out for us, the silk girls.”

“For once, they can do without you,” he said. “I must run now. I will be waiting for you there. Please come.”

As Harry left the general store, Nora deeply immersed herself into shopping. She paused by the Belding’s Silk thread cabinet, since the silks were such a big part of her life.

“Mr. Spencer, can I have the golden thread and some marshmallows,” she said while still thinking about Harry’s proposition.

Nora walked to the Bel in the November chill. She threw off her coat in the dorm room and sank on her bed, confused about Harry. Mathilda was out with John.

Mathilda doesn’t have a problem dating John, why do I struggle with Harry, Nora was thinking out loud. Her mother’s last words before she left for Belding kept ringing in her ears:

“My dear Nora, beware of young men hiding their true intentions with you under cover-up stories; they will be asking you out to the movies to get what they want. Don’t trust anyone. Morals are loose nowadays.”

Was mama right, though? Nora questioned her mother’s experience and her old-fashioned ways.

"Mama you're just out of touch," Nora remembered a recent telephone conversation from the Spencer's store.
Nora was afraid of being overheard if she had called from the dorms at the Bel.
Back at the Bel, Nora entered Doris' office by the front lobby. Doris was busy doing paperwork and she looked funny wearing her eyeglasses.
Nora sat in the chair in front of Doris. Doris looked up surprised; it wasn't the usual custom for the girls to visit with Doris in her office.
Nora was hesitant to speak.
"You want to talk to me, dear?" Doris encouraged her protégé to speak up.
"I know Doris, you're single and you probably wouldn't understand me," whispered shyly Nora.
Doris straightened up in her chair and looked deeply at Nora's face.
"I may be single, but that doesn't mean I never had a boyfriend," she said.
The office was functional but appealing to the eye just like the rest of the dorms.
"I can't attend high tea on Sunday," Nora breathed heavily.
Doris walked to Nora and put her hand on her shoulder.
"Look at me, Nora," she said. "It isn't a sin not to attend high tea. You know it's not mandatory."
"I know, but I don't want to disappoint you, Doris," said Nora teary-eyed.
"Nora, you're acting up, what is going on?" Doris asked.

Nora had been secluding herself ever since that dance with Harry at the Rose Ballroom. She didn't talk much with any other girls at the dorms or at work.

"You know my friend Harry?" Nora paused.

"Yes, the newspaper writer, you danced with him at the ball," said Doris. "What about him?"

"He asked me out to the movies this Sunday during your high tea," said Nora sadly.

Doris sat back in her chair behind the desk.

"Oh, darling, and you're troubled because of that," Doris smiled. "And I was getting worried that you were sick or something. Most of the other girls are dating."

Nora was on the defensive and continued to argue:

"But mama said to beware of young men," Nora said. "I don't know that much about Harry."

Doris felt joy inside for another woman.

"Listen to your heart, Nora," said Doris. "What is it telling you?"

Well-brought up Nora was surprised to hear Doris encouraging her.

"Mama would never approve, you are different Doris," said Nora.

Doris was overjoyed, as she could see admiration in Nora's eyes.

"Don't forget darling that I come from a different country with even more strict rules for ladies," she said. "And look where it got me. Yes, I am in America and doing what I dearly love to do. But I am alone. I don't have a partner or a friend."

Nora felt lighter.

"I love you dearly, Doris," Nora said.

She walked around the desk and kissed Doris on her cheek and left the office. Nora had never been to a movie theater before.

Harry was waiting for Nora in front of the Empress Theater as the first snowflakes fell on the sidewalk. He was wearing his cap and tweed jacket. Harry was watching Nora walk down Main Street past the lanterns and the jewelry shop to the Empress Theater.

"Am I late Harry?" Nora asked.

"No, let's go inside to warm up," he said. "It is chilly outside." The grandiose theater was known as the "picture palace" of Belding because it was so gaudy; it was an extravaganza in the style of art deco. Nora stepped carefully on the plush red carpeting in her Mary Jane shoes. She admired the marble-lined hallway and the crystal chandeliers.

Harry took her coat to the coatroom, and they lounged in the lobby munching on Baby Ruth bars. The sounds of someone playing the organ filled the lounge.

"Oh, my, there is also a billiard room in here?" she gasped.

"Yes, you can find everything in here you have ever wanted," said Harry.

An usher took them to their red plush seats in the ninth row. Although the movies were silent, they were a treat for the majority of the population. The theaters of the 1920s up until the start of depression in the early 1930s attracted millions of Americans to the silent movies in the opulent palaces.

The ushers also served for crowd control.

This all was so new to Nora; she couldn't get enough of the film atmosphere.
"Oh, I wish I was more than just a silk girl," she whispered into Harry's ear. "I wish I could be like Marion or Greta."
"I like you the way you are, Nora," Harry said holding her hand.
After the movies, they walked the boardwalk along the Flat River back to the Bel hand in hand.
"I must tell you something, Nora," Harry said seriously stopping.
Nora looked at Harry, as he took of his cap and held it on his chest. A chill crawled down her spine, and suppressed fear rose in her.
"I will be leaving for Europe soon," he said.
Nora swallowed heavily and looked at Harry.
"The war is tearing Europe apart, Harry," she sobbed. "Why would you want to go there?"
Harry feared this moment ever since he found out he would be going to England as a war correspondent for Toronto Star. Mr. Hiram Belding in his Toronto office had the necessary connections and arranged for Harry to write for the Toronto Star.
"I will be writing from London as a war correspondent," Harry said. "It is a great opportunity for me to get out of Belding."
Nora broke into tears. She quickly turned away from Harry and ran to the dormitories. When Harry caught up with her, Nora pushed him away and slammed the door shut in his face. She ran up the stairs and fell on her bed crying out loud into the night. Luckily,

Mathilda was out with John, so Nora cried out even louder. She pounded her small fists on the bed.
"I hate the war," she sobbed. "I hate the war."
She couldn't sleep all night staring into the star lit sky.
The next morning at the silk mill, she punched in late and the floor manager Carrie was upset with her. Nora cried through the shift and she could hardly see the Grecian Doubler machine for her tears.
"You cannot work like this, go home early," Carrie said.
Nora left work early, but she didn't go directly to the dormitories. Instead she went to the Spencer general store to talk with the owner Earl and to buy the "Belding Banner."
Mr. Spencer noticed his regular customer Nora was upset.
"What is wrong, Nora?" he asked behind the counter.
"This is wrong," Nora threw the Banner across the counter. The big headlines screamed, "U.S. to enter War in Europe: Housatonic sunk by Germans."
Mr. Spencer shared Nora's pain; his own son signed up to join the forces in anticipation of the US entering the conflict between Germany and the Allies.
"My friend Harry from the Banner is leaving for Europe as a war correspondent," she sobbed. "He says it's an opportunity for him."
Mr. Spencer put his elbows on the counter and supported his head and lowered his eyeglasses looking at Nora.
"My son sees it too as an opportunity to help Europe," he said. "I see it in a different light. People are dying

there every day. Maybe we can talk him out of it. Do you want me to try when he brings in the papers?"
Nora, threw a few candy bars and crackers in her bag and the paper.
"Please, Mr. Spencer, do talk to him," she pleaded.
The next day when Harry brought in the papers, Mr. Spencer was standing behind the counter cleaning his eyeglasses. Harry liked to hang around the store too. Mr. Spencer offered him coffee as he opened the paper and found a short article with Harry's photo. It was an announcement about Harry's promotion to war correspondent with the Toronto Star.
"You're in the news, Harry," said Mr. Spencer. "That is not usually a good sign. You know mostly criminals make the papers, not decent folk like you and I."
Harry was drinking his coffee.
"Your son too was in the paper, Mr. Spencer," said Harry politely. "He will be joining the forces, once the U.S. officially enters the war."
It was silent in the store, that was usually like a beehive with constant chatter of the town folks, ringing of the telephone or the cash register.
"It is none of my business, Harry," said Mr. Spencer, "If you leave, the town will lose a good reporter, and I will lose a good customer. Your friend Nora was in here crying that you are leaving her for the war."
Harry was still sipping on his coffee thinking about the spin of the events since the Sunday movie and his announcement to Nora.

"Like I said, it is none of my business, but if I had to choose between a girl and a job, I would go for the girl," Mr. Spencer said. "She really likes you."
Harry was torn inside out clinging onto his cup of coffee.
"Mr. Spencer, I have to go and serve the country the best I know how, and that is with my pen," he said. "It is less dangerous than your son's enlisting."
"That wasn't my point, Harry," said Mr. Spencer. "My point is that you're leaving your heart here in Belding, and you're making a pretty girl unhappy."

Mathilda was back at the dorms combing her hair in front of the mirror getting ready for dinner. Mathilda sat with Nora in the beautiful dining room under the crystal chandeliers. The room was lively with girls' chatter after a long day of work at the silk mills. It was time to unwind. One of the girls played the piano. Nora finally stopped crying and sat quietly at the table staring blankly in front of her, while Mathilda was all fidgety, nervous to talk.
"I haven't seen you in a while Nora," said Mathilda. "I've been going out with John."
"Yes, I've noticed," said Nora. "I haven't seen you around. I wonder what the chef has for us tonight. I haven't had anything decent to eat all day long."
Mathilda examined Nora's face closely.
"You look kind of tired," Mathilda said. "I have to tell you something."
"Yes?" Nora said.

"John asked me to marry him," said Mathilda. "We are getting married."

No, Nora was not ready for this. She stood up, looked around and then sat down again. She carefully placed the napkin on her lap and sipped tea from a hand-painted porcelain cup.

"I am happy for you," Nora waged every word. "I suppose you will be leaving the Bel and me with Doris behind."

The dinner was served and the piano music stopped. Nora dedicated herself completely to the dinner rather than to Mathilda. Avoiding her completely, Nora picked through the mashed potatoes, vegetables and the chicken.

"Excuse me, Mathilda," she said.

Nora walked back into the kitchen to talk to chef Josiah who always had Bourbon hidden in the cabinet. It was their secret.

"Can you mix me a mint julep, Josiah?" she asked and walked through the kitchen to the small patio.

Nora inserted a cigarette in a long cigarette tip like a true lady.

Josiah wasn't surprised; he read the Banner and he knew about Nora and Harry from Doris. It wasn't the first time, Nora asked him for a mint julep or a gin rickey with tons of lime.

"He'll come back," said Josiah downing a julep too and lighting up.

"I just don't want him to go," said Nora sipping on her julep. "You don't understand that."

She finished both her drink and her cigarette and walked back into the dining room to re-join Mathilda.

"I hope you're not upset with me," said Mathilda.
Nora shrugged her shoulders and chased away the thought of being upset over another woman's relationship with a man. She continued to poke the fork into the cold mashed potatoes. Nora pushed away the plate and the cup of tea.
"I am not hungry today," she said. "I got to go to bed early. I am getting up early to make up for today. I won't lock the door. Just come in and don't turn the light on."
Nora crawled into her bed long before the town clock struck 10 p.m., the official bedtime for the silk girls housed at the Bel.
She didn't hear Mathilda come in, as Nora drifted into her dreams about Harry. It was warm in the room from the steam heat and the stars were shining brightly.
Nora woke up more rested in the morning, and went downstairs for breakfast by herself. She didn't want to wait for Mathilda, that way she could avoid her chatter.
"You have a phone call, Nora," Doris shouted from the lobby.
"Who is it?" she snapped back.
"It's your mother," Doris said.
"Tell her, I am not here," Nora said. "I do have to go to work, you know."

Harry was waiting for her on the sidewalk in front of the silk mill. Nora was surprised; he had never done that before. She noticed his luggage that resembled a chest or a trunk.

“Will you come with me to the station,” he said scared. “I am leaving on the 6 o’clock train to New York Grand Central Station. I already have the tickets.”

“What do you mean the tickets?” Nora asked.

“I want you to come with me to New York,” he said lovingly. “I did not mean to hurt you. I love you.”

In awe, Nora ran to the Bel to pack her clothes.

“You could have said something,” Nora said. “I would have gotten ready.”

They boarded the New York Express line to New York Grand Central Station at the Pere Marquette Depot in downtown Belding.

They comfortably settled in the passenger railway carriage with plush seats and three-section windows. Although, Ford’s Model-T was in its boom, the trains were enjoying their “Golden Age.” They were designed for comfort, not speed before the streamliners took over. The couple had some 20 hours of travel ahead of them.

Harry nostalgically looked back at the depot when the train pulled out from the depot on its long journey to New York City. Nostalgia settled in both Harry and Nora’s hearts, not knowing what the future held for them.

As the night descended on the countryside, the duo laid themselves to rest. In the morning they had breakfast in the Pullman lounge car, where they would stay until the end of the trip.

"When will you come back, Harry?" asked Nora with tears in her eyes.

"Well, it depends on how soon the war ends," he said watching out the window.

"I will stay in Belding. I want to make some money before I leave for home," said Nora.

"You won't leave," said Harry. "I have something for you."

Harry pulled out of his pocket a small box with the insignia of Belding Jewelers.

"Will you marry me, Nora?" he asked getting on his knee.

He put the beautiful Art Deco ring with Burmese ruby on Nora's finger and kissed her.

"Yes, I will," she said. "I will wait for you to come back as soon as you can."

Back in the railway carriage, they picked up their belongings as the train was already approaching Grand Central.

"I bought you a return ticket," said Harry. "I knew you would want to go back to Belding."

"Yes, I told Doris and Carrie that I would be back soon," Nora said.

They hugged and kissed farewell.

"I will pray for you to return every day," said Nora. "Please come back."

"I will come back to you, Nora," said Harry. "My heart stays with you forever."

Harry quickly left into the chaos of the Grand Central Station.

Upon arrival back in Belding, Nora fell into the depression of loneliness. But she visited more often with Doris.
"You never told me about your trip to New York," said Doris.
Nora showed Doris the ring with the Burmese ruby.
"Oh, my, you're engaged now," said Doris. "Congratulations. Come and give me a hug, my dear."
They were sitting in the parlor by the French doors.
"Now, all you have to do is wait for Harry," said Doris. "He will come back. He loves you. I saw it in his eyes that night in the Rose Ballroom."
"I know he will come back, but I have to live in the meantime," Nora said. "My 21st birthday is coming up."
"Then, we shall celebrate together," Doris shrieked with joy. "In a saloon."
Working class taverns were knows as "saloons" with swing doors and bar-rooms proper that offered games such as: Faro, Poker, Brag, Three-card Monte and dice games. Some saloons even included bowling, can-can girls, theatrical skits or plays to face off increasing competition until the prohibition in 1920.
On Nora's 21st birthday, the two friends, a single girl and a single matron, went into the local watering hole, Frank & Norm's Tavern. They were women pioneers carving out their own space in the saloons of industrialized America.
Even though most customers at the time were men, the tavern had a "Ladies Entrance." Doris and Nora

used it to get in just in time to catch the new theatrical skit, "Parlor, Bedroom and Bath."

The tavern was full of men drinking bourbon. But, the two women knowledgeable of cocktails from big cities, ordered a Mary Pickford with white rum, pineapple juice, Grenadine and a Maraschino cherry. They happily watched the loud crowd and laughed. This was soon to become their secret; sneaking into Frank & Norm's through the "Ladies Entrance" and hanging at the tavern on Saturday nights way past the Bel's curfew at 10 p.m.

"Have you heard from Harry?" Doris asked.

"Well, I mostly read his war stories syndicated in the Banner," said Nora sadly.

"But, certainly, he writes to you or not?" asked Doris.

Nora pulled a letter out of her pocket, folded several times and re-read a million times.

Dear Nora,

I hope this letter finds you well. I write this during my brief stay in London, before I head back out to the trenches on the Western Front battlefields. The Allies are facing off the German Spring Offensives. The Germans began bombarding the British lines. We have a new foe: gas. But, don't fear for me.

I do plan on returning after the offensives are over and we stand in victory over the Germans, so please do make wedding plans for the fall.

If this doesn't end well, you will have my ring forever.

Please bid best wishes to Mathilda and John.

Yours forever,

Harry

Nora sipped on her Mary Pickford and leaned toward Doris folding back the letter into the tiniest square possible.
“There are more gross war details, I don’t want to get into that,” said Nora.
“We have a wedding to go to, my dear,” Doris diligently reminded Nora.

Mathilda and John got married that summer in the park on the banks of the Flat River. After that, Nora lived by herself at the Bel. She eagerly read the newspapers and listened to the radio for news from the Western Front every evening before bedtime.
She grew increasingly quiet at the dinner table with lively chatter from the rest of the silk girls. Nora grew restless in summertime and went for long walks on the boardwalk dreaming about Harry. She played with her ring with the Burmese ruby.
She visited often with Mr. Spencer at the general store. That summer afternoon, when she got out of work, she headed directly to the store. It was a hot summer day, and the doors were wide open.
Mr. Spencer was reading the Banner behind the counter and greeted her joyfully.
“Good news, Nora,” he waved at her with the paper in his hand.
“What is it, Mr. Spencer?” Nora was breathless and eager to hear any news from the Western Front.”
He showed her the big headline leading in the Banner: “Battle of Amiens starts 100 Days Campaign”

"I don't understand Mr. Spencer," she said.
"That means the Allies started the campaign to crush Germany for good," he said. "Our boys will come home soon. Now, it's only a matter of time to bring them down. The Germans are done."
Always skeptical Nora didn't share Mr. Spencer's joy about the progress of the war in Europe.
"But, are you sure we will win?" she asked Mr. Spencer.
"As sure as the moon will come out tonight," he said smiling, "and the stars. We have a noble cause. We didn't start the war, the Germans did; they must be defeated."
Nora picked some Baby Ruth candy bars and crackers, and stalled around the store.
"It's a nice summer evening, why don't you go out for a dance in the park with the other silk girls," Mr. Spencer encouraged. "There will be a band playing tonight. You don't want to miss out on life. The boys coming home soon."
Mr. Spencer's soon wasn't soon enough for Nora. She went to the dance in the park since John was playing at the band shell.
It was time to make wedding plans for her and Harry. Nora called mom to come over and help with the wedding plans. Together they visited local seamstress Lulu who also had a bridal shop.
"Are you sure about this guy Harry?" mom asked. "Darling don't you want a dress from our eastern boutiques? They don't know what fashion is around here."

"Mom, I want Lulu to make my wedding dress," Nora insisted.

"What about the wedding reception and our guests from the East? They will have to travel," mom argued.

"They can travel, they have plenty of money," said Nora. "Dad got a new car, right?"

"Oh, yes my darling," said mom. "I forgot to tell you; he got a red Duesenberg."

Seamstress Lulu was chatty and happy all the time. Nothing other than fashion trends ever entered her mind. She usually found out about the world outside Belding from her customers. Once a year she travelled to Chicago fashion shows to see new trends.

Nora picked the material: white chiffon, and silver beads, hundreds of them that would be sewn in Art Deco bold geometry.

"You will look so beautiful," said Lulu. "Harry will love it."

From then on, Nora spent most of her time preparing for the wedding. From time to time, Doris and Nora went to the tavern for a few Mary Pickford cocktails.

Nora was already at the tavern, as Doris walked in, not her usual self. She slowly sat down. At first, Nora thought that Doris was just tired after working also the shift at the hospital. She ordered a Mary Pickford for Doris to cheer her up feeling guilty about her own happiness in anticipation of her own wedding.

Doris dropped into the chair heavily. It was hot inside the tavern as well. The men, as always were rowdy after a full day at the factories.

"I had a rough day at the hospital," said Doris quietly sipping on her drink.
"What happened," asked Nora quickly. "Is it that doctor again? Has he been bugging you?"
Doris just waved the thought of the doctor away like a fly.
"Don't I wish it was just the Doc," Doris said breathing heavily. "It's more serious than that."
Nora now realized that she hadn't seen Mathilda around lately, not even at the silk mill. The last time she saw her was at the dance at the bandshell in the park. That's been a while. Mathilda seemed a little pale to her, but Nora thought that was her natural complexion.
"Is something wrong with Mathilda?" asked Nora fearfully.
Doris lit up a cigarette and offered one to Nora, who took it.
"Mathilda is sick," said Doris trying to catch her breath, "Very sick."
"And I thought she had been neglecting me because of her marriage," Nora said. "I haven't seen her at work either. I've been busy with wedding plans. What is wrong with her?"
Doris recalled that afternoon when John walked with Mathilda into the hospital. Doris had trouble recognizing her; Mathilda was skinny and pale like a corpse. She was twisting with each bout of cough. Doris noticed the blood on the pretty white handkerchief.
"What is wrong with Mathilda?" Nora asked.

"Mathilda has the White Plague," said Doris breaking down into tears.

Nora paused in shock recalling reading about the White Plague in the South.

"That's not here, they have it in the South," argued Nora. "I will go and see her."

"You can't," said Doris. "The Doc sent her to a Tuberculosis Sanatorium in Virginia."

"You're telling me this now," Nora was shocked. "You knew all along. That's why you didn't talk about her. You're not a friend."

Nora stormed out of the tavern, not knowing where to go. She was crying and stumbling on the boardwalk along the Flat River in search of peace. She had no one left; Harry was in Europe on the Western front and Mathilda was in a Tuberculosis Sanatorium. Nora was convinced that she could have saved Mathilda if she had known about her disease.

But there was no cure for tuberculosis at the time. Nora remembered reading about it in the Banner. "No cure for tuberculosis."

Nora went back home to the Bel restless as she threw herself on the bed hopeless in tears. After a while, she heard a faint knock on the door of her corner bedroom.

"Come in, I don't care," she cried burying her face in the pillows.

Doris walked into the room and sat in the armchair by the window with the view of the boardwalk and the Flat River. Doris ordered hot tea, and chef Josiah brought it upstairs on a pretty silver-plated tray with some cookies.

"Josiah, you can set it on the nightstand," said Doris. She touched and caressed Nora's short hair that curled onto her shoulders. Nora, sobbing out loud, didn't turn around.

"My Mathilda," Nora cried out loud.

She didn't have enough energy to throw Doris out. Doris sipped the hot Darjeeling and carefully put a lemon slice in her cup, and another one in Nora's cup.

"My dear, have a cup of hot tea," she soothed Nora. "It will do you good. You will get a good night's sleep. Morning will find you well."

Nora usually looked forward to the Thursday summer concerts at the bandstand in the park on the Flat River after a shift at the silk mills.

Floor manager Carrie asked about Mathilda, since she hadn't been to work in a few weeks. It was the end of summer, and it was hot. The silk girls were wearing comfortable summer blouses and skirts seated behind the "Doublers" machines.

Belding was getting ready for the biggest event of the year the "homecoming celebration" on the Labor Day weekend. The town was decked out in red, white and blue.

"How is Mathilda doing?" asked Carrie. "I've heard that she has been transported to a sanatorium in Virginia."

"I want to go and see her," Nora looked up from her "Doubler" machine at Carrie.

"You can't," Carrie said. "You have to enjoy life, There's music at the bandshell in the park tonight."

"How, can I enjoy life," argued Nora defiantly. "Harry's on the Western Front, and Mathilda is sick in a sanatorium."
Carrie paced around Mathilda's station with her arms crossed on her chest.
"Look, I've lost a child to tuberculosis," she said. "You have to continue to live on."
Nora struggled to understand Carrie's words.
"Are you trying to tell me that Mathilda is going to die?" she asked Carrie.
"Go to the bandshell tonight, John is playing," Carrie said wiping sweat from her forehead. "He might need you. Don't be selfish. Stop thinking about yourself."

Back at the Bel, Nora changed from work clothes into her summer fling dress, yellow with white stripes and black trim. She took the boardwalk to the East Riverside Park and breathed in the late summer breeze coming from the water. The park was already filling up with townsfolk. In this town, everyone knew each other and each other's business.
Nora walked to John who was in the bandshell getting his trumpet ready. He blew a sad sound on the horn, when he saw Nora approaching. She stood by his side as he continued to play a sad tune. Nora listened to the "Jazz on the River." She didn't have the courage to ask him about Mathilda. She stepped down from the bandshell and took a seat on one of the park benches. Nora cried the entire concert listening to the tunes of Jabbo Smith.

After the concert, John came to see Nora holding his trumpet case and sat beside her on the bench. It was a long hot summer night in the park.

“John, I am very sorry about what had happened with Mathilda,” she said. “I really am.”

John cried and put his head in his hands.

“She was pregnant too,” he said. “I will lose both of them. There is no hope.”

“Are you going to see her?” Nora said. “I can come with you.”

John shook his head in tears.

“I am going to see her tomorrow,” he said. “You can’t come with me. It is not safe to visit.”

The sanatoriums of the 1920s were known as the “waiting rooms for death.”

Mathilda was in the Catawba Sanatorium in Roanoke, Virginia. The sanatorium had a rule: “If you expect to get well, you must work for it.”

Nora nurtured deep sympathy for death due to Harry. She feared for him every day that passed by without any news from the Western Front.

Mom did give her better news from the East Coast when she called the other day.

“Daddy says we will win. The 100 Day campaign was a big success,” mom said. “There were some casualties.”

“How do I find out who died?” Nora asked.

“You just wait, dear,” mom said. “Harry will come home, along with the Spencer boy.”

Nora went to the "homecoming" parade that she pretended was the homecoming for her Harry. The "Belding Boys" band played without John.

Doris and Carrie joined her on the sidewalk to watch the parade pass by. One entry was by the wounded veterans of WWI. Their friends and family carried a banner:

"End to WWI is coming soon."

Nora and the girls marveled at the different automobiles in the parade; all signs of the new roaring era marching in. Nora wished she could have a car; a nice Ford Model T affordable for everyone. She was determined to buy a car as soon as Harry gets back home.

The "Belding Banner" had their own entry with marching newspaper boys throwing free copies of the paper and flyers. She noticed the big banner:

"Harry, come home soon."

For a brief moment in time, Nora was able to forget all about that deep sadness in her heart. She waved crazily at the people in the parade. All three women decided to join in the parade with the Red Cross entry led by Doc from the hospital.

"I am glad you have found us," said Doc. "This is a great parade."

After the parade, there were public picnics in the parks around town. Chef Josiah from the Bel had prepared their picnic hamper with stuffed eggs, celery stuffed with cream, salted radishes, homemade lemon-limeade, coconut layer cake, cheese sprinkled with paprika, slices of watermelon and chicken.

The "Belding Boys" played jazz at the bandshell.

"You know they are missing a trumpet," said Doc. "John had to go to the Catawba Sanatorium in Virginia."

They were all seated around the bench enjoying the late summer festivities. Nora stopped eating her stuffed egg and took a sip of the fresh lemonade breathing in the summer air.

"Doctor, is Mathilda going to die?" Nora asked.

Doc paused before he took a bite out of the big sandwich. He had previously taken off his straw hat and set it carefully by his side not wanting to mess up the picnic spread. He was holding a fresh copy off the presses of the Banner depicting "Victory after victory on the Western Front."

He took a deep breath before he spoke weighing every word.

"Dear, Nora, we can't always win all the battles on all fronts," he said. "We cherish the ones that we have won, and honor the ones that we have lost. Let me leave it at that."

The rest of the evening glided by into the soft and gentle night.

"Are you coming with us for a few bourbons?" asked Doc.

"I'd rather not," said Nora. "I have some reading to do and I would like to work on the wedding invites. I am sure you understand."

Back at the Bel, Nora could hear the loud conversations coming from the taverns and the hotels. Nora wrote an invite for Harry as well. It was a beautiful ornate invitation on hand-made paper:

Dear Harry,

I hope this letter finds you well on the Western Front, that I've been hearing so much about. Doc and Mr. Spencer know a lot about the war. I try to stay away from the war news.

I invite you to our wedding. Mom and I worked hard to find the right place. We settled on the Rose Ballroom. I had Lulu make my wedding dress from chiffon with beads. I am looking at the ring with the Burmese ruby you gave me that evening at the Grand Central Station in New York. I am kissing it right now, and I am sending you a kiss as well.

I hope you get this letter in time. Mom and dad will drive to Belding in dad's new red sedan. I got my driver's identification card for 25 cents while you were gone. We'll buy a nice car when you come back home to me.

Love,

Nora

It was a Sunday afternoon at the Bel inside the parlor, where the high tea ritual took place. It was fall again, and the tea was in harmony with the season.

Nora watched the leaves fall with a nostalgia after the summer gone by. There was a lively chatter ringing through the hallways and lobbies at the Bel.

Doris was pouring tea in the beautiful fragile hand-painted porcelain cups.

"Darjeeling or Earl Grey," she asked Nora.

Doris was always the perfect "tearista" for the Sunday afternoon high tea ritual. Before the tea, they prayed for the end of war in Europe and the success of the 100 Days Campaign and for Mathilda to get well.

That afternoon, Doc appeared in the French doors leading to the parlor. He was stalling a bit, as he gave his hat to the butler.

"Are we allowed to come in?" he asked smiling. "I have a friend with me. Can he come in to?"

The girls looked up as Doris walked over to greet Doc. Nora was surprised that someone had the guts to break the Sunday ritual. She looked toward the French door. And there was Harry standing by Doc's side with a big smile, holding his hat.

Nora got up and ran to him. The two hugged forever to the shock of the girls.

"Oh, this is better than a romance movie from the Empress Theater," one girl cried. "I wish this happens to me too."

Chef Josiah was standing in the back with Mr. Spencer, and the town folk. Nora was blushing and holding tight onto Harry, while Doris stepped back to blend in with the folks.

"Thank you, Doris," Nora said. "You are a true friend and you know how to keep a secret."

"Look outside the window, my love," said Harry gently leading Nora to the large windows.

"You didn't, Harry," Nora cried.

"I did for you, my love," Harry said.

The folks ran out the Bel to admire Harry and Nora's brand-new Ford Model T automobile. The car had a swag on the front.

"I will always love you, Nora."

A few months later, the new Ford Model-Ts automobiles flocked to the Hotel Belding for Harry's and Nora's wedding in the Rose Ballroom. John

played with the “Belding Boys” on his trumpet a lonely tune.
The Catawba Sanatorium took in another soul.

40 Hunks

The old dilapidated grey bus was jumping up and down on its rickety wheels on the dirt road. It was dragging a partially ripped bumper. The shaking motion was making the driver in his black cap sick. He should have gotten used to it by now. It was the same route, he had taken over the last five years. He praised the dry route through the Sonoran Desert because the driver’s job gave him enough money to feed his family back home in Quiriego.
The passengers were quiet after almost 30 hours on the bumpy road. He could hear the snoring behind him. The arid land around was occasionally disrupted by a shrub. In the best case, a vulture would scavenger on a dead rat or a snake. The heat outside climbed over 115 Fahrenheit as Jose turned up the music. Since there were no radio stations around, Jose always made sure he had his cassette player with him, lots of water, crackers and several red fuel containers. He bought the cheap red containers in the US during one of his many trips.
They were crossing the Sonoran Desert west of Nogales. Jose felt the pocket of his jeans for a piece of paper. He pulled it out to look at it for the 100th time as they were nearing the border.

It was the letter from the US Department of Agriculture giving him permission to cross the border to the US with the 40 men sleeping behind his back. Before they boarded the bus, Jose had to make sure they were the right men. Most of them didn't have any IDs, so he trusted them and tried to match up the names with the list from the government.

The list wasn't exact, but Jose knew once they entered the US territory, they would be assigned a permanent work guide. From there on, it was none of his business what would happen with these men. The guides were correction officers borrowed from the regional correctional facilities in the US.

The border patrol in Nogales searched the smelly bus and studied Jose's driver's license and the piece of paper.

"How do you know who's who?" barked a sweating guard with an AK47 across his shoulder, at Jose.

"Vaguely. I know that I have 40 men," said Jose also sweating.

The guard boarded the bus and walked in the aisle examining each face, holding the piece of governmental paper in his hand. He stopped and looked closely at one man. The men were wide awake now. He leaned over the hulky man taking in his odor.

"Who are you?" he asked with his face distorted in an evil grimace.

Jose walked up to the two men in the back of the bus.

"Hey, amigo," he said to the guard. "They don't speak English."

The guard shoved the piece of paper with the list of names in front of the hulky man ignoring Jose.

"Show me, which one are you?" he ordered strictly breathing down the hulky man's neck.
"Amigo, they can't read either," said Jose. "I'll show you which one he is. Give me back my paper."
But the guard hid the hand with the paper behind has back and grabbed onto his AK47.
"Look at him, and tell me who is he," the guard insisted. "You don't need the paper."
Jose was scared.
"Does this gringo asshole know who this man is?" Jose thought to himself.
"Put down the gun," said Jose looking back and forth at the hulky man and the guard.
The hulky man looked up at Jose with a serious face smoothing the pocket, where he kept his knife. Back in Quiriego, when the bus was loading, the hulky man came up and asked if he could get a ride showing Jose his knife. That was an extra man unaccounted for on that governmental piece of paper. And this was a big man, who must have been in trouble with the law.
Out of the boarding crowd, Jose picked a smaller guy and pushed him aside.
"You're going to stay home, and I'll take you on the next ride," Jose said. "What's your name?"
"Antonio," the small guy said fearfully as he stepped back.
Jose motioned the hulky man to approach him.
"From now on, you're Antonio, and remember you owe me for this," said Jose. "When we get to the US, you're going to pay or I will talk to gringo."

Jose was standing over the hulky ripped man who gave him another stare with his hand on the pocket with the knife.
"Stand up, Antonio," Jose challenged him. "The gringo wants to look at you."
Antonio stood up in his entire bulky stature hovering over the other men."
The guard looked at both men, turned around and marched out of the bus and waved his hand for the bus to proceed to the customs for search.
The men had nothing to claim other than their body odor.
"This smells like shit," said the customs officer searching the bus. "Open that box down there."
Jose opened the bottom part of the body of the bus next to the rear wheels. The heat was pounding on Jose's neck. Inside the storage bin were just his red fuel containers, old clothes for the road to change and a water cannister.
"Where are you going with them?" asked the customs officer.
"Michigan," said Jose rubbing his neck. "The men will work there in the fields and orchards for a few bucks. They're cheap labor for you; your folk won't do their work."
"Don't get smart on me," said the officer. "You can go now. When are you bringing them back?"
Jose shrugged his shoulders staring into the sun and then into the officer's aviators.
"When the season's over," he said.
On the US side, a gringo work guide was awaiting them. He had a USDA tag on his brown uniform. He

climbed on the bus, and pulled out a folding seat close to Jose. He was carrying a big black duffle back with him. Jose extended his hand to the gringo work guide, who poorly masked his fear of the 40 men.
"I am Jose, you?" he said.
The work guide didn't respond and turned his head away from Jose. He got immediately on the phone with the central farm.
"We're heading out," he said. "I need to count the heads. There's supposed to be 40 men aboard. I need to count them to make sure I don't have 50. We already looked in the storage; just fuel containers, no extra men."
Jose ignored the guide who walked to the back of the bus counting the men.
Antonio got up as the guide approached the back of the bus. His shirt was ripped in the back and he had leather bracelets on his wrists. He grabbed the handle bars below the ceiling of the bus, and swayed in front of the work guide.
"How may I help you, gringo?" said Antonio in broken English. "How many times are you going to count us? There are 40 men on this bus. That doesn't include you and the driver. I want to keep it that way until we get there."
Antonio looked at the work guide and ripped off his name tag and threw it on the floor.
"There you go," he laughed. "You're nobody. You white piece of shit. Remember that."
Antonio fell back heavily on the torn seat with white fuzz coming out. He pulled some of the fuzz out of the seat.

"I'll stick this into your mouth, if you don't stay quiet," threatened Antonio.

The guide returned to the front of the bus by Jose, who was now whistling to a tune on his cassette player.

"Man, you got a rough crowd here," said the guide. "Who is that big dude?"

"Nobody, just like the rest of them," said Jose. "Leave me and them alone. I need some rest."

Jose pulled the bus to a stop at an Indian gas station in the Mohave reservation.

"Out everyone, we're taking a break," said Jose. "We're going to be driving all night long. I need a break. Here, guide Mike will be watching you. Don't try anything on him. He's armed and dangerous, like all gringos. Stay here, and you're not going to get hurt. I have to fill her up too."

When the men left the bus, Jose locked it up.

"I don't want anyone doing anything crazy, understand?" said Mike to the men stretching their limbs.

Jose pulled in at this Indian gas station on purpose; he knew the men had no place to run in the Mojave Desert.

"You got smokes, man," asked one of the men.

Mike was scared, now that he saw Jose leave him just with the Mexican men.

"I'll give you smokes, but you're going to leave me alone or else," he said showing the Mexican his gun. "Here, have some."

He gave them two packs of Marlboro cigarettes per instructions from the central farm.

"Don't screw around with those men," said the producer. "Remember, I want them alive here; they have to work. Don't start any fights."

Guide Mike regretted taking this job over the cushy deal at the correctional facility. He got paid more here, but the scare from the Mexican men was real. He stepped back watching over the men, as he spoke to his wife on the phone.

"You know, Laura," he said. "I don't know if this was such a great idea."

The men were pacing around the reserve gas station and smoking. One of them asked Mike if he could go inside the station. Mike who kept talking with his wife just waved his hand to signal that's okay to go in.

"You get more money, Mike," she said. "We need the money."

Mike lit up his own cigarette to fight his own fear. He's going to have to be with these men for their entire stay in Michigan.

"You can't leave them for a minute," producer Harry warned him during the interview at the beginning of the year. "You're going to have to go out into the fields with them."

The new directions from the US Department of Agriculture were clear and strict.

"Forty men in, forty men out per batch," the directive stated. "No more, no less."

Mike thought, the corrections facility with a fence was bad, but this was worse; the men were loose. Was he supposed to count them like sheep?

In the meantime, Jose filled the bus up and walked inside the gas station to get him some snacks and coffee.
The Navajo girl greeted Jose. She preferred Mexicans over the white man.
"You're back Jose," Avlen smiled. "It's another season up north, right?"
Jose walked to the counter and leaned over it, looking at the girl. Avlen was the oasis in the desert and a reprieve from the load of dirty men he was carrying. Over the years, she hasn't changed much. Avlen still had long black hair flowing over her shoulders.
"I am glad you always stop over here," Avlen said.
"There's nowhere else to go with those 40 men," he said. "I have to guard them, like they're mine."
"You have that gringo to help you," she smiled.
"He does, but he is afraid of them." Jose said.
"Who's that big guy?" Avlen asked looking outside the window on the porch.
Antonio, leaning over a post, was smoking.
"You didn't have him last year?" she smiled at Jose.
"You're right I didn't and he shouldn't have been here this year either," he said downing his coke and spitting on the floor. "He's nothing but trouble."
"Can you stay for a bit?" Avlen raised her head and looked Jose directly in the eyes.
"Not, now," he said. "They have to be on the farm as soon as Friday."
Antonio walked inside the gas station store looking around the shelves.
"You got booze," he asked the scared girl.

Jose straightened up from the counter and looked at Antonio.

"No, booze on the bus," he said strictly. "When we get there, you can talk to the producer. Not here. We're heading out."

Antonio grabbed Jose by his shirt and tore it apart as he lifted Jose up on his feet and dragged him against the counter.

"I said, I want some booze," Antonio pulled out his knife and put it to Jose's throat. "You girl give me some whiskey or I will slash his neck."

Avlen quickly grabbed a bottle from behind her and handed it to Antonio, who opened it and drank from it, still holding Jose.

"That's $20," Avlen said to Antonio.

Antonio let Jose loose and turned him to Avlen like a puppet.

"You pay her," he said. "I am going back on the bus."

Jose gave Avlen $20 shaking his head.

"Don't call the police," Jose begged. "I'd get in trouble that I let him loose."

He waved to the girl and left the gas station store. Mike was smoking nearby shaking his head.

"I saw what happened," he said. "Do you want me to call the police?"

Jose shook his head as he boarded the bus.

"No, I want us to get to the farm as fast as possible," he said. "You deal with him at the farm with the producer. I don't want to have anything to do with him. If he disappears, I won't look for him."

The central farm was waiting for the cheap labor transport from Mexico. The apple trees needed pruning, and there was still snow on the ground in what seemed to have been a never- ending winter.
The men didn't even have coats or boots. Most of them have never seen snow before. They had been complaining of being cold on the bus, that had no heating.
"We're going to be there soon," said Jose.
The hunk got up and walked to Jose and touched his shoulder. He spoke in Spanish so the guide wouldn't understand them. He was hovering in his 6'5" height and 250 pounds over Jose in his driver's seat.
"Hombre, I want you to drop me off somewhere before we get to the farm," he said.
Jose was watching him in the rearview mirror; his big chest with twitching muscles. His ripped sleeve was hanging over his right biceps. Antonio slid his big hand over his right pocket where he kept the knife.
"You drop me off before we get there, understand Hombre?" he tightened his grip on Jose's shoulder.
Mike spoke lousy Spanish and understood only Hombre from the entire conversation between the driver and the hulk. The correctional facility didn't pay for Mike to take Spanish classes. He knew only what he had picked up from the cons.
Jose kept his eyes on the road as he felt the tightening grip.
"I will drop you off in the next village," said Jose in Spanish. "We will stop for a bathroom break and you will disappear."

Big Antonio grabbed a guy from the front seat and motioned him to take his place in the back.

The bus pulled into a gas station in the Northwoods area close to nowhere.

"Everyone take a break," said Jose. "You too Mike. Go and buy yourself pop for the road."

Jose pushed Mike out of the bus and saw the other men to the dilapidated gas station with the convenience store.

"You go, I don't want to see you again," he said to Antonio.

Big Antonio flashed his eyes on Jose, and showed him the shining blade of the knife.

"I want money to go," he barked. "You say a word; I'll find you and kill you."

Jose gave Antonio $100 and kept the other $100 for himself.

"Is that all you have, you pig?" he said.

"You leave or I am calling Mike," said Jose. "I have a gun in the bus. Go."

Jose watched Antonio run off behind the dilapidated building and off into a nearby park. He had no jacket, and it was snowing up north.

Jose felt relieved that the hulky bastard had left. He was almost sure he had seen the hulk's photos on a "Wanted" poster around Quiriego in Mexico.

The men piled back in the bus with Mike as the last one boarding. He took the seat next to Jose and searched his face for an explanation.

"Where's the big guy?" he asked Jose.

Jose started the rattling motor on the bus. The bus jerked forward to a deafening noise; Jose was hoping

they were going to make it to the central farm. After a few jumps the bus continued on the county road. Jose looked down at Mike seated on the small folding seat next to him. Mike was playing with his phone.
"Do you want me to call the central farm?" asked Mike.
"Hell, no. You call the farm and I'll throw you off the bus," said Jose. "No one will ever find you out here in the boondocks."
"You're bluffing," said Mike.
Jose stopped the bus on the road side. He stood up facing the passengers and shouted in Spanish.
"Should I throw this gringo off into the woods?" he asked the men.
There was some shuffling of the stinking bodies, now chilled down with the northern cold, and 3,000 miles of shaking on the bumpy roads. Jose grabbed Mike by his jacket and pulled him up to stand in front of him.
"I repeat; should I throw this piece of white shit into the woods?" Jose asked again.
Mike dropped down on his knees and pleaded for his life.
"No, save me," he handed the phone to Jose. "You can have the phone. I am not calling anyone. Just don't leave me here to die."
Jose took the phone from Mike and pushed him back on the folding seat.
"You stay put with your mouth shut," Jose slugged him. "And pray for your life."
Jose opened the storage bin and got his handgun out.
"See, I have a gun too," Jose said. "And I know how to use it."

A silence settled in the bus, as Jose started the rattling motor again, and the bus headed out deeper into the woods of the state game area.

“We have an emergency,” yelled Father Ralph into his phone.
“What’s the emergency,” asked Julio sheepishly working in his shop on a tractor.
“Forty men are coming our way,” he said. “They’re locked up in a bus without shoes or coats. They’re transporting them to the central farm.”
Julio stopped working on the tractor.
“Slow down, Father,” he said. “Tell me again what’s going on? They’re bringing 40 pigs into the farm? That can’t be right; the farm has no animals, just apple trees.”
Father Ralph blushed in anger over his poor English and raised his high-pitched voice.
“I didn’t say anything about pigs,” he yelled. “40 men are coming from Mexico locked up on a bus without coats or shoes. I need help, Julio.”
Julio knew what this was like; living like an animal and hiding from the US authorities. Long time ago he stayed illegally with his family in the country picking apples on a farm. The farmer helped him get his permanent permit to stay. It took years before Julio could walk without fear into a store or a church. He was still afraid of the phone ringing.
“I am coming over,” Father Ralph slammed the phone.

He drove to Julio's humble home on the outskirts of the small Midwest town of Peoria surrounded by cornfields and farms.

Julio opened the door carefully and then let Father Ralph in. Huddled in his coat, Father Ralph repeated the story about 40 men without coats aboard a rattling bus on their way to the central farm.

It was a freezing early spring, and the winter had taken its toll on nature and on people. Coming from the southern warmth, neither one of them, have ever gotten used to the harsh climate around the 45th parallel.

"We'll have to organize an emergency drive for the men," said Julio back on his constant state of alert. "Otherwise the men will freeze here, and they won't be of any help. I'll spread the word, and you do the same."

The men arrived the next morning on the frozen central farm shaking with cold, thirst and hunger. They only knew the heat coming from the Sonoran Desert along with the "dust devils." The producer showed them into the large barn with half-empty storage crates with Evercrisp apples. It was cold in the barn too. The producer known to friends as Harry was saving money on everything from heat to labor cost.

Jose watched the process along with work guide Mike carefully.

"We were expecting 40 men," said Harry looking at the government list with names. He noticed one name was crossed off. "You know the drill; 40 men in, 40 men out at the end of the season. No tricks or I will get in trouble with the government."

Holding tight onto Mike's shoulder, Jose immediately responded.

"Antonio couldn't make it, he stayed at home sick," said Jose looking directly at Mike.

Producer Harry looked at the work guide shaking in his brown work uniform.

"Where is the 40th man?" he asked Mike holding onto the list. "Antonio, right? Where is he?"

Mike straightened up under Jose's pressure on his shoulder. Jose pressed the gun in his pocket against Mike's thigh hard, so Mike could feel the barrel of the gun digging into his body.

"We only had 39 at the border in Nogales," Mike said with a shaky voice. "There was no 40th man. I counted them personally."

Harry looked at the former corrections officer, his new work guide.

Mike was shaking under the barrel of a gun that was pressing into his pants and the lyrics from the song "Barrel of a Gun" that played on the bus that sleepless night kept ringing in his ears:

"Do you mean this horny creep, Set upon weary feet, In need of sleep, That doesn't come?

Mike nervously shuffled his feet; he felt cold sweat dripping down his back on the cold barrel of Jose's gun.

"You will make sure that no man disappears from my farm," Harry said. "You will watch them like your own kids with your own life."

Mike backed off and sat down on an empty apple crate. When he signed up for this deal, the government didn't tell him what he was getting into. He figured nothing can be worse than watching cons at the correctional facility.

"We need coats and shoes for the men," ordered Harry into the phone to Father Ralph.

Jose, tired after the 30- hour bus drive, turned around to leave the cold barn. He waved to the men, who looked desperate and cold. Jose gave them two $20 bills to divide among themselves.

"I'll see you in October," he said. "Be good, amigos."

Harry offered him coffee from the big coffee pot set up on the table in the back of the barn. The farmer's wife bought donuts by the dozens on sale from the nearest store. They weren't fresh, but they were food.

"Are they going to be okay, Harry?" asked Jose sipping his coffee.

Producer Harry was a tough man, a fourth-generation farmer hardened by work in the fields from early morning into late night hours. The family owned more than 1,000 acres of fields and apple orchards.

"Yes, they'll be okay. Except I don't like this new thing with the work guard. It's like in a Nazi work camp. We're in America."

The new regulations coming from the government required the work guard to protect America against the influx of the illegal immigration from Mexico, Central and South America streaming into the country by thousands.

Jose finished his coffee and took a donut on the long road back home to Mexico.

Harry loaded the men on a wagon and took them to their quarters at the Three Bees Orchards in the middle of the apple trees with a large storage shed. The orchards were protected by a wire fence from the deer.

The new labor order reminded Harry again of the Nazi work camps; the wall at the Mexican border, and now this work guide in the brown uniform was more like forced labor.

He turned to work guard Mike.

"I am sorry about that harsh greeting back in the apple barn," Harry said. "I just didn't expect you. At least not so soon."

Mike shrugged his shoulders as he sipped on his coffee and started to unpack his large duffle bag.

"I'll be sleeping with the men?" he asked Harry.

"Well, you have to watch them, day and night," said Harry. "You get paid for that by the government. I don't have another place to put you in."

Mike recalled the interview.

"You will be with the men all the time," the interviewer said. "Once you take them over at the Mexican border. They will be your responsibility, not the farmer's. You remember that. You're getting a good pay for this. Keep that in mind."

Back at the correctional facility, at least he didn't have to sleep with the cons. He didn't eat with them, either.

Harry handed him back his phone from Jose.

"Here's your phone back," he said. "Call me, not the police, if you have any problems. Remember, don't call the police. I am the police on my farm. I don't want to see anymore uniforms here."

They all slept in a large pole barn with cold draft coming from the outside. The morning woke them up in their bunk beds with the farmer's wife bringing in hot pots of coffee.

They walked outside, where Father Ralph and Julio were waiting for them by the big green church van.

"Grab a coat and boots," Julio said in Spanish. "Hurry you're going out into the orchards."

The men, regardless their size, picked anything that could remotely fit in the freezing March morning of a new day.

Mike was standing by the van in his new work coat, his wife bought for him, along with the boots. He was feeling somewhat guilty as he watched the men fight over a better pair of boots or a coat that wasn't torn. He pulled his hat over his ears, as they headed out on a wagon into the vast orchards.

The drive past the creepy orchards with bare black and gray limbs was endless. The old two-track road had deep holes were the water was frozen. The frozen water puddles gave Mike the shivers again when he noticed some rotted apples got trapped in the puddles and frozen over.

It was just like that Mexican hell that bred these men, he was supposed to watch for government money. They finally reached the end of the road and the beginning of the work area with ladders, saws and axes.

The first day in the orchards was one of the longest days in Mike's life. Although, he didn't have to work, he had to keep warm by moving around. Sometimes, a Mexican worker, would ask him to hand a tool. He did it to stay warm. The other thing was that he didn't understand the men speaking Spanish.
"Are you talking about me?" he barked at a duo working together late in the afternoon.
Of course, they didn't understand him, so they went on chatting and working. He grabbed his thermos from the wagon. He poured himself a generous cup and spiked the coffee with a splash of bourbon from the flask. Mike looked at his watch; one more hour and they're done.
Tomorrow, he was taking the men to the nearby catholic church and to the store, so they could stock up on supplies. Producer Harry gave all of them a miserable advance, so they wouldn't eat from his table.

The church in Peoria was bigger than anything else; the men were seated in the back, as Father Ralph gave them a blessing for the season. The church bus took them to the store well-stocked for campers.
"Don't let them buy a lot of booze, or I won't be able to get them out into the fields," warned Harry. "Just enough to get by."

The store clerk eyed Mike closely. Her dad owned the only store in a radius of 20 miles.

"You brought in another batch from Mexico?" she said.

The clerk spoke about the men like she talked about bulk food stocked in the back.

Mike looked at the woman, who knew what hard work was.

"You got yourself a cushy deal watching Harry's men," she said grimly. "I wish I could do something like that."

Mike wished he could slap the woman behind the counter.

"They're not Harry's men," he corrected the woman. "They're Mexicans."

"Hell, I know who they are," she said turning red. "What difference does it make?"

Mike could tell that the village of Peoria was used to having the Mexicans around.

"They work and buy your food, right?" said Mike turning around the leave.

The men with bags of food boarded the church bus to the farm. Julio left a TV for them in the main quarters, that served for sleeping, for eating and entertainment all at once.

A full hard week was ahead of them. The men sorted through their new torn belongings fighting over a better piece of clothing without holes. They ignored Mike, who crawled into his corner. He stretched on his bed listening to the Spanish discussion.

"At least they're not plotting like the cons at the facility," he thought.

But then again, he really did not know that because his Spanish wasn't good.

Jose was singing a tune as he drove back home through the Indian Navajo reservation. He was planning to stop by to say hi to Avlen at the gas station in Coconino. Jose pulled into a screeching stop. He lit up a cigarette and walked inside the convenience store. Instead of Avlen, a guy was behind the counter.

"Where is Avlen?" he asked the young Indian.

"She left for to work elsewhere," he said.

"To do what?" Jose was surprised. "I just wanted to say hi to her."

"She's a guide somewhere in the Canyon now," the guy said. "She got scared. A large man was threatening her."

Jose had a deep suspicion.

"What did the man look like?" he asked.

"He was a big man with big muscles," said the Indian. "He liked Avlen and kept coming back. She hated him and ran away from him."

"What happened with the big man?" asked Jose.

In spite of the desert heat, Jose froze as someone grabbed him by the shoulder, and turned him around. Jose was facing Antonio towering above him in his 6'5" height.

"So, you're back you skunk," Antonio said. "You have a wife back in Quiriego. What do you want with Avlen?"

Jose twisted out of Antonio's grip disgusted with the huge man who had the same smell on him like when he dropped him off.

"Why the hell did you come back here to the desert?" Jose challenged the hulky man.

Antonio looked down at Jose.

"Why did you come back, you married skunk," he said. "I like Avlen, like you do. Only I am not married."

The Indian was watching the two men who started to fight. Jose hit Antonio in the stomach, and Antonio smashed him back in his face. Antonio kept kicking Jose who curled up by the cooler. Antonio kicked the cooler, and all the cold pop fell out of it. Antonio opened a can and poured it all over Jose's face.

"You be happy, it's not gas," said Antonio turning around to run. "Next, time I'll set you on fire and this place too."

Jose picked himself up off the wooden floor. He was all sticky from the spilled pop.

"You want me to call the cops?" the Indian asked fearfully.

"Like which ones?" said Jose. "We're in your land. Just forget it. I am going home."

Jose walked out to the bus to find the tires slashed.

"That damn, SOB," he said. "I am going to hitch a ride home. I'll be back in the fall."

Jose gave the Indian the remaining $50 and decided to leave the bus behind to have it fixed.

It was high summer in the Midwest orchards. The heat was cracking the dry earth open, and it was hurting the trunks of the old apple trees. The heat was different than in the Sonora. There were no "dust devils", but the humidity from Lake Michigan was hanging in the air.

"If I sweat anymore, I am going to die," said Mike to his wife.

Lately, he was calling her less and less. It was close to the busiest time of the year; apples needed to be harvested fast because of the dangerous heat.

They already took few Mexican men to the hospital for heat exhaustion, and one fell of the ladder.

"No more injured men," Harry yelled at Mike. "You are responsible for them: healthy or sick, dead or alive. I need them alive and well picking apples before they return home."

After the rough spring, came even a rougher summer. It was hot in the storage barn where they slept with apples and flies. One night, Mike felt a Mexican man creeping over his sleeping body and sliding his hand in his pants.

"Get off of me, you Mexican creep," said Mike fully awake from the horror of being raped by a smelly Mexican from Quiriego.

He called Harry in the morning about the incident.

Producer Harry entered the large barn that smelled of dirty sweaty men, who were working on his apples. They were just eating breakfast getting ready to go into the orchards. The tall and tan producer with dark

hair and a mustache commanded respect among the men, unlike Mike or Mikey, as the men called him.
"What's going on," he looked at scared Mikey.
The men stopped sipping coffee and watched the two gringos intensely.
"One of them tried to rape me last night," cried Mikey looking at the men.
Harry, a conservative fourth generation farmer, with six kids and old values, hated homosexuality as a vice which belonged to the weaker. He froze when Mikey informed him about the rape.
The men ranged in age from 17 to 40; they were all tanned with dark hair, well-built from the hard work in the orchards. Some were faithful to their women back in Mexico, while others entertained themselves at the adult movie theater by the freeway.
"Show me who tried to rape you," said Harry angrily standing in the middle of the barn.
Mike walked to the man sitting on a bench drinking his coffee. He pulled him up by the collar of his dirty t-shirt. The man was not afraid. He stood up and faced Mike.
"He's lying," he said.
Harry looked at the two men standing in the middle of the barn. He realized they were wasting precious time.
"Speak up, amigos," Harry encouraged. "Is he a faggot?"
A strange silence settled in the heat of the barn. Harry took off the belt from his pants and walked to the Mexican. He pushed him against the wall.

"Take off your shirt, you dirty bastard," Harry said. "I am going to beat it out of you, until you straighten up."

The men could hear in the silence of the morning, the leather swish against the man's tanned and sweaty skin. Somewhere, a horse, whinnied into the heat of the morning.

"I'll show you Mexican bastard," Harry was all red and exhausted, as he finally stopped. "You're not going to get paid for today."

They headed out on the wagon into the orchards, speechless about what they had just witnessed; a gringo man beating up a homosexual horny Mexican.

In the afternoon, the Mexican men grouped up and beat up Mike and let him lay under an old apple tree amidst fallen rotted apples unconscious. Mike missed the ride to the barn and woke up under the full moon in the middle of the night. He walked back to the big barn. The men were breathing heavily after a long hot day at the orchards.

Mike quickly packed up his duffle bag and left the farm walking on the county road. In the morning, a trucker picked him up.

"Where you going man?" the trucker asked. "You look like a wreck."

"I am going home," Mike said sweating. "Drop me off in the nearest town."

The nearest town was 100 miles away. The trucker offered Mike coffee.

"You sure, you don't want to go further?" he asked Mike again.

"I am sure," Mike said. "Leave me here."

At the rest stop, Mike threw away his brown work uniform and changed into jeans and shirt. He watched the truck leave out of the rest stop, and he let his cell phone ring.
Later, Harry walked into the barn and watched the men get ready for work.
"Where is Mike?" he asked the men.
Nobody knew where the man in the brown uniform was.
"Darn, the fricking government with their rules and guides," Harry said.
"Let's get out there and finish the job."
Harry didn't question the men about Mike's disappearance anymore. They remained tight lipped about the beating in the orchards and the barn.

Jose picked the men up in late October, as the air was beginning to chill and the early frost was settling on the branches. He was bringing back across the border 39 men instead of 40.
"Where's the 40th man," a border officer near Ciudad Juarez questioned as he stared into the governmental list of names.
"I counted them, you only have 39 men," the officer barked at Jose.
Jose gave the tired gringo officer a hard look and felt for his handgun in the pocket of his pants.
This man knew nothing of the hardship of the 39 men aboard going back to the Mexican hell in Quiriego. The officer knew nothing about what had happened at the apple farm or with the farmer in Peoria.

"Where's the guide? You damn SOB," yelled the border officer at Jose.

"Leave, I have a long way to go," Jose stood up, pulled the gun and pushed the border officer out of the bus.

The officer backed off. He knew better; one guide or a Mexican man more or less didn't matter.

Jose turned up the cassette player with "Barrel of a Gun" playing.

"Do you mean this horny creep, Set upon weary feet, In need of sleep, That doesn't come?......"

He was dreaming of Avlen working somewhere by the Canyon. He was hoping Antonio had never found her.

Thirty-nine men with some pocket change remained on the bumpy bus heading back to Mexican hell.

The Writer, the Nun and the Gardener

Zita touched her left cheek and ran her finger on a newly-formed pimple overnight. It will soon flare into a nasty red bump that may get infected. She smoothed her jean skirt tightly hugging her thighs covered by floral tights. Her straight brown hair was long. She always sat by the windows in any class to tame her phobias. She looked outside the window at the falling leaves. The harsh winter would come soon, and as always, she wasn't prepared for it.

Teacher Mr. Bob Kotias was going over it again; the reproductive organs and sexual functionalities or dysfunctionalities. She had just turned down a date, and Mr. Kotias was having too much fun with his sex education.

The only reason Zita took the class was her mother Dona, who insisted on it.

"You will soon be dating, you need to know some things about your body," Dona said.

"But, why can't you explain it to me?" asked Zita at the suburban home in Green Heights.

When Kurt asked her out again, Zita snapped, "I am not dating yet. I am not ready."

Kurt didn't live far from her in the middle-class neighborhood. When they were kids, they played together, since she was the only child in the family.

"Go and play with Kurt," Dona said.

Kurt, too, had pimples and a lot of them. He had dirty blond hair, straight nose and blue eyes. He was tall and well-built, so he was on the football team.

In the boredom of winter, Kurt asked Zita out to go to the movies. This time, Zita couldn't resist as the days were getting shorter and shorter; she had read all the books she could.

It was busy inside the movie theater. Most people were suffering from the lack of sun like Zita was. Kurt bought popcorn and looked at her pretty figure with pleasure.

"I can buy some chocolate too, if you want me to," he said tempting her.

"Yeah, right, you want me to be fat or what?" Zita snapped.

Ever since her hormones kicked in, Zita had trouble with weight. The constant dieting cycled with overeating.

"We can run around the hood together," he said.

The thought of running around the neighborhood in Green Heights startled her. The people loved to gossip about each others' diseases and faulty relationships; who had sex with whom and let's not forget that dry drunk next door, who beats his wife.

"You want to stir the gossip soup, ha?" she laughed.

"It will be good for your figure," Kurt said as he leaned toward Zita and put his arm around her shoulders.

They entered the darkened cinema and sat in the back row watching the loud previews, eating the popcorn. Zita had popcorn all over her and her fingers were salty and cheesy.

When Kurt touched her, she felt a strange sensation in her skin. He took her buttery cheesy finger and licked it. He kissed her from her right ear to her cheek and to her lips. Zita didn't resist. She gave in to the sweet warm sensations inside her body.

Neither one of them knew what the movie was about. They didn't need to. They had their bodies to discover.

"How was the movie?" mom Dona asked.

"Perfect."

Kurt was in Zita's sex education class and sat in the back with the other guys.

"How was Zita, Kurt?" they picked on him.

"Nothing, happened," he laughed. "We just went to the movies."
"You mean, you didn't get laid?" the guys laughed.
"It was our first date," Kurt was offended.
"So, what, how long are you going to wait?"
Kurt turned away annoyed and opened his tablet to stare into the drawings of reproductive organs.
Teacher Mr. Kotias was explaining all the possibilities of human reproduction without consequences. Finally, the guys started to pay attention, while Zita was looking out the window. The maple and oak trees were almost bare now with black trunks and branches. The trees were wet from the drizzling rain. The teacher brought her back to attention.
"You really shouldn't have sex without a condom," he encouraged. "I never did that, and so I never got into trouble. You can get them anywhere, even at your local grocery store."
"How much are they?" Kurt asked. "I am on a budget."
The class burst into laughter.
"A lot less than not having one and getting your girlfriend pregnant," said Bob.
"What if I am careful?" Kurt continued to the smirking of the class.
Zita turned around and looked at Kurt.
"You know what, can you just take this somewhere else," she said.
"No, let him be," said Bob. "This is the type of dialogue we should be having."

"You really need a condom if you're planning to have sex," Bob said.
"Ok, chief, you got it," Kurt said.

They went running together on a Saturday morning around the hood not caring about the neighbor talk. It was cold and close to the holidays. People were heading out to malls to participate in the "shopping wars" between the local retailers.
"You going shopping?" Kurt asked.
"I hate shopping," she said.
They stopped briefly to catch their breath. Both rubbed their knees and legs.
"You want to do a 5K run? I'll take you to a campus that I know of," Kurt offered.
Zita was pleasantly surprised the offer wasn't to see another movie and eat more popcorn. She had to watch her weight before the holidays.
"I would love that, when is it?" she asked.
"I'll pick you up next week," he said. "We have to drive there, it's out in the country."

Dona watched Zita get ready for the 5k run in the evening. The house smelled of chili and fresh baked bread. Everything was where it should be. They all ate dinner in the well-lit dining room together discussing Zita's first 5K run.
"I am really excited for you, Zita," dad said. "You're finally coming out of your shell. You'll lose weight and you will socialize. It's a good cause. Are you going with Kurt?"

Not only did dad know about the run from the local paper, but he already knew about Kurt.
"It's a fundraiser for autism program at the Dominican nuns," said dad. "You're going to love it. Was that Kurt's idea?"
Dad poured himself and mom some pink wine.
Zita's cheeks turned the color of the wine. The fire in the fireplace was making her hot.
"Yes, it was. I had no idea that nuns organized runs," Zita said all embarrassed.
"Smart guy, that Kurt," dad acknowledged. "And you're a poet, you made that rhyme."

It was a crispy morning. Zita watched the countryside from her passenger side window. The long alley took them to the secluded campus. As they pulled into the campus, Zita realized she would never find her way back home from this labyrinth of dirt roads, pathways and fields.
The starting point for the run was by the cornfields.
They headed out together past the trail markers like deer tracks, cherry trees, birdhouses and onto the open meadows. On their run, they spotted deer and rabbits.
They stopped by the picnic table to take in the view of the autumn rolling on the hills and valleys and listened to the brook.
"I will always remember this," said Zita, "thank you for taking me out here. I would have never found this on my own. How did you find it?"
Kurt looked directly into Zita's eyes.

"It's my hiding place, and I wanted to share it with you," he said.

The peace was inspiring and touching both of them.

"You're not afraid that the hood will find out," Zita asked as she reached for Kurt's hand.

Kurt kissed her hand and put it on his chest close to his heart. Zita could feel his heart beating fast. Was it from the run or the excitement of being together?

They sat on the picnic bench and kissed for what seemed like eternity. Kurt touched her breasts, but Zita stopped him. They had to finish the run.

Back at the main camp, the Mother of the order, welcomed them with warm bread and tea.

"I am Mother Karla. Thank you for participating, eat with us," she beckoned. "How did you find out about us?"

The round cafeteria with big windows overlooked the well-groomed gardens. It was full of runners, orchards and flower beds.

"I don't know, a friend mentioned this lovely place," Kurt said smiling. "We'll come back."

Zita admired the arts gallery with the atrium, waterfalls and ferns. She could smell incense coming from somewhere. The sisters, dressed in white, were moving around silently and humbly holding onto their rosaries.

She could hear the piano and the harp playing from the artists' studio. It was soothing and it spoke to her.

"What will you do with your life, my dear?" asked Mother Karla.

Zita was still undecided. She always thought that she had plenty of time to grow up. She was artistic, but constantly discouraged from the arts. Most kids at school have decided by now.

"I am still thinking about what I want to be when I grow up," she smiled. "And that's not a joke. I like a lot of things: arts, writing, movies and plays."

Mother Karla smiled:

"You remind me of myself long time ago," Karla said. "I still love all those things, only in a different way, in a more meaningful way closer and deeper."

The runners were leaving now rushing out of the solemn mystical space dominated by the Sisters.

"You're more than welcome to see all our galleries," said Karla. "Winter is a peaceful time here and the arts flourish."

The lonesome melody on the harp followed the two into the car and back home.

"Have you seen those two running together?" Wilsa asked her husband Bob.

The two were having Sunday night dinner at home preparing for a long work week ahead.

"Who are you talking about, Wilsa?" Bob asked annoyed by the sheer thought of work at school tomorrow and the upcoming discussion about neighbors' kids. He knew damn well who Wilsa was talking about.

"Well, honey, you should start paying more attention," she said. "The neighbor's boy Kurt has been hanging around my girlfriend's daughter, Zita."

Bob stretched lazily at the dinner table and searched for the remote.

“No, you’re not going to watch TV at dinner,” Wilsa snapped and banged the knife against the table. I want to have a discussion.”

Bob knew there was no way out of this without fighting, which he didn’t want to do. He decided to go along and fuel Wilsa’s gossip.

“So, what?” Bob smiled.” You hung around me too, until you got me. And now you have me forever. Maybe, that’s what the two of them want too.”

“Well, that’s not going to happen, because Kurt is going overseas to study,” Wilsa said wistfully. “They’ll never tie the knot. Distance separates lovers, not relationships.”

Bob wondered what did he really like about Wilsa. He’s been married to her for what seemed like forever. Evil thoughts distorted her pretty facial features into a grimace.

“It doesn’t matter that the parents don’t want the two together, they’ll find their own way, just like we did,” Bob said. “And by the way, Wilsa, it’s none of your business. Don’t you have to get ready for work? I do.”

“You’ve never told me that Kurt was in your sex class too,” Wilsa said.

“What difference does it make? Leave me alone tonight,” Bob said and left for his office.

The kids were wild after the weekend as Bob entered the classroom bustling with activity.

“Alright, let’s take it easy, kiddos,” Bob said. “We’re back to reproduction, evolution of human species and relationships. It kind of all goes together.”

Mr. Bob Kotias, sporting a brand- new Polo pullover sweater, walked in the aisles between the desks and returned to the front of the classroom to face the adolescents at their best.

"Does anyone have anything interesting to share that would fit our theme?" he looked at Kurt in the corner, and then at Zita by the window.

Nervous silence took over the classroom shocked by Bob's nosiness. The kids fidgeted and looked at each other.

"Okay, if no one wants to share we will write a paper about your sexual and human evolution over the weekend. The paper will be due next Monday."

Kurt got angry, upset about another thing to do. The football season was in full swing, and he didn't have time to sit and write papers.

"If I talk now, will you drop the paper assignment Mr. Kotias?" Kurt pleaded. "We have practice. You know I got to get a scholarship to go to college. Come on Mr. Kotias, can I talk?"

Bob smiled to himself; he used an old tactic on the kids that has always worked in the past. It was the paper scare. He knew the kids hated writing, and writing a paper with a sex theme was the worst kind of punishment.

"Go ahead."

"You all realize, I am doing this for the sake of all of us, so you can come to the football game instead of writing another paper," Kurt said.

"With my new girlfriend, we found there is a world beyond sex, even though we both can't stop thinking about it," Kurt said. "And I don't think abstinence from sex is healthy at our age. We have to express ourselves both emotionally and physically, otherwise

I wouldn't be playing football. I just wanted to get laid, but I didn't."

His face turned red, then pale and then red again, as he watched Zita's scared reaction.

"Maybe writing about it is better than talking about it after all," Kurt surrendered totally embarrassed in front of Zita and the rest of the gang. "I don't want to say anything else."

Bob looked at the class. He immediately realized wife's Wilsa's bad influence on him, and tried to correct that.

"I agree, the paper is a better route for all of us," Bob backed off. "It doesn't have to be long. You will exchange the papers sealed in envelopes with whomever you want and read them. You don't have to sign your names."

Monday came way too soon. Kurt volunteered to go first to get it over with. He opened the envelope. Chance had it that he got Zita's letter to read:

Even though, I want to get laid too, I also have a responsibility to myself and to my boyfriend. The fact of the matter is that I am afraid of sex or a relationship. I am also afraid of real life; you know the one where the parents fight over every shitty little thing at the dinner table before they go to bed. Mom because of her glamorous job at the City Magazine has not time for me or for dad.

Last weekend Kurt and I ran the 5k run at the Dominicans. Peace and serenity came over my heart and I realized I belonged there. Kurt is leaving for the university anyway and I don't want to struggle my

way through the community college just because it's cheap.
I will enter the order as soon as I can. That's all I have to say about human relationships and my evolution.

Kurt dropped the envelope all red and looked at Zita. He hovered over her angrily.
"What kind of bullshit is this?" he yelled and walked to Zita. "Are you out of your mind? We didn't even have sex, yet."
Zita stood up Facing Kurt.
"And you never will have sex with me," she said. "May I leave, Mr. Kotias."
She left the stunned class frozen in disbelief. Bob dropped into his chair behind the teacher's desk.
What have I done? he thought.
"Mr. Kotias, look what you've done with your experiments," Kurt said. "Look at the consequences of your sex tutoring."
Kurt left the class without asking for permission. In vain he searched for Zita, first in the hallways, then in the front yard and the parking lots. He realized; she was gone. She was gone forever.
Zita didn't answer the phone calls. She left the home phone ring, and she blocked the calls from Kurt on her cell phone. Zita arranged with the high school office to finish the year online. She would never set her foot in that classroom again.

"You know, Wilsa, I feel really guilty about what happened last month," said Bob. "I didn't want to talk about it then in front of you. But it has been bothering me. I have to talk to someone about it."

Wilsa was eager to hear what bothered her well-balanced husband. He had been walking around like a ghost.

"I broke a relationship without knowing about it," he said sadly.

"What? You?" Wilsa laughed. "Nah, you don't know how to do that. You're an honest man, Bob."

He told Wilsa the story with the papers about human relationships exchanged between the students.

"Zita would have never told him if it wasn't for my stupid paper assignment," Bob said.

Wilsa was taken aback. She could feel the pain he was going through. After all they were both Catholics, and they knew the full power of guilt.

"Bob, it would have happened anyways: their breaking up," she said.

"Yes, and I enabled it, so it happened in my class," Bob said. "I can't believe what I did."

"Well, maybe honey, you can go to confession," Wilsa said. "It will make you feel better."

"I didn't sin," he said. "I was just unknowingly meddling in other people's lives. You're the one who usually does that, not me."

"You're being sarcastic, that's not you either, Bob," Wilsa said. "You will get over it. Zita wouldn't have written that message, if she didn't want Kurt to know. She could have made up anything."

"But, she didn't. She was honest," he said.

"Well, she's going to be a nun; she had to be honest," said Wilsa. "Nuns don't lie."

Wilsa went over to Dona's house just two blocks away. She always enjoyed visiting with Dona. But now she had to go there.

"You want some coffee?" dainty Dona asked.

"I am not taking up your time, am I?" Wilsa acted polite.

"No, I just got done," Dona said pouring the coffee into two cups.

Wilsa looked around the house. Everything was in perfect order. Nothing displaced or misplaced. Paintings were carefully hung on the walls with the piano along the right side of the wall by the French door. Photographs in frames showed the happy family at different times in life. Wilsa liked the one where all three of them stood on a merry-go-round at the park on a hot summer day with the dolphin mister in the background sprinkling drops all over the three. Dona seemed always happy and ready to chat.

"So, what's new with you?" she asked Wilsa. "I haven't seen you in a while."

Wilsa sipped her coffee and looked directly at Dona.

"Dona do you know why Zita is taking online classes?" she asked.

Dona didn't hesitate for a moment.

"Oh, she just feels more comfortable studying at home at her own pace," she said. "Why?"

"Oh, just wondering if you know what she wants to do after she graduates?" Wilsa asked.

"She is going to the community college for the time being," Dona said. "We can't afford anything else. But that is okay for now."

Wilsa was nervous, now that her suspicions that her friend not knowing anything about Zita's escape into the order, proved to be right. She didn't tell Bob where she was going, and it was probably up to Zita to tell her own mother.

Zita just walked into the living room and saw the two women chatting. She knew Wilsa was teacher Bob's wife, and Bob knew about her future profession.

Mom cannot find out yet, thought Zita. Not now, and not from Wilsa.

"Hello, Zita," said Wilsa sweetly. "I hear you're going to the community college."

"Yes, I am," Zita said. "I need time to decide what I want to do with my life."

Zita sat down with the other two women on the tan leather sofa. She always admired her mom's love for natural materials. This put Wilsa at a disadvantage of not being able to face Zita directly.

"Your husband is a very good teacher," said Zita. "He always gets what he wants from his students."

"Yes, he does that with me too," sighed Wilsa realizing that she won't be able to tell Dona the secret about her daughter.

She will have to keep it to herself for who knows how long.

"Do you have a boyfriend?" Wilsa attempted once more to find out Zita's secret. "I mean you're going to college after all."

Zita stood up and walked to the armchair, now facing Wilsa directly. Mom was sipping her coffee and munching on nuts. The tension between the three women was hanging in the air.

"Well, Zita tell her you run around with Kurt," Dona encouraged. "But, he's just a friend, not a boyfriend."

But Zita zipped her lips shutting out both women determined not to say a word.

Mother Karla was the only person who mattered at the moment. She was the only person who understood Zita.

"Kurt is just a friend and I have other plans," she said looking straight again at Wilsa.

The three women changed their conversation to the upcoming holiday shopping season and to wars between the stores. Zita hoped everything would be forgotten within a few days or weeks as time went by.

"I got to get going," Wilsa stood up and left the two to themselves.

"Honey, it seemed like she wanted to tell me something before you came," Dona turned to her door.

Dona sensed something must have happened at school before Zita's big decision to finish school online.

"Mom, everything is fine," Zita said. "I am better off studying online. The guys were obnoxious and Mr. Kotias was nosy."

The next day Wilsa waited patiently for Dona to come home. As soon as Dona pulled into the driveway,

Wilsa appeared on the sidewalk walking in her sweats.

"Hi, Dona," she walked to the car.

"Hi, Wilsa, doing your regular walk?" Dona asked.

"Yes, but I need to talk to you," she said quickly before she would change her mind. "I wanted to tell you the other day but Zita came."

"Not here. It's cold, come on in, Wilsa," Dona said.

"No, I won't. I have to keep on moving," said Wilsa shivering and scared.

"What is it?" Dona was frightened now.

"Zita will enter the order; she told the class in front of Bob," said Wilsa teary-eyed.

Dona paused and leaned against her small car breathing heavily.

"What are you talking about, what order?" she slammed her small fist against the car.

"The Dominicans, they are catholic nuns," said Wilsa knowingly as she turned to resume her walk.

Dona cried in the master bedroom for hours. She had just found out from the neighbor that their only child will lock herself up away from the world in a convent. How could Zita do that to Mike and her? She had no right to do that.

"Mike, you have to make her stay," she begged. "Please, talk some sense into our daughter. Don't let her go."

Weeks of quarrels between Mike and Dona followed. Nothing mattered more than saving Zita from the order. So, Dona was determined to do just that; save her only daughter from the tenants of the thorny prison.

The image of the thorny prison haunted Dona from that day when Wilsa dropped the bad news on the driveway.

Months later Dona found herself knocking on the convent door. A nun in white garb opened the heavy door looking at the disheveled worldly woman in tears in front of her. The sun was high in the sky and the day was warming up. The light breeze was bringing in the smell of the budding roses from the convent gardens.

"What can I do for you, my dear," said the nun.

"Can I speak with the Mother of the order?" Dona asked scared as she stepped back.

"My dear, you have to have an appointment to speak with Mother Karla," said the nun. "And she is not here today."

Back at home in Green Heights Dona decided to confront Zita to make her change her mind. She will use force if she needs to, but her only daughter was not going to enter a convent.

Zita was studying for the finals in her room surrounded by books and papers. Dona entered her daughter's sanctuary and sat on her bed.

"Zita, why didn't you tell me?" she asked.

"Would you really care, if I did?" Zita was defiant and turned away from her mother.

"Zita, you can't go," she said. "You're the only one we have."

"You will have dad for yourself," Zita was determined not to give in.

Dona hugged her and cried tears all over Zita's neck. Kurt Cobain's music was playing in the background.

Yes, Zita was a true Generation X young woman. Zita freed herself from mom's desperate hug and turned up the music louder. She loved Nirvana and "Heart-Shaped Box." Cobain remained her idol for years.
"Mom, please leave my room," Zita plead. "I made up my mind a long time ago."

Dona drove again through the long alley of beautiful crab apple and oak trees. The crab apple trees were now in their late pink and white blossoms, so the petals were all over the dirt road leading to the Dominican sprawling retreat center. Dona passed the red barn on the right with the apple orchard in full blossom. The labyrinth of dirt roads took her to the main building. She knocked on the big heavy door again.
Mother Karla opened the door and welcomed the woman into her quarters. Sitting at a big desk with a cross behind her, Karla folded her hands and looked up at Dona. A rosary was intertwined between her fingers and wrapped her right wrist.
This time, Dona was more composed. She dressed appropriately for a battle with what was become the new mother of her only child. Dona put on her best suit, a striped navy-blue jacket and skirt, and a white silk blouse. Golden bracelets were dangling from her left wrist, and Dona made sure she put the diamond ring on the correct finger of the left hand even though it was a little big.
An hour before Dona's arrival, Mother Karla went through a different ritual of preparing for a guest. She

prayed for a successful outcome. Karla put on her white garb. It will be a mother against a Mother battle.
"What brings you here," Mother Karla said watching Dona closely.
Without wincing or fidgeting, Dona went straight to the point looking directly into the Mother's eyes.
"I will not let my only child become a nun," said Dona firmly. "There is no way, my child will be a nun; not while I am alive. It will happen only over my dead body. I will fight this. You lured her into doing this. She would have never done this on her own."
Dona leaned back into the leather armchair crossing her slender legs. Mother Karla leaned forward over her desk toward Dona playing with the beads of the lavender-colored rosary on the first decade. She inched her fingers toward the cross on the rosary.
"Why would I lure your child to the order?" asked Karla.
Dona stood up and walked closer to the big desk breathing heavily into Karla's face.
"You coaxed her into this with your lies and deceptions," she attacked Karla.
Dona slammed her small fist in front of Karla's face on the big desk. Karla stood up too and walked around the desk to stand face to face with Dona. Karla put her hands against her wide hips:
"First of all, I am a woman of the cloth. I do not deceive or lie," she said. "It is my highest duty to tell the truth to anyone who is seeking it. Are you seeking the truth?"

Dona was sobbing out loud now. She was trying to catch her breath before speaking again. Then, she collapsed back into the leather armchair.

"You're stealing my daughter from me," she wept. "You're a thief."

Mother Karla pulled a chair to sit in front of Dona. She put her arm on Dona's shoulder and lifted her chin.

"Look at me," she said. "Your daughter made her own decision. I did not coax her into anything. She sought us out shortly after the 5K run on her own."

Dona was shaking her head in disbelief and pushed away Karla strongly. The Mother of the convent, where everyone quietly obeyed her iron rule could not believe that this worldly woman was fighting her on her own grounds. She walked back behind her desk and sat down. On her rosary, she inched her fingers to the next decade.

"Hail, Mary please give that woman peace," she prayed silently. Dona's sobbing penetrated her prayers. The clock struck five p.m. Soon, the evening prayers would come.

"You will have to leave now, my child," Mother Karla said gently. "Your daughter can change her mind any time before the vows. She has not committed to anything yet."

The fight between the two mothers ended abruptly. Dona gathered her purse, tablet and the cell phone. She slammed the door behind her; she slammed all the doors she had to go through in order to get out of the convent that was like a labyrinth.

On her way back through the blossoming fragrant alley, Dona, used to accomplishments in her glamorous editorial job, realized she had achieved exactly nothing with Mother Karla. She jammed her foot on the gas pedal and sped through the fields back home.

Zita's room was empty. Dona opened her closet and noticed Zita's favorite clothes were gone. She ran into the basement and searched for Zita's suitcase; it was gone along with the winter coat even though summer was on its way. Her Nirvana CDs also disappeared. She only got a message on Zita's cell phone.

Mike just got home from work and sat at the dining table opening his first beer.

"What's wrong, honey?" he asked. "You look like you've seen a ghost. How was your day at the magazine?"

Dona sank into the chair across from Michael.

"Our child left home," she said crying.

"Why are you crying? She probably just went running," he said stretching out his hand. "Don't worry. She'll come back."

Dona cried all the way to the fridge. She stopped as she noticed an envelope on the fridge with a heart-shaped magnet. Dona tore it open and read loud:

Dear Mom and Dad,

I know this will hurt you greatly, but it wasn't my intention to hurt you in any way. In the fall, I realized I wasn't meant for the real world or for Kurt. If I stayed, I would only keep on hurting more and more

people, including you two. And I love you too much to do that.
It was my decision, and only my own decision, to enter the Dominican Sister order. I've had that calling for some time. I didn't rush into anything and it wasn't out of fear.
I am grateful for all the days we spent together. Thank you for all that you have lovingly given to me.
Do not look for me, I'm everywhere around you; in the air you breathe, in the dirt you walk, in the flowers you smell and in the heat of the fire in the woodstove.
Forever yours,
Zita.
A photograph fell out of the envelope; it was the three of them on the merry-go-round in the park on a hot summer day with a mister in the shape of a dolphin in the background. Water drops were in the photo.
Dona ran to her bedroom and locked herself up. Mike knocked and knocked, and then gave up. As he walked down the stairs, he could hear Dona's loud sobs.
As weeks went by, Dona grew accustomed to the feeling of emptiness. She stopped the numerous attempts to reach her daughter. Zita's phone number did not exist anymore. She waited for letters or messages; none ever came.
Summers turned into fall and winters, and these turned into years.
Kurt called Dona several times inquiring about Zita, if she had changed mind. He was already back home from the college overseas, but he hadn't forgotten his high school girlfriend.

"How is she doing, Dona?" he asked occasionally. "Is she okay?"
Kurt was the only lifeline from the past to Zita, so Dona always answered unlike other phone calls. She stopped talking to Wilsa, since she was the messenger of the bad news.
"I don't know, Kurt," Dona said. "We haven't heard from her in five years."
As winter arrived with first snow, Dona finally received an ornate envelope with the insignia of the Dominican Sisters order.
It was an invitation to Zita's final vows at the convent. Dona was shocked to read the signature: Sister Theophane. That was Zita's new name forever.
"This is the last time, we will see our daughter," said Dona.
"No, you don't know anything about it," said Mike. "These Sisters can come out into the public."
"I don't want to see her anymore after this," said Dona.

Veni Sancte Spiritus played in the background of the chapel with huge organ pipes in the front. Then, the Sisters sang psalms. Mike and Dona sat in the back of the chapel. Dona noticed that Kurt was sitting in the front.
Their beautiful daughter dressed in a white bride's gown with a wreath of yellow roses on her head, now Sister Theophane, walked alongside Mother Karla to profess the vows in front of the priest. Mother Karla stepped aside to make room for new blood. Sister Theophane prostrated on the wooden floor in front of

the priest and then recited the vows and received a ring. As such, she was the "Bride of Christ."

Over the last few years, four women have taken the solemn vows. Dona noticed their pictures in the hallway; all young women forever locked up. The smell of incense permeated the space under the cupola. Other sisters sat in the pews were reliving their own profession of vows. Known as the "Brides of Christ" they all officially released their enslavement to the world.

Dona remained in a state of shock and in silence as the music continued to accompany the ceremony on this New Year's Eve.

"I am so glad you could come," said Sister Theophane to her mom and dad who walked up to congratulate her. Dona was sobbing out loud cutting into the music.

"Why did you do this to us?" asked Mike. "Look at your mother, she will never get over this."

Mike watched closely as Sister Theophane was shaking with fear of the upcoming days after taking the solemn vows.

"Congratulations," said Kurt. "Is this really what you wanted?"

Kurt was going through his own discernment of what had happened. Dona accused him several times of introducing Zita to the Dominicans during that ominous 5K run.

"If you hadn't taken her out there, Zita would have never known about it," Dona snapped at him.

"There's one thing about running in the nuns' fields with me and another to decide to join them for a lifetime," Kurt snapped at Dona.

Kurt, now equipped with his landscaping degree from England, was back for good. He wasn't excited about his job at the University Extension office.

Zita's decision to enter the sacred private life of Sisters hurt him more than he cared to admit. Zita never really disappeared from his life. She grew distant, yes, but she was always present in his heart. He forever cherished that memory on the bench on the trail run overlooking the rolling hills.

"Dona, I had nothing to do with your daughter's decision to enter the order," he said in a phone conversation.

"But, the two of you were dating right?" she said. "Something set her off into that convent. It was you."

Dona shifted her own guilt of putting her glamorous magazine job ahead of her daughter onto Kurt. She delegated guilt ever so wistfully even on Mike.

"You with your job and beer," she yelled at Mike once. "We've never even noticed; she was drifting away from us."

"Come and join us in the community room," Mother Karla said blushing. "We have a banquet ready for our guests."

They filed along with other guests into the large well-lit round community room with a panoramic view of the gardens and the campus. Everything was covered with snow, and the silence of the winter entered their hearts. There will be no laughter between these walls, Dona thought.

But there was already music and joy ringing throughout the buildings, and prayers chanted to welcome the new Sister.

Years went by faster than minutes on the clock on the wall, Sister Theophane went through more rigorous discernment. One Saturday afternoon, she decided to take a walk on the trails. She just followed the one that seemed familiar to her. There were the cherry trees on the left and the deer track on the right. The trail went a little up the hill and into another curve before the opening on top of the hill.

She stood by the bench under the big tree overlooking the rolling hills. The essence of that afternoon a long time ago came back to her. Theophane could feel Kurt's touch. She forgot completely what he looked like. They were too young back then to savor their memories.

Saddened by the moment, Theophane headed out on the trail looping back to the convent gardens. The gardening team was working along with other sisters. It was the Saturday work day. And the community was getting ready for another event.

Theophane was so immersed in her discernment and studies, that she forgot what the event was.

"Hello, Sisters," she said. "What's the rush?"

"Mother, we have another 5K run coming," said one novice. "Have you forgotten?"

Theophane looked into a distance bringing back that 5K run many years ago.

"When is it?" she forced herself back into reality.

"In two weeks," said the novice.

Theophane realized that in two weeks, she would become the Mother of the Order. Karla passed away two months ago, and a directive came from the administration that Theophane will be taking over.

"You have only a few weeks to get assume the Motherhood of the Order," the note stated. "Stay humble and pray."

This time the ceremony was very private; no public was allowed. The chapel was full of other nuns and clergy.

Theophane kept her sister name that she learned to love and to respect it. She would be leading the lively campus with many work teams.

On a Monday, Mother Theophane went to introduce herself to the gardening team. As a girl she loved to garden. Later she had no time because of the constant studying and the discernments.

"I want to express my deepest gratitude for your work that glorifies these gardens," she said to the team. They bring so much joy to all of us."

She noticed a tall tanned guy in the back.

"Who is your team leader?" she asked. "You've done such a great job on the trails. I was out there on Saturday enjoying the autumn glory."

The tall guy in the back stepped up front with a cautious smile. His dark hair showed signs of gray on the temples. He had a dark mustache and a hat in his hands. He seemed somewhat familiar.

"I am happy to be working here with the other guys," he said. "It's my pleasure to meet you."

Theophane wasn't sure about this tall guy with the mustache. The eyes like deep wells reminded her of a similar set of eyes. It must have been her imagination. In the evening Theophane studied for the upcoming workshop on relationships for troubled couples.

An urgent knock on the door startled her and took her away from the workbook.

"Come in," she said.

The tall guy with the mustache entered her office. He changed into different clothes and looked different than out in the open air. The stuffiness of the building was choking here a little bit, and she coughed out loud. Mother Theophane couldn't understand her own anxiety.

"Mother Theophane, do you have a minute for me?" he asked inquisitively.

Theophane felt fear in his voice as well.

"Of course I do," she said as she leaned back into the chair. She looked at the clock on the wall. It was 8 p.m. well after her office hours.

"I didn't catch your name outside," she said.

"I am Kurt," he said breathing heavily.

Theophane tried to conjure up the Kurt from her past, from her high school class. No, this couldn't have been the same man. This guy was old. She looked at her wrinkled old hands, and realized her own age. She grew old too in the convent.

"I once knew a boy by the name of Kurt, but that was back in high school," she smiled.

Theophane looked at the gardener closely, and closer yet. She searched in his deep eyes for traces of the past. She found that twinkle, that sparkle that lit up her heart. Theophane realized that she had already looked into these eyes before.

“We ran on those trails out there together, Mother Theophane,” he said. “You were Zita then.”

Theophane stood up and walked closer to look at the gardener. She felt goose bumps on her arms.

“We stopped and kissed at the bench by that big oak tree overlooking the rolling hills,” Kurt said. “I was never able to forget that kiss.”

He gently drew Theophane closer to him, and closer yet. He could feel her tears rub against his cheek. Kurt found her lips and kissed her. She didn’t resist, not for a moment. After a long kiss, they set their next date in one of the austere retreat rooms.

These rooms served guests from far who sought out the campus for their personal retreat journeys from the world. There was still time before the trail run next weekend.

When they met again in room 11 at the end of the long hallway, the old excitement of something forbidden came back. This time the forbidden was multiplied by years of abstinence from sex for Theophane. She was still a virgin. There was only a single bed in the room with one window overlooking the gardens, a desk with a chair, the cross on the wall and an armchair. The wind was lifting the leaves and howling behind the window.

She came in her evening clothes intentionally, not wearing her Mother’s white garb. Her hair was tied in a bun under a white cap. When Kurt entered the room, Theophane was still looking outside the window. He took off her cape, but left her green silk shirt on, to enjoy her beautiful body by the light shining in from the clear night. In the moonlight, she looked like a fairy from the nearby forest.

"You've cast your magic spell over me many years ago, and you're doing it again," Kurt said as he laid her on the bed.

He dropped the silk nightshirt on the wooden floor and was lost in her arms forever. He covered her body with his and touched every inch of her soft skin. Theophane shrieked at first with pain as he entered her, but as the pain ceased and pleasure took over, she moaned and whispered his name.

Kurt played with her breasts and sucked on her pink brown nipples, while she hugged his wide shoulders. The two moved in unison for a brief moment in time. Then, they laid side by side, their hands intertwined for hours. Kurt left before dawn. They repeated their date in room 11 several times before the 5K run, since they couldn't get enough of each other.

Mother Theophane couldn't go about her regular business the way she used to.

"Mother, are you listening to me?" Sister Kate asked her. "Where do you want me to be on the trail?"

"Yes, of course I am listening," she said. "Wherever you want to be."

The other day, Kurt begged her to leave the convent and marry him. She couldn't sleep ever since he proposed to her in room 11 down on his knees by the star and the moon lit window.

Theophane walked the hallways of the convent like a ghost. She hadn't slept for weeks in a row. She handed the workshop for troubled couples over to Sister Kate.

"I can't focus," Theophane said. "I am not well."

"You need to leave for a while, go somewhere secular by yourself, so you know," Kate suggested. "You'll come back refreshed and feel better about everything."

"Know what?" Mother Theophane snapped back in fear how much did Kate exactly know about her and Kurt.

Mother Theophane realized that Kate was right; she did need a break from the secret relationship with Kurt and from the walls of the convent. She decided she would visit retired Dona at the Commons by the lake.

The drive on the Lakeshore Drive offered her respite from the overwhelming guilt; not only did she sin as the Mother of the convent, but she sinned on sacred grounds. The guilt was growing exponentially with time. She stopped at one of the beaches, now closed for the season. Theophane walked on the boardwalk toward the lake with the wind and mist hitting her face. She pulled the veil more over her face and wrapped the white habit tighter around her.

Theophane hasn't seen or spoken to her mother since she accepted her final vows years ago.

The upscale Commons complex on the lake fit Dona well. She had a large audience here just like back at her fancy job with the City Magazine. Dona moved in the Commons shortly after dad passed away.

"Oh, you're here to see our writer in residence, Dona," smiled the cute receptionist. "She's been waiting and talking about you ever since you called her that you're coming."

Mother Theophane smoothed her white garb and lifted her head.

"You mean she's not angry at me?" Theophane was surprised.

"Go and find out for yourself," said the receptionist.

When Theophane entered the suite with large windows, she immediately spotted Dona seated in the armchair by the French door leading to the deck. She was writing on her I-pad, but lifted her head to greet the visitor.

"Mom," cried Theophane as she walked to her mother.

Dona got up slowly straightening her aching back. She wore her Sunday dress to greet her daughter.

"Mom, you're not angry at me?" cried Theophane as she hugged her mother tightly.

The two women cried and hugged each other. Then, they sat down in the dining room with windows overlooking the lake.

"I made some chili and homemade bread," said Dona. "I know you like it."

Theophane looked around mom's condo. The walls were painted blue and lavender, a color combination mom loved.

"How was your drive?" Dona asked.

Theophane was flabbergasted by mom's behavior; Dona was acting like nothing had ever happened between the two women.

"I was waiting all these years for you to call," said Dona lovingly.

Theophane ate mom's chili and found the photo she loved; the three of them on the merry-go-round with the dolphin mister in the background.
"You still have that picture?" Theophane said.
"I wouldn't lose it for anything in this world," Dona said. "Too bad we can't go outside, it's too cold. But summers are nice out here."
The mother and daughter talked for hours about the years that had gone by.
"You know that my former colleagues at work have great grandkids by now," Dona said. "I've never even had grandkids."
Theophane wasn't ready to tell mom about Kurt. She thought she might never tell her. Kurt didn't know that Theophane was outside in the real world.
"Mom, I want to tell you something," Theophane said. "But, I can't."
Dona looked at the troubled face of her lovely daughter. She couldn't believe that nuns had secrets too, just like real people. Maybe even worse, because everything they do is so clandestine. Her daughter was here for a reason, and not just to visit with her old mother.
They were back in the living room and mom was staring into her I-pad.
"What are you working on, mom?" Theophane asked to cover up for the previous statement, waffling back and forth.
"A memoir," said Dona. "You were going to tell me something about your secret life."
Thiophane's cell phone rang. It was Kurt.

"Where are you, I've been looking for you," he said urgently. "Can we meet tonight?"
"Yes, I will see you tonight," said Theophane.
Dona kept writing on the keyboard, as Theophane got up to leave. Dona was surprised.
"Who was that, and you're not going to tell me what happened at the convent?" said Dona looking up.
"I can't," Theophane said.

Back at the convent in room 11, Theophane was wearing her green chiffon night shirt, so Kurt could see the contours of her body and her breasts. They made wild love and laid on the single bed for hours. Theophane got up and looked outside into the night.
Theophane had two rings now; the one she accepted at her final vows and the other one she had accepted from Kurt. She will have to get rid of one, but which will it be?
She still loved the convent, and she wasn't ready for a secular life with Kurt. But Kurt was the only man she had ever known and loved, other than her dad.
"I will always love you," Kurt said touching her naked body as she laid back in bed.
The days of her indecisiveness became harder and harder; she was tortured between the power of the vows and the power of love. Theophane confessed about her torment to the chapel priest, leaving him in shock.
"I cannot help you, but you should leave the convent if you have had any sexual contact with this man, you

cannot stay any longer," said the priest. "Did you have sex with this man?"

"I haven't," Theophane lied. "Those were my sexual fantasies; it was in my dreams only; nothing physical happened."

"Go, and repent," said the priest, "Stop your fantasies right now or the devil will get you."

As Theophane walked out of the confession booth, she realized how much she had sinned again.

That night, the devil disguised as the pastor appeared to her in her dream.

"You've been lying and lying over and over again," he challenged her. "You don't even know the difference between the truth and a lie. You will burn in hell."

Theophane woke up shaking from her nightmare sweating a cold sweat. She realized she wasn't in room 11, and that Kurt wasn't lying next to her; and that the devil was gone for now.

Theophane put on her white habit for the day and went into the chapel to pray for forgiveness and discernment. The preparations for the 5K run were in full swing. The designated trails were already marked with yellow tape and different stations were set up along the run.

"Are you going to run, Mother Theophane?" Sister Kate asked.

"Yes, I think I will," Theophane said.

Theophane was still in good physical shape and she loved the outdoors. On the day of the run, hundreds of runners came to the campus trails. Chatter replaced the usual silence around the campus.

"You're not going to run, are you?" asked Kurt.
"Yes, I will. I need some fresh air," she said. "You're not running?"
"I wasn't planning on it," he said. "I thought we could be together while everyone is out on the trails. We could make love. Everyone will be gone."
Theophane fought the proposal hard standing outside in the cold wind. She had already told Sister Kate she'd be running. In the morning, she prayed for forgiveness.
"What time are they heading out?" she asked.
"In about an hour," said Kurt. "I want you. They won't be back until later. We're safe."
"I'll see you at 10:30 in room 11," Theophane said still undecided.
The runners headed out and so did all the sisters except for the sick ones, who stayed inside a different building. The campus was quiet again.
Theophane entered room 11 first and changed into the chiffon green shirt. Kurt came soon, and for the first time, they made love in broad daylight. They both wanted that, so they could see their naked bodies joined in the act of love. They indulged in each other with passion and lust.
But someone else wanted to see lust as well. The chapel pastor was already in the room waiting for the two to make love. He hid in the closet and watched as Theophane changed into the green chiffon shirt. He watched them closely during the foreplay and fondling, and into the act of love.

He waited for them to leave first, and then priest Greg sneaked out of room 11 with a wistful smile on his face.

The 5K run was a tremendous success raising close to $300,000 for the Dominican Sisters order. The money was much needed for the various programming at the campus, since the cash flow from regular donors wasn't as steady as it used to be.

The main mass on Sunday was held in the chapel led by priest Greg to thank all the runners and the donors.

"This is in thanks to all the runners who benefited our cause, without them we would not be able to continue our mission," he said bowing to all. "I would like Mother Theophane to come up and say a few words."

Theophane's face turned red, why didn't he say something ahead of time, why did he put her on the spot like this. Surely, Father Greg must have known it was her in the confession booth.

"That sly dog," she said to herself.

But, Mother Theophane kept her composure as always. She steadily walked to the speaker's stand and raised her head to the audience.

"I would like to thank everyone who made the 5K possible: the runners, fellow Sisters, the gardening team and the sponsors.

A festive reception followed in the round dining room with the panoramic windows. A fancy buffet was spread out in front of the guests and the campus residents.

Theophane headed toward the table reserved for the gardening team, but someone's hand touched her shoulder. She was afraid to turn around. She didn't want to know who was behind her. A man's voice whispered into her ear.

"I know what you did on the day of the run," the male voice whispered. Don't turn around. I saw you both in room 11."

Theophane's feet froze to the wooden floor and she couldn't move. When she finally turned around, no one was behind her. The guests were loud and no one noticed the incident.

Theophane looked at her plate; she loaded it with everything she loved from cheeses to charcuterie, and wild game. Exquisite wines were imported from Burgundy domains in France like Clos Vougeot Grand Cru. A bottle of it was already set up at the gardening table. She joined the team.

"You look like you've seen a ghost," Kurt joked. "Here have a glass of Clos Vougeot. I know the priest shouldn't have put you on the spot, but you did so well."

Theophane sat by the window and stared helplessly into the bare garden. The team chatted about the success of the run.

"I am going to join the Sisters for the meal," she said and left the gardening table.

But Theophane couldn't find reprieve by the Sisters' side either. Their chatter, much like the gardeners, was meaningless compared to what she was facing.

"May I join you," a male voice asked.

Theophane, startled, realized it was the same voice that whispered into her ear by the buffet table. Father Greg seated himself opposite of Mother Theophane and looked directly into her brown eyes clouded with anger and fear.

"Dear Mother, did you enjoy the run?" he said slyly.

"I couldn't participate, I was sick and tied up with my studies," she lied.

Father Greg smiled understandingly and carved through his rare steak carefully watching the reddish pink juice flow out of the meat. He was a lover of meat, and before he became a priest, he loved women too. He liked Theophane for their similar life paths.

Back then, when she entered the confession booth, Father Greg immediately knew who it was. He longed to touch her, but the wooden wall separated them. When he found out about Kurt, he was more jealous than anything else. Secretly, he followed them around until he found out about room 11 and their clandestine meetings.

He was full of lust, when he watched them make love. Father Greg will never forgive the two for giving into their love and putting it before God. He was too scared to do it himself.

"I am sure you were sick," he uttered. "Are you feeling better now? Or how can I help you? Maybe you need to confess."

Sister Kate leaned toward Father Greg and said lovingly:

"Mother Theophane never sins, she's nothing but perfection," said Kate. "She is a shining example for all of us."

Theophane was burning red, her stomach was upset, and her mind was racing.

She ate quickly.

"Would you like some wine?" Father Greg asked. "Wine is good for your mind; it makes you forget things you want to forget and remember the things you don't ever want to forget."

"To this year's success of the run," Father Greg raised his crystal glass. "And to Mother Theophane in her new duties. She's been doing so well uniting everyone on the campus."

Theophane sipped on the wine, but stopped eating.

"Can you pour me another glass," she asked the priest. "I want to forget everything that has ever happened."

She left the table and went straight into her Mother's suite. She prayed by her bed and then lay quietly. Theophane looked at the photo of the three of them on the merry-go-round with the dolphin mister that was hanging on the wall.

"Why did I ever enter the order?" she asked herself out loud. "I've sinned more than an ordinary woman."

The next day she found a letter in her mail from Father Greg. He was threatening to tell on her to the order's administration.

"Either you repent, or I will tell on you. As a sign of repentance, you will meet me in room 11 tonight at 9 p.m., and I won't say a word."

Theophane entered room 11 at 9 p.m. exactly and Father Greg was already inside sitting in the armchair by the window. She walked inside in fear.

"What do you want from me?" Theophane asked scared.

"You're going to give me what you gave to other men, your body," he said, "or I will tell on you."

Theophane was burning inside with anger at the willful priest. She slapped him on his right cheek, while he threw her on the bed and coerced her into having sex.

From then on, neither one was sure of the other's silence. A secret battle between the priest and the Mother of the order began. Theophane went into the confession booth.

"I confess to having sex with one of the employees, as well as to having involuntary sex with you," she said. "Please forgive me."

She left the booth without absolution. From then on, Mother Theophane refused to see Kurt in spite of his numerous attempts. She stopped answering the phone and closed herself into further studies.

In vain did Kurt try to meet with her. Theophane turned down every attempt and became withdrawn even from the community of the order.

It was Sister Kate who first noticed that no one has seen Mother Theophane neither at the morning, evening or Sunday masses. She panicked and searched for her in her Mother quarters. Kate ran to Father Greg to seek guidance about what had happened.

"Dear Sister Kate, Mother Theophane must have gone back into the real world," he said. "She was struggling in here."

"No, she would never do that," Kate argued. "She loved it here. She had friends here: me and Kurt. She would never leave us or the order. She must be here."

When Kurt couldn't find Theophane in the campus buildings, he headed out on the trails. He took the one with the cherry trees and deer tracks trail markers. He was shaking with cold as he walked the curve to the opening with the bench.

And there he found her, laying on the ground by the bench. He touched her white forehead and cheeks. As he searched for her hands under the heavy coat, he noticed blood stains on the snow. He pulled her hand out of the coat, all bloodied. The blood was already cold, and she wasn't breathing. Kurt found a slit on her left wrist. In vain, he tried to bring her back to life.

Two days later, they all gathered at the small campus cemetery by the big pile of dirt. The casket was already inside the hole in the ground. The wind was blowing from the west and the snow on the ground was already two feet high.

Father Greg led the funeral mass.

"Mother Theophane wasn't meant for the order life. It was the superficial secular life she secretly led that took her away from us. May her soul rest in peace. May she be forgiven."

Kurt remembered the last words as he walked away from the cemetery, down the long alley without looking back.

White Nights

Father Samuel couldn't sleep well. He never slept the entire night. Sometimes he blamed it on the full moon that flooded his bedroom with white light in the rectory. At other times, he wasn't tired enough or too tired. Sometimes he could hear the mice scratching in the attic.

Once he walked outside into the nearby woods to seek solace. Lately, he couldn't manage his loneliness.

What he used to seek out, was now seeking him. Sam tried to escape into writing, talking and various engagements in the community, and projects. He had a long running relationship with bishop Arwen of Irish origin.

He hasn't always been a priest. His speckled past drew away from the parish some families who wouldn't put up with the dichotomy of the act of a divorcée becoming a priest.

He felt guilt listening to people in the confession booth every Saturday afternoon. What would he have confessed to if he had been in place of the guy, he was just listening to?

"Father, I have sinned," a man whispered reluctantly. "I drank heavily and beat my wife."

Sam had to lean forward so he could hear the guy on the other side. He could smell the manure on him.

He tried guessing who it was. Sam liked to think he knew everybody, even the visitors who showed up for Christmas and Easter only known as CEOs. Sam used a few tricks to memorize the people who were not paying into the church coffers.

After all he had a plan. He wanted to impress the bishop and himself.

His favorite trick was: "Visitors please open your books to page one. Whoever opened the book to page one was an immediate suspect of not being a paying member. But even the regulars liked to play tricks on Sam, and they opened their books to page one. In fact, they have not memorized the words to the "Nicene Creed."

For generations they have heard it over and over again, and they still didn't know the words:

"I believe in one God, the Father almighty, maker of heaven and earth, of all things visible and invisible."

The words and their meanings just never clicked with them, because they didn't believe in much. On some days, beer and a piece of salami were sufficient, on other days the soul needed to be healed. And for that day only they would become "soul seekers" seeking themselves inside the confession booth.

This farmer was seeking his soul in front of another soul seeker- the troubled priest.

Sam could make out only a little of what the farmer had said. The whisper was so soft that it was like a murmur.

"Can you speak up please, I can't hear you," said Sam wryly.

"What if someone out there hears me?" the farmer worried.

"You're the last one today, I close soon," said Sam already thinking about the evening ahead of him after another long week of asceticism. He had fishing plans.

"I regret what I have done and I won't do it again, "said the guilty voice.

After giving him absolution, Sam remained in the booth. He could hear the heavy tread of the farmer's boots as he made his way down the nave of the church toward the enormous door. The door had a huge metal bar. Sam could hear the large door bang behind the farmer.

The village with only a general store, a gas station and a pub were still a farming community in spite of the encroaching development on the corn fields and apple orchards.

"We will preserve our farmland," the township proclaimed.

The parishioners were a fine mix of "yuppies" and hardcore characters like farmer Joe who had just left the confession booth. Sam finally recognized him by the heavy tread of the boots. Joe was 6.5 feet tall and weighed 250 pounds which made him into a feared giant.

The village talk had it that Joe beat his wife. He was a fourth-generation farmer on 20,000 acres of farmland-the largest plat in the township.

Joe acted properly; he did everything that was expected of the largest landowner to do. He sat on the township board, on the school and the church boards. In spite of the gossip, he was a respected man lacking self-control.

Unlike Father Sam, he had no choice of what he wanted do. He inherited the land, therefore he had to farm it. When farming got tough with the dumping of the cheap apple juice from China in the late 1990s, his two brothers decided to get out of working with soil and apples. They went to work for the largest milling company out by the Shimnicon Corners. At that time, Joe too had to seek his soul at the confession booth, after beating one of them close to death.

"You will never cross the threshold of my house," he yelled that winter when they fought over the buyout money. "Where do you think I am going to get two million bucks?"

The brothers left anyways, and Joe owed them money. Joe sold off land for development and paid off some of the debt, while making enemies with other farmers.

However, Joe was a big contributor to the church coffers not by his own will, but by the testament his mother Elena had changed after his father died.

"You will pay one-third of your income from farming to the church annually," the will stated.

"How can she enforce it?" wife Helen fought every Sunday. "It's more than the 10 percent tidings required."

"Shut up, the papers are also filed with the church," Joe said. "It's in the church's trust. Those two idiots have no idea how much money is being blown out into the coffers."

Sitting behind a big hardwood table, Sam felt relieved after the long week. It was more of what was ahead of him rather than behind. It was the upcoming week of All Souls Day.

It was fittingly nasty outside with rain and drizzle. He himself felt dead as he looked at the bare trees outside the rectory. He heard the wind howling down the chimney to the woodstove.

It was also Halloween time, and Sam felt like dressing up. When he was leading a normal life, Sam used to dress up even as an adult. Anything worked for him. But he has been dressing up in his chasuble and changing it according to the seasons of the liturgical year from the ordinary green to the festive red and white.

He was thinking about the last 11 years of his life as a priest. Unlike the previous priest, the parishioners liked Sam even with all his baggage.

A few years ago, they were surprised to see him with his grandson on Christmas Day. They had forgiven a long time ago, because Sam was the people's priest. He liked being close to the people as well as close to Irish Bishop Arwen some 50 miles away.

Sam knew how to play both sides well. It was his natural capability to cater to all without distinction.

Sam tried hard to leave the mess of his previous life behind the heavy gates of the church and behind the doors of the rectory. He struggled as a married man.

There were all those things a married man had to do. Out of all of them he failed to do the number one thing, and that is to please his wife Gloria.

But it was the years that had taken a toll on their marriage. Sam forgot why he married Gloria in the first place. It may have been love at first site, but it also could have been a lot of other things and sex wasn't the least of them.

After years, he got enough of sex as Gloria was getting fatter. She was no longer the class beauty he had met so long ago, that he couldn't remember what attracted him to this woman.

Beauty and sex are elusive. They arrive, stay for a while and then they fly away like a balloon. Never to be recaptured in the same form. The longing and the temptations come again, but they are different. Love and sex caused him a lot of problems in the past. Sam vowed not to let that happen again when he was ordained that sunny Sunday afternoon in June. It was a pompous ceremony with hymns and chants.

When the fanfares were gone, Sam felt proud that he had proven that he can be a different man. He felt even more proud when he was alone than at the celebration.

At first loneliness intensified that elation of success, but after years of wearing the chasuble it changed. Sam couldn't define it. It was a constant struggle between lying to himself or lying to others.

Lately he had trouble believing his own lies.

"I love being a priest," he repeated over and over again in front of the mirror.

Then he asked himself, "What do I like about it other than myself?"

Sam reached the age of wisdom, and his bucket list was getting longer and longer. Sam didn't long as much for material things, as for a real bond with a human being. He had a lot of friends among the parishioners. For the most part, they were a funny bunch.

He imagined himself flying away in a balloon. Up, up and away. Away from it all. Away from the mundane drainage of ordinary days.

Suddenly, Sam realized while daydreaming he forgot to open that ornate envelope that someone left on the drawer in the hallway. Impatiently, he opened the letter with the bishop's insignia. He was shaking now, because Sam respected the higher clergy.

It was an invitation to the annual conclave in the mountains. He had never been invited before. That fact stirred suspicion in Sam. Yes, he had the seniority, but he was just on ordinary village priest.

"We request your presence."

That's how the letter ended. Sam quickly looked at the date; of course it was coming up on the All Souls Day feast on November 2.

"No, I am going to get out of this, I have to serve," he thought to himself. He already scripted his homily, and he always carried the "Book of the Dead."

And this was the only feast he liked with a passion for the beloved dead close to his heart. His aunt, who helped pay for the seminary studies, was one of the beloved dead.

Sam decided to call the bishop in the morning. That night he couldn't sleep because of the vision of the conclave in the mountains, and he could hear the mice scratching.

As a regular man, Sam heard weird things about the clandestine conclaves. He imagined rituals going on during these secretive gatherings high in the

mountain yurts that resembled Turkish nomad tents. He had goose bumps all over, and the chill crawled down his spine.
Some never came back from these conclaves; either they got lost in the mountains or chose not to come back.
What was discussed at these conclaves or why were they called to them? Those were the questions that were chasing in Sam's head.

"I cannot come," said Sam on the phone to the bishop. "I have a service that day."
"But my dear Sam you can come after the Feast of the Dead," said the bishop firmly. "We shall wait for you."
"But I don't know how to get there," said Sam. "I have no directions."
"Someone will pick you up after the procession of the lights," said the bishop.
There was silence on the other end of the phone. Sam looked at his feet. He was a short man, so he had small feet. In the 80s, he wore high heels to make up for the height he never reached. He liked walking around barefoot, even though the floor was cold and impersonal just like the rest of the rectory. Sam pulled out of the closet one of his oldest shirts. It resembled a rag. He got attached to it, because the shirt was with him all the time. Sometimes he wondered what was he going to do without it once it falls apart.
"You'll buy a new one," said secretary Kim.
It was one of the few things he kept from his previous life along with some photos and books hidden in a

box in the last drawer of the dresser. The shirt with holes covered up all the treasures underneath.

Sometimes, Sam would get down on his knees other than to pray to comfort himself by looking at the old pictures. Most of them haven't yellowed yet, because he kept them in the dark. Wherever he went, he took the box with photos with him, and his favorite books. Sam liked having the photos just thrown in the box without any organization. That way he kept himself in suspense of what was he going to find next.

"Why does Arwen want me to go to that conclave?" he kept asking himself over and over again. "He must have plans for me."

Sam needed to show off in front of Arwen to get a promotion. Sam was going to show off with a large project.

"I will help you reach your goals," once Arwen said over a lobster dinner before the Super Bowl game. "I want to see more of you around here."

But that was five years ago, and Sam was too new to understand Arwen. Sam started the expansion project last year to please the bishop. He had already proven that he can raise money, and a lot of it.

The folks around Shimnicon Corners were not cheap. Of course some money, like farmer Joe's, was forced by wills and testaments. People were angry over their non-obedient children, so they gave their money to the church.

Sam had no problem with money. After all, he was using other people's money for the good of all. He knew well-spent money would heal souls. What he really needed was to heal his own soul. The answer could have been in that box of old photos.

On the evening of the All Souls Day mass, Sam looked outside the window. He could see the glass stained windows of the church depicting saints from the rectory. His favorite saint was Saint Paul because of his stature. St. Paul was depicted in one of the gothic windows that Sam loved to stare at.

Today, Sam was scared before the mass. He felt the flutters in his stomach and the tightness in his throat. It was a dark night with only a yellow light filtering through the windows.

The church was full. He carried the "Book of the Dead" in total silence. Sam was overwhelmed with fear. There were so many people in the church, who had lost loved ones, and Sam traveled their journey from the beginning until the end at the funeral mass. He took pride in knowing these journeys and comforting many. Sam cried with the people. Often, during the mass Sam broke down crying due to emotions: past, present and future. The tears flowed freely down his cheeks without him trying to control any emotions.

As he stepped up front, Sam looked at the people dressed mostly in black. They also had candles in their hands for the procession to the cemetery to follow the mass.

"We will light the candles in memory of your loved ones at the end of the mass," said Sam to comfort himself with the vision of light.

It was cold in the ornate church. He wanted it that way, because it was cold outside. He practiced for the sermon many times. He noticed some people crying. Sam looked at the young widow in the sixth pew to his left. He felt a pain in his chest over her story. But he felt the same pain over his own life story, even though it wasn't marked by death but by deceit and lies.

"We all have memories, some are good and some are difficult, but we treasure them and keep them in our hearts," he started off choking a little bit. "I had a dear aunt who inspired me on the path to church. She was a holy woman."

People were quiet and listened to Sam what he had to say on the dreary feast of the dead.

"Some dead are with us more than they have ever been in life," he said.

Farmer Joe, thinking about his mother, shrugged.

"I am sure I will remember her more than when she was alive for all the money she gave to the church ripping me off."

Sam sometimes wished he could get into each person's head to see what they're thinking about his words. He liked to think that he had impact on people, and the confessions often confirmed that.

"I am a better man now because of you Father," the words rang through his head.

He descended from the elevated altar area to be closer to the people.

"Call out the names of our beloved dead," Sam invited and watched who's going to name who first.

Joe jumped up first, "My beloved mother Elena."

People named their beloved for longer than Sam had expected. After 20 minutes he had to stop the "valley of tears."
The ushers lit up people's candles and a procession formed inside the church to the cemetery. The cemetery was glowing in lights that were flickering in the wind. They proceeded to the cemetery on the narrow pathway under the pine trees. They stopped at the center by the large celtic cross.
The procession prayed for the dead and everyone left into the warmth of their homes.
Sam left the cemetery last after looking around at the crosses with knots and the monuments. From the short distance, he could see the lights shining through the stained-glass windows as a car parked in front of the rectory.
"I'll be right out," he said to the driver.
He prepared his luggage earlier in the day. He was ready to take off into the unknown as he sat on the back seat behind the driver.
"We can go," he turned around and looked at the stained- glass windows were Saint Paul's silhouette was standing out.
He imagined St. Paul bidding him farewell. His mind was playing the usual tricks on him.
If he hadn't entered priesthood, this wouldn't have happened to him. He should have stayed secular and troubled. He should have been nicer to Gloria. Why was he so mean to Gloria? Has she forgiven him?
After all Sam was only ignoring her. They were living like roommates. Sam tried to remember when and why he stopped sleeping with Gloria. He looked

through the window into the dark veil of the night. They left the city limits long time ago.

"Can you tell me where exactly are we going?" Sam was scared.

"That I cannot," said the driver muffling his voice with his hand in a glove. "Bishop Arwen gave me directions not to say anything that would reveal his intentions."

"Yes, what exactly are those intentions that you are dragging me somewhere into the mountains?" Sam said. "What are the bishop's intentions with me?"

Sam leaned closer towards the driver's seat. He noticed the driver was a big man wearing an overcoat and a standard driver's cap that shaded most of his face.

"Sorry buddy, I forgot to introduce myself," Sam quickly switched the tone of his voice from scared to condescending. "I am Father Sam."

"I know," nodded the driver. "I know everything about you and you know nothing about me. Let's keep it that way."

Sam pushed himself back into the seat. He noticed the driver was watching him in the rear-view mirror. Sam straightened the collar of his black shirt and snuggled deeper into his black wool long coat. He was cold and the heat in the car wasn't turned on. He tightened the black scarf around his neck and mouth.

Why did he stop sleeping with Gloria? It wasn't because she was getting fat, and that he was getting used to it. He liked simple pleasures of immediate satisfaction during and after sex.

Sam tried to trace that exact moment when he stopped sleeping with Gloria. And now the song "Gloria in Excelsis Deo" was resonating in his ears. He had always loved church music. Especially the innuendo in some of lyrics. Sam didn't have a great voice, so he never chanted the words like some priests did.

His strong side was the gift of the gab that pleased everyone including Arwen. Arwen wasn't naïve, but he trusted Sam. Ambition was the guiding light of trust for Arwen. Ambition stays on guard, when other desires sleep.

During their Sunday dinners together, Arwen couldn't help but ask himself why he liked Sam so much. He knew about Sam's speckled background. Only once he asked Sam:

"Why did you get a divorce?"

There was a long silence in the Bishop's chambers. Sam was playing with a snow crab claw, as he picked up a glass of white wine. Arwen had good taste in wine. He didn't hesitate to buy a bottle of Louis Latour Batard-Montrachet Grand Cru for $152 to accompany the Sunday dinners.

Sam was looking through the pure gold color of the wine. He sniffed the aromas of honey and vanilla. The structure of the wine was much like Gloria's body and skin: smooth, generous and well-built.

"Excuse me Arwen, but I do not want to talk about the break-up with my wife Gloria," Sam took a sip of the wine, and looked Arwen straight into the eyes.

"We will never talk about it," said Arwen.

Sitting on the back seat, Sam closed his eyes and saw Gloria in front of him. Her well-built body was that

of a baroque statue. Even now in the cold car, Sam could feel the heat rising up in his body as he visualized touching Gloria's breasts and playing with the nipples until they hardened up into spikes.
As he threw her on the bed, Sam knew Gloria would resist in the beginning until she would give in to his soft touch. Sam was falling deeper and deeper into the vision of his lovemaking. He was no longer cold, but his hands were sweaty. He felt tiny drops of sweat on his forehead.
He awoke startled as the car came to a stop. He looked outside. It was still the same dark, only some three hours later.
"We're here," the driver opened the door for him.
Sam looked around in the dim light cast by ground lanterns. There were several paths leading from the circular plaza labyrinth without any signs surrounded by the woods.
"Is this a test?" Sam asked turning to the driver.
"You're on your own," said the driver as he climbed back into the car.
"Wait a minute, I don't have a flashlight," Sam said. "Arwen didn't say anything about a flashlight."
"Use your lighter," shrugged the driver as he lit up a cigarette.
"I don't smoke," Sam felt anger rising in his body. "You son of a bitch, give me your lighter."
Sam snagged the lighter from the driver and turned his back on him. He was just standing in the middle of the maze not knowing which path to take. He heard the car leave, and it became darker yet. He grabbed a piece of paper from his pocket to look at the

directions he had printed out earlier at the rectory. It stated:

“Find the compass in the grass made from shrubs pointing to the north. Take the path coming from it. It will take you to the “Bishop’s Yurt” with my insignia. Just walk in. Arwen.”

Sam crumpled up the paper. He discovered the compass made from the shrubs. Sam remembered seeing a clock like this many years ago on his trip to Geneva. The designers of this clandestine conclave sitting high in the mountains of Shabbawa did not leave anything to a chance. That’s why Arwen hired them. The path from the compass led into a unicursal labyrinth much like the one where king of Crete kept the Minotaur.

In the daylight, Sam would have happily searched his way to the “Bishop’s Yurt ” while meditating over Gloria. But now, it was cold and Sam did not know what Arwen was up to.

He clearly remembered the day, he decided to leave Gloria. It was a hot summer day of the equinox in June. He was at a catholic conference that took place under a tent. Sam was sweating in the heat of the day. But he was also sweating over a decision he would have to make soon.

“You cannot serve well the God and your family,” said the renowned speaker. “At some point you will have to make a decision.”

Sam struggled over the decision to leave Gloria for years. Even though love dwindled, there was something he liked about being married. It was the stability of a material everyday relationship that he cherished.

But he was torn apart by the daily struggle that lacked meaning to him, while it meant the world to Gloria.

"Let's go shopping Sam," she begged.

"No," he was resolute about shopping on Sundays.

"You never listen, do you?"

Gradually, Sundays turned into fighting days. Gloria would gossip about the people in church out loud to hurt him and his beliefs.

"Did you see her?" she attacked. "She looked like a Barbie doll in that fluffy skirt."

"Don't be jealous, leave her alone."

Sam was sitting at the dining table, waiting for Gloria to bring out the soup and to dish out more poison. He noticed that the bottle of wine was almost empty. Gloria sat next to him and cried.

"You don't like being here anymore," she said whining.

Sam looked around their suburban house. Gloria was wrong. He loved their home with all the comforts of a secular life. Sam had his place on the sofa, his favorite show, his favorite beer and his favorite sport. But there was something deeply missing in his life when he looked past the yellowing curtains into the garden.

"Did you know that our priest will be retiring soon?" she quipped. "Maybe if we switch churches you could become a pastor."

"What makes you think I want to preach?" Sam was getting angry.

Gloria still in her church clothes was sipping on her wine. She nodded her head towards the door.
"You know what, if you want to leave me, please leave now," she was crying now.
Sam took a deep breath and looked at Gloria while sipping the hot soup. Then he put the spoon aside.
"You know what Gloria, I will leave," he said. "I will leave you to your gossip and fake world of illusions."
He left the table for the bedroom. Sam snagged off the hanger his old rugged sweatshirt which he loved more than anything else. He added some books and photos.
"Goodbye Gloria," he said as he turned around. "You knew all along it wasn't meant to be.
What followed was a painful battle with counsels, and most of all with himself.
"Have you tried working this out?" asked the counsel, who was an old friend of the couple. "You were married in front of God; and I quote 'for better or worse'. So now that the good years are over, you're pulling out Sam. Why?"
Sam fidgeted nervously standing in front of the counsel. Now, that he had officially left Gloria, he had nowhere to go. He placed himself in the 'worse' years.
"I want to be a priest, God has spoken to me," pleaded Sam as tears rolled down his cheeks.
"Well, isn't that convenient Sam," said the counsel sarcastically. "Can you prove this God's call to me."
Sam burst out in tears.
"I cannot prove it even to myself, let alone to you," he cried.

"You're looking for an easy way out Sam," said counsel Bill. "You know you love Gloria, you're just afraid to admit it. Give me five good reasons why you're leaving her.
The two men were sitting across from each other in Bill's old-fashioned office filled with books and antiques. Gloria was sitting somewhere in the middle between the two resentful men. It was a late summer afternoon, and a fly made its way into Bill's office. Sam's shirt and pants were wrinkled from the suitcase that he had just thrown underneath the motel double bed. He also forgot to comb his thick dark hair.
"You don't exactly look like you're ready to leave her Sam," said Bill. "Give me your five reasons."
All of a sudden, as the past dissipated, Sam couldn't think of a single reason why he would want to leave Gloria. She was the breadwinner, the banker, wearing the pants in the family. Gloria had always let him follow his dreams, except for the one of becoming a celibate priest. Sam worked as an assistant arts teacher at the Catholic High School before he got his calling.
"You can get a certificate online for $20 and preach right away," she would respond to his arguments that God was calling him.
"Not in catholic religion," he said. "I cannot be a married man."
Sam turned to the counsel with wild white hair. He stood up and approached his desk. He took Bill's mallet from the desk, and slammed it several times. Then he slowly beat it once:

"Here are my reasons: number one, I hate being tied to one woman, one house, one belief, one job and one set of standards."
Both, Bill and Gloria stared at Sam in total disbelief as he slammed the mallet the second time:
"Number two, I hate conformity and all the lies that come with it; you have to work hard so you can make it. Make into what, ha?"
Sam was furious as he looked around him.
"How many clients did you have to screw over Bill to get to this point to make it?" Sam stepped closer to Bill. He was in his face now. Bill pulled away.
Then the mallet hit the table again for the third time.
"Number three, I hate money, and the pain it brings regardless whether you have it or not."
Sam looked at Gloria.
"I despise you for your love of money, never making any time for me. Just your bank job, that's what you're all about. Your eyes are turning green from it."
Sam leaned over Gloria's head so he could smell her cheap perfume.
"You have turned into a green monster over the years," he said.
Sam was now fuming trying to catch breath. He wanted to slam the mallet on her head. Instead he slammed it back in front of Bill's wide-open eyes.
"Number four, don't stare at me like that when I am angry. Don't look at me at all. Number five, don't question me in front of God's eyes. Have you no belief?"
Sam looked up at the ceiling, then he bowed and fell on his knees.

"God, show them that you're calling me, please show them," he broke down crying.

A deadly silence filled the room with only the fly buzzing behind the curtains. Bill stood up and looked outside the window as he took a deep breath.

"Sam, you need psychiatric help," said Bill. "You've lost it."

The door slammed, and Gloria was gone. After the showdown in Bill's office, the divorce didn't take that long. According to the hired psychiatrist Sam was deemed unfit for a marriage. Later, the marriage was finally annulled by His Holiness.

After years in the seminary, Sam got used to the ascetic way of life. All those years, he never regretted for once leaving Gloria and his comfortable life in the suburbia. Sam trained himself to be humble.

"They declared you crazy, ha?" asked a fellow seminarian.

"They did, I have papers to prove it," said Sam. "It was the only way out."

Now, as he was standing in front of the bishop in the Yurt, Sam rubbed his forehead.

"Sorry, Arwen, I couldn't find my way here," said Sam. "And that driver just took the longest route in the middle of the night."

Arwen was sitting in an armchair accompanied by high-ranking clergy from all over the country. It was cold in the big tent, even though the heat was on. Arwen seemed entertained.

"Bring us some Chardonnay," ordered the bishop.

"Have a seat my dear friend," Arwen beckoned. "You've been waiting for this for a long time. I've always known you've wanted this since the first time I set my eyes on you."

Sam sat down exhausted next to Arwen. He wondered why was Arwen all dressed up ceremoniously in the middle of the night in the middle of nowhere. Arwen put on his white ornate chasuble on purpose. Even the green-painted yurt had stained glass windows, as it blended well into the wooded surroundings. It was white and spacious. There was a cross and a small altar in the main octagon facing the east.

"We shall wait until sunrise," said Arwen holding up his wine glass.

Sam too grabbed his glass and looked through the liquid gold at the rest of the clergy. He missed Arwen's deep searching look. They ate crab legs, artichokes and wild rice. By now, Sam was hungry and he was getting increasingly impatient.

But impatience was the story of Sam's life. He was impatient to get married, to have children, to get divorced and to get ordained. And it was all in that particular order. Sam never enjoyed the presence of the moment, always waiting for something new to happen in his life. He treated life like a menu in a two-star restaurant. Since there was not much to choose from, Sam always went for the next best thing, whatever that may have been.

After he got tired of his teacher's job and demanding Gloria, he went for the next best thing. He didn't want to deal with regular life and its never-ending 9 to 5 requirements, and thereafter. Sam was sure he got the calling when Arwen touched his shoulder inside that speaker tent a long time ago. He remembered Gloria yelling at him.

"I don't believe you," she screamed. "You just want an easy way out now that the kids are big."

Arwen was engaged in deep conversation with the other priests, who were also all dressed up. Sam missed the solitude of his rectory. The previous priest left a well-stocked bar in the rectory. Sam stopped drinking when the mid-life crisis hit him 15 years ago. Before that, he was a moderate drinker searching for answers in rye liquids like whiskey. After he became a priest, he switched to wine, which was not allowed but encouraged in the catholic denomination. Christ and the apostles also drank wine. But, this time around, Sam watched his drinking never to cross that forbidden line. He watched the priests and Arwen get intoxicated.

"This must have been planned to the last minute," he thought to himself. "They're not going to be able to announce whatever they want to announce."

The first rays of the rising sun hit through the stained-glass windows uncovering a remarkable vista of the Shabbawa Mountains. The peaks turned silver in the morning mist of the sunrise. The water was evaporating from the rich brown soil under the pine trees. Skiing runs and trails cut through the woods creating remarkable patterns. Some peaks already had snow. The morning in the mountains was a testament to the secretive announcement.

Arwen stood up steadfast, still holding his glass of wine. He raised it along with the clergy.

"Here is to the next bishop of the Shabbawa diocese," Arwen said. And then the wine glasses clinked a hundred times over and over again. The ringing of the glasses spread outside the yurt and over the mountains.

The archbishop came out of his hiding. Arwen did this on purpose, so Sam would be kept in secret as to what was going to happen at this conclave.

"Do stand up, dear son," said the archbishop.

Sam's knees started to shake. He expected a lot of things, but not this. Sam felt he couldn't stand up to face the archbishop or bishop Arwen. Slowly, he got up out of his chair, his palms sweating. He felt sweat on his forehead and trickling down his spine into his pants. He could now smell the incense, and the morning coffee. The sun blinded him, so he couldn't see the archbishop anymore. Sam stared into the stained-glass window depicting St. Paul, his favorite saint. The archbishop had a face of gold from the sun. He was handing him something, as he made the sign of a cross on his forehead.

"We will make it formal in the cathedral," the archbishop said. "For now, you have this."

It was a scroll of papyrus paper with the logo of the Archdiocese of Kawanah. With deep interest, Sam looked at the logo. It was a sword with a ring on it. The wording became blurry, as Sam bowed his head and knelt in front of the archbishop. The archbishop put oil on his head.

"You will await your official appointment in silence without sharing with anyone under the sun or the soil," said the archbishop.

Sam with his head bowed did not see the archbishop leave. He remained kneeling until he heard a car leave. He dared not look up at Arwen. Sam could hear the shuffling of the feet as the clergy left the main chamber in the yurt. He could smell Arwen before he put his hand on his shoulder. Arwen always smelled of incense, foreign lands and unknown pleasures. Sam noticed the sun rays were now hitting the mosaic floor. He studied the pattern of the mosaic on the floor. It was a perfect pyramid in the middle surrounded by stars, the moon and the heavens. Sam tilted his head back, and attempted to look at Arwen. Arwen had a distinct look in his eyes. Only his body was present inside the yurt. He touched Sam's head and made the sign of the cross on his forehead.

"In silence, you will await your official appointment when the time comes," said Arwen. "No one outside this conclave shall find out about this. You will stay by yourself for three more days, pray and meditate over this."

Everyone had left the yurt. There were no phones; Sam had to hand his phone over to Arwen. However, there was plenty of food, drinks, a radio, books and notebooks. Sam had difficulty breathing. He heard the furnace turn on, and a warm wave flooded him.

When he finally crawled into his bed, the super moon flooded the yurt with cold, silver light. Yes, Sam got what he wanted, even though he didn't know he was looking for it. Strange fear of the unknown settled in his throat.

Under his eyelids, he felt the future; the cardinal was placing the mitre on his head. It was heavy with a sturdy construction. He lowered his head, so the cardinal could place the mitre firmly on his head still full of dark hair. The choir was singing, “Gloria, In excelsis Deo.” The incense was everywhere.

As he looked at the crowd in the pews, he spotted a well-known face. Gloria was sitting in the third pew to the right. She was holding a handkerchief to her face, and wiping off tears from her eyes.

Because of the choir, he couldn’t hear her sobbing out loud. She was dressed in purple and white. The sun rays touched her red hair gently.

“It will be over soon,” Sam thought to himself, “Finally she will leave my life forever.”

Sam was wide awake now, as he felt his head for the mitre that was placed on it. Instead he held a thick lock of his hair. He could feel the distance of the dream.

He got up and walked through the narrow passage to the observatory dome. He watched the magnificent Perseus showers while searching for answers in the stars and in his love for astronomy. He got what he wanted, but not the way he wanted it. It looked like more of Arwen’s accomplishment than his own. Surrounded by the secrecy of the entire deal, Sam wasn’t sure if he could live up to what was expected.

“This will stay in complete silence with you,” the archbishop’s words rang in his ears again.

Wow, he couldn’t keep the secrets from the confession booth that he heard on Saturdays. Everybody knew of Joe’s ordeal and his hate of his mother’s will of money to the church. Sam made no secrets of that.

"And even though some of you may not want to give to church, you should consider the will of your mother," he preached from the altar. "You cannot wander astray from that, or you will end up in hell."
Sam noticed that he increasingly used the word hell to scare the oblivious parishioners.
"And you know that gossiping is a sin that will land you in hell," he said with a grimace on his face.
Sam himself was the worst gossiper around. Now, that he was scheduled to leave the Shabbawa Mountain retreat soon, he had to tell somebody about his promotion.
"I'll tell it to the stars what had happened here," he thought.
He struggled sleepless into the wee hours of the night. The morning coffee didn't taste that great, or the soggy toast. The unofficial promotion left a bitter taste in Sam's mouth. He quickly packed up and stood outside the yurt brushing away the thoughts of his promotion.
The obnoxious driver was back in his cap.
"Hey, did you have a good time," he laughed as he opened the car door. "Got any chicks under your covers?"
Sam felt offended as the next holy man named by the archbishop himself.
"How dare you speak to me like that?" Sam yelled with his face in the driver's.
"Because I can," laughed the driver, "without me, you're going to stay here forever or at least until Arwen blows his whistle."

Sam climbed into the car disgusted with the driver's behavior. He would have time to think on the way home. The car took several turns left and then right descending from the mountains on the slippery road. The tires screeched as the driver got the car out of a slide on the hill.

"You don't have to worry, I can't tell my way back," Sam said urgently. "You're wasting our time trying to confuse me."

Sam knew the rules of the labyrinth; only one route would lead them out of the maze of trails and two tracks.

"You realize, I will never see you again," said the driver sarcastically.

"I hope not, you scum bag," Sam was glad they were back in front of the rectory.

"Goodbye."

It was quiet inside the rectory. Sam immediately noticed a letter on the dining table. There was his phone lying next to the letter. It was full of messages. Arwen did not delete them. He didn't have to. Sam had decided back in the mountains while watching the Perseus showers.

It was a Saturday, and time for confessions.

"Father, I have sinned," said a man with a heavy voice. "I beat my wife when I was drunk."

Here we go again, thought Sam. If he was looking for answers, he got them right there.

"Joe, I can't give you absolution, because you are unforgiveable," said Sam breathing heavily. "You're like me, you will never learn. That's why we don't belong here."

"But, Father, I promise to repent, I will not beat her again," said Joe crying.

"You will have to let somebody else know," said Sam. "I am done here."

Sam stepped out of the confession booth, and threw his black gown on the closest pew. He walked down the church nave toward the big gate.

Sam turned around and gave one last look and a bow to the altar. He pulled out of his pocket the letter that was laying on the table, quickly reading the message again.

"I'll be waiting for you when you get back from Shabbawa."

Gloria.

When Layla met Corey

Layla recalled that day when she met Corey at the Little Blue Market in Vicksburg. She was spending her summer break in the Midwest USA near the Great Lakes. She was excited as always to come to visit with her relatives.

Soon she learned to speak the language of her new peers in the private school in the nearby Irish community of Leiland. Her first love was the school with her friends and faith.

The Little Blue Market stood out among the tidbits of joy consisting of Shopkins, ice cream shakes, chocolates and cornfields.

One summer afternoon after school, Layla headed out to the park with aunt Madeleine. She called her lovingly “Maddie.”

For the longest time Layla did not know the name of the boy, who came to play with his mom to the same park. They played on the slides and swings and in the colorful iron kingdom in the woods by the Bear Creek.

He had a nice smile and was about the same height as Layla. However, the boy was a lot shyer and careful about not getting dirty in the needles of the pine trees.

Layla glided down the slide and climbed the ladder to the kingdom steeple. She swung on the rope high into the air, even though she was wearing a yellow skirt that flew around changing her into a butterfly.

Layla loved to wear dresses and skirts to the great joy of those around her. The times in the first two decades of the new millennium were meant for jeans and pants for all; men, women and kids.

Her height didn’t show that she was prematurely born. The boy in the red, blue and yellow kingdom made of scrap iron, seemed younger, but mature enough to play with Layla.

“Look, Maddie,” she yelled from the steeple. “I am the queen here, and he is the king.”

Maddie was writing in her diary and looked up at Layla.

"You need a crown, Layla." she said. "We can get one in the afternoon."

A week later, the two kids ran into each other at the same park.

"I want to see him again," she begged before they headed out.

"We don't even know his name," said Maddie. "How are we going to look for him?"

It was a hot summer midweek July afternoon at the park under the pine trees on top of a hill. The boy with his mother were already there. The boy was perched up high on the first level of the playset.

Layla quickly climbed up to join him. The boy stepped back a little, surprised at Layla's speed. They sat next to each other on top of the slide deciding whether to go down or not. They remained high on top of the kingdom.

"What's your name?" Layla asked.

"I am Corey," he said as he turned his head to mom down on the bench.

"I am Layla," she said. "That is my Aunt Maddie."

Corey looked at the girl and below at Maddie.

"I don't have an aunt," he said. "I have a mommy."

Maddie suggested they meet at the Little Blue Market next week, since Layla had been talking about the boy from the playground so much.

"When do I get to see Corey?" she asked. "I want to see him now."

"You still have Christmas in July before we get to see Corey," said Maddie. "It's your favorite thing."

Christmas in July at the private school was Layla's favorite summer activity, because she never got to spent the real Christmas in America. They watched a Christmas movie in school, baked cookies and made presents for each other.

"We're going to see him right this afternoon?" Layla asked eagerly.

They drove past the cornfields to the Little Blue Market with tire swings and a barnyard.

"We don't have cornfields back in France," Layla said. "I love corn."

They arrived at the Little Blue Market just in time to get the superman ice cream in all its pretty colors and flavors. They sat underneath the pergola with their cold treats.

"I love the banana flavor," said Maddie. "It reminds of the bananas I could never have at home."

Layla was eating her ice cream carefully not to get her yellow dress messy or stained from the blue or red of the superman ice cream.

"Maddie, where do they make this ice cream?" Layla asked.

It was hot and the ice cream started dripping from the cone. Layla licked it making a bigger mess.

"This is so delicious," she said, "wherever they make it."

Corey finally arrived at the Little Blue Market in mom's van.

"Sorry, if we're late," said Corey's mom. "I am Renca."

The afternoon at the farm was like a feather in the summer breeze; the kids were playing on the swing set made of tires. The women chatted about their lives in the country.

“I come from a big city, but I love it here,” said Renca. “It’s so peaceful.”

The animals were hiding from the heat in their sheds; the chickens were running across the yard from the chicken coop. Earlier, they all had peaked inside if there were any eggs.

The heat pounded hard since there were no trees on the farm.

Maddie smiled thinking about her faraway origins across the Atlantic Ocean.

Many years later, Maddie had trouble drawing her memory back to that hot afternoon at the Little Blue Market. She could feel that same heat, but Maddie could not think of what had happened.

“We’ll see you again, next week,” said Renca.

“Come to the fair with us,” Layla said.

They didn’t have fairs in the old country of Europe. Since, it was time for the Vicksburg Fair in August, they set their next date at the fairgrounds in town. Layla loved fairs. For Layla, fairs were like butterflies or feathers at the Little Blue Farm.

It was hot at the fairgrounds in town. There were no trees here either, unlike in the park where Layla met Corey. Layla was careful not to get her white dress dirty from the dirt paths through the fairgrounds.

They parked in the grass and hitched a ride on a horse-drawn wagon by the huge Belgians into the magic of the fair. Layla was delighted to find out the horses' names: Dolly and Colby.
She had never seen horses that big, not even on TV or in her fairy tale books.
"Maddie, how come the horses are so big?" she asked with wide eyes glued to the horses.
"They are draft horses used to pulling big loads," said Maddie.
"Do you think they're hot like us?" asked Layla. "Do they have enough water to drink?"
The fairgrounds with animals and people were trapped in the sweltering heat of the August afternoon. The sweet smell of Elephant ears and cotton candy filled the dry air. The Midway was filled with people seeking reprieve from the heat.
The barns with pigs and poultry smelled in the heat.
They were meeting with Renca and Corey by the lemonade stand near the rides. Layla kept peaking around the stands and booths until she finally saw Corey and mom coming down the Midway. Corey had a blue t-shirt on and brown shorts. He was sporting a new haircut and ran to hug her.
"I can hardly wait to go on all the rides," Layla pulled Corey's hand.
The two hopped from one ride to another. Layla's white dress was dirty now and she almost lost her sandals on one of the rides.
They had ice cream in the little park by the Midway and watched people.

"Come one, come all," a carnie was inviting to a ride on the carousel.

The carnie strapped them into the seats on the carousel and they flew high into the air above the ground. The people on the ground below were small, while Corey flying by Layla's side was bigger and bigger. At times he flew ahead of her, sometimes behind her.

When they got off the ride, they watched the little pigs' races and rooted? for the winning pig. Layla's pig Tommy Lee won, and Layla received the much-coveted checkered pink and black flag.

Corey's pig Stallion won too, and Corey received a black and white checkered flag.

"Now, you each have one flag from the fair as a souvenir," said Maddie.

"We don't want to leave yet," said Corey.

"I don't want to leave at all," cried Layla in her dirty white dress. "I want to stay here forever."

The boss fat lady sporting a Stetson noticed the two kids by her pig stalls.

"You both won," she said. "What's wrong?"

"I want to stay here," said Layla crying and holding on tight to Corey.

The boss lady in the Stetson turned to Layla.

"For heaven's sake you can come back tomorrow with your friend," she said. "Just don't cry here in front of the other kids."

She turned up the country music, so the kids couldn't hear Layla sobbing.

Layla wished she could stop time right there by the pig race arena. All in tears, Layla went to sit down on the bleachers. Corey joined her and took her hand.
"Please, do not cry," he begged.

It was the end of summer and time to say goodbye to Corey. Layla had already packed her suitcase with everything under the sun. Maddie was sitting on the floor helping Layla close the suitcase. They couldn't fit anymore toys or clothes in the luggage.
"I am still not done packing," Layla said. "I don't want to leave. I forgot some of my toys."
"We can't fit it all in, we'll keep it for you here," Maddie said.
They arrived at the Little Blue Barn at the same time as Corey and mom. Layla and Corey had their winners' checkered flags with them.
"I am taking mine with me to France," said Layla holding back tears.
They swang on the tire high up in the air.

Many years later, Layla was working at a bakery in Paris to make money for her university studies. It was a hot summer in Paris, and Layla dreamt of the cool breeze coming from Lake Superior at the Straits of Mackinac by that big bridge.
"Mom, I want to go and work in that cute candy city," she said one day after arriving from Paris.

"What candy city?" asked mom. "Paris is not good enough for you?"
Layla threw her backpack in the corner and sat at the dining table inside the old stone house in a small wine village.
"I made enough money for the air ticket to America," she said. "Look."
Layla opened her purse and showed the colorful money to mom.
"I want to be in that candy city at least for the summer before the school starts in the fall," she begged. "Please mom. I am a big girl now."

After landing in Montreal, Layla took the bus from Montreal to Detroit.
"I will be getting off in Mackinaw City," she told the bus driver.
It was a long trip before they reached the Straits of Mackinac and headed across the Big Mac suspended bridge swaying in the breeze between the bridge towers. When she was little, Layla visited the cute candy city with Aunt Maddie and Uncle Bob during her summer stay in America.
Layla barely remembered that last trip to the candy city with all the sweet shops.
It was their second trip to the pretty candy city right before the bridge, and it was also Layla's last one to America for years to come. Money was tight on both sides of the ocean, and no one could afford the private catholic school in Leiland anymore. Months turned into years; Layla grew up from a little girl to a pretty

young woman. She forgot the name of the boy with whom she played on those old tire swings at the barn market.

But the cute candy city stayed with her all those years while attending schools in France. Layla took English classes so she wouldn't forget the language of that faraway land with little racing pigs and colorful ice cream.

When she got off the bus by the Star Line docks in downtown Mackinaw City, Layla didn't know what to expect. There were hundreds of people on the sidewalks. Layla realized she was hungry and she walked into the restaurant she remembered so well, "The Pancake Chef."

The waitresses were still wearing white shirts and black pants, and there was the big buffet island in the middle of the restaurant. A middle-aged waitress with the name tag Nona came to her table. She looked familiar to Layla.

"I know you," exclaimed Layla. "You wanted to study culinary arts in Romania as soon as you got out of high school here in Mackinaw City."

The woman looked in disbelief at the pretty fashionable girl who spoke with an accent.

"I did study in Rumania," she said. "How did you know?"

Layla sporting a light blue summer dress smiled while looking at the menu.

"You waited on us a long time ago," Layla said. "You came back to Mackinaw City and you still work here. What happened?"

"Just for a while," Nona said. "My husband and I are going to open a restaurant here soon."
Nona looked at Layla's suitcase.
"You came for a visit to Mackinaw City?" asked Nona.
"No, I'll be working at Marshall's Fudge and Candy Co. on the corner," said Layla. "I can't wait. I missed this town so much. I had dreams about it back in France."
Layla stayed in the studio apartment above the fudge shop overlooking the docks and the Main Street with its Frontier storefronts. She had to fight with both of her parents back in France to make her dream of going back to America come true.
"You're crazy," dad screamed at her when Layla first mentioned Mackinaw City. "Other people dream of Paris, and you dream of that cold hole Up North," he yelled.
"Daddy, you've never been up there," she fought hard. "It's my little candy town."
When Layla had finally arranged everything for her stay in Mackinaw City, the parents gave up.
"It's your fault that she found out about it all," screamed daddy at mommy.
"And never forgot about it, right?" mommy fought back. "That's my fault too."
Layla worked happily at the Marshall's Fudge shop packaging candy, fudge and desserts. She wrote a letter to Aunt Maddie and Uncle Bob to come and visit with her.

"Maddie, what was that boy's name?" she asked one evening when they went all out to dinner at the Irish pub.

Maddie was fearing the moment when Layla would ask that question. She had asked her that in letters before, but Maddie lied that she had forgotten the boy's name.

"My dear Layla," Maddie said touching Layla's hand. "I have no idea who you are talking about."

Then, they walked in the Straits park with the lighthouse and watched the lights on the "Big Mac." From the park, they took a short stroll down Main Street to Mama Mia's pizzeria and to the bridge museum above the pizzeria.

They sat at the soda fountain on red chairs.

"I have to work tomorrow all day," said Layla. "You don't have to leave until Sunday evening right, Maddie?"

Maddie never forget the name of the boy or his mother, even though they haven't been in contact for many years.

"Don't even mention the name of the boy in front of Layla," were the strict directions coming from parents in France. "Layla cried over him for months; she has forgotten now."

Maddie and Bob stayed in the same resort on Lake Huron they had stayed many years ago with Layla.

"Are you going to tell her?" asked Bob, who was concerned about Layla's stay in America. "You know her parents did not want her to come here. She still has to finish her education."

Layla had that Sunday off from working at the fudge shop. She was looking forward to spending that day with Aunt Maddie and Uncle Bob. But mostly, Layla wanted to find out more about the boy from her childhood.

She suggested they take the ferry to Mackinac Island for the day to bask in the July sunlight.

"We never took you to the island because it is so expensive," said Maddie as they were seated on the top deck of the high-speed ferry.

Layla wore an expensive boutique dress from Paris since they all wanted to eat at the Grand Hotel on the island. They took the horse buggy to the hotel from Jack's Livery & Stables.

They got their expensive seating by the window overlooking the Big Mac suspended bridge.

"I love that bridge," Layla said. "Remember when we went to the museum above Mama Mia's pizzeria?"

"And we've never been to the Grand Hotel before," said Uncle Bob. "It's a special treat for all of us."

"Did you miss America when you were in France?" Aunt Maddie asked.

The trio shared many special bonds since Layla started coming to America for the summers as a little girl.

"I mainly miss the boy, whom I used to play with," she said teary-eyed. "Do you know his name Aunt Maddie?"

"It was Corey," said Maddie reluctantly. "I do not know what happened with them. I've never seen them again. We were hoping you had forgotten about him."

The Mackinac Island was a paradise for Layla.

"Can we stay here forever?" she asked. "I don't want to go back ever to France."

They walked the island and shopped the pretty shops with souvenirs.

"Maddie will you help me find Corey?" Layla begged as they boarded the Star Line back to mainland.

"How would I do that?" asked Maddie concerned. "You have to work tomorrow, and we have to go back to Vicksburg.

"Please, promise that you will help me find him," Layla insisted.

"I promise," Maddie said. "Have a good week. We'll come back next weekend to see you."

The trip back to Lower Peninsula was troubling due to Layla's main concern about the boy from her childhood.

"Even if we find him, what next?" said Bob. "We shouldn't have allowed her to come back here. Corey's parents could have moved out of the area; America is a big country."

"I could place an ad in the paper," Maddie suggested. "But we don't really want to find him."

Layla was working the evening shift at the fudge shop, when a young man asked her about the bridge museum above the Mama Mia Pizzeria.

Layla looked up from her work because she thought she had recognized the voice.

"Have we ever met?" she asked the young man. "Your voice sounds familiar."

"And you have an accent," he said. "Where is that coming from?"

Layla blushed.

"I am from France," she said. "But I used to go to a private school in the Lower Peninsula."

Layla searched for a clue in the young man's face, anything that would help her remember. He had those big blue eyes and dark hair, that she had seen before. He was a lot taller now than she was.

As he paid with a credit card, Layla noticed the name Corey. As soon as she saw the name in writing it dawned on her:

"I used to know a Corey back when I was little," she said. "We used to play on a tire swing set at a barn market. Then, I had to leave for France. We went to the fair together in Vicksburg."

Corey was shocked; he too had long time forgotten about Layla. He took a deep look at the young woman in a white apron.

"That barn doesn't stand there anymore," he said. "It's long gone, along with the Superman ice cream. I miss it. I would have not recognized you, but your name tag says Layla."

Layla had tears in her eyes.

"I'll be done soon at work," she said quickly. "We can meet at Mama Mia's, if you want to."

"I'd love to do that," Corey said. "See you there in about an hour?"

"Yes, I will see you there at 8 p.m. downstairs," she said.

Layla was scared of the rendezvous, and so was Corey. Years have gone by without them staying in contact.

When she was finally done at the fudge shop, Layla changed from her work clothes in the backroom. As she was changing, she could hear the sirens of emergency vehicles.

Layla ran out of the store to see what was going on. There was a raging fire with flames shooting into the sky.

"Where is that coming from?" Layla asked a co-worker.

Then they could see it clearly from the corner of Central Ave in front of the fudge shop. People were running around in panic and screaming:

"Mama Mia's is on fire."

Layla ran down Central Ave to the pizzeria. The fire got the best of the place with many false storefronts and false ceilings. The 100-year-old building with the museum were destroyed within a few hours.

"Did everyone make it out?" Layla cried to the firefighters.

"Yes, everyone was evacuated," said the fire chief.

In vain did Layla search the area for Corey. She went back to the fudge shop to ask about him.

"Was Corey here looking for me?" Layla asked.

She kept getting the same answer: "No one by that name has been here looking for you, Layla."

Aunt Maddie called her as soon as she had found out about the fire at Mama Mia's and at the Mackinac Bridge Museum.

"Layla, I spoke with your mother," she said sobbing. "She saw the fire coverage on the Internet. You have to return to France as soon as possible. Mom got you a ticket for the first flight out of Detroit to Paris tomorrow."

"But, what about Corey?" Layla cried. "I have already found him. He's here in Mackinaw City. I talked to him."
"You will have to forget about him just like about America," said Maddie. "We will miss you, but it's best for all of us. That fire was more than an omen for you not to stay here."

Waiting for Snow

It was January in the new year of the Earth Pig, and there was still no snow on the ground. Green stalks of grass and weeds were peeking out of the ground and laughing in the wind at the parked snowmobiles with no riders. Other equipment too was idling.
The eager machines just sat still waiting in the front and backyards. Mother Earth was refusing to cooperate on one side, on the other she released her wrath on the coastal states.
The Midwest was sleeping its winter dream dipped into deep dry freeze and after the holiday blues. A man in the tiny community of Paris put some water in his coffee maker. The year-round Christmas tree was still lit and cast colorful lights on the modest kitchen with a broken cabinet underneath the kitchen sink. He stored a bucket with a rag there for his chores; now this was a habit from the old country in Europe.
The first morning cigarette of the day was the best one. He deeply inhaled and let out the smoke in gray

circles. One wall of the mobile home was an entire mirror divided into three separate sections. He often walked to the mirror wall to look at himself. But just before looking in the mirror, Colin had to look outside. He pulled aside the checkered racing flag that was covering the window overlooking the front yard with a view on Paris Road.

Colin had to move through a set of obstacles to get to the window. These were large train layouts taking up the entire living room. Colin's mom called it a fire safety hazard, so would the firemen.

The green and yellow grass lacked the coveted white cover. Colin carefully stepped outside on the wooden steps to make sure there was no snow. He went to the green snowmobile with the new permit and a full tank of gas.

Paris sat on an extensive trail system close to a county park. The community had a motel, a pizza parlor and a general store "Papa's;" all located on the trail.

Colin, always wearing a train conductor's black hat, called himself "The Trainman."

With untied shoelaces, Colin thumped his feet on the frozen ground. He pulled off the cover from the idling machine. He purchased the permit from his last modest paycheck. Colin could have bought beer or more tobacco, if he had known there would be no snow. That frozen morning in January, he wished he had bought beer and tobacco instead of that stupid permit.

Since, the cigarettes were getting more and more expensive, Colin had switched to tobacco. He rolled his own cigarettes with Tin Star Gold tobacco available at the gas stations. The closest gas station was six miles away in Big Rapids. He couldn't even ride there to get his stash.

Colin thought about calling the weatherman from the local TV station to ask him what's going on. He covered back up the snowmobile and walked inside the mobile home puffing on his cigarette. As Colin opened the fridge, he realized he was running out of milk and ground beef.

The new owner at "Papa's" bought the general store last summer. The old store sat on the main drag through Paris. He also owned the ice cream shack next door.

"Hey, Colin, what's up?" he laughed touching his round belly. "I got some hot pizza and fresh coffee. You look frozen, man."

"Yeah, man, I had to walk a mile in the freeze," Colin said. "Give me some of that hot coffee. I couldn't ride my snowmobile."

Hayden, the owner, kept a table and four chairs behind the last aisle of groceries. The last aisle was a space where Hayden hid everything from the customers; from buzz balls to hemp, and marijuana.

The two sat down with large mugs of coffee. Memories abounded at the old store with three previous owners. Hayden put up some NASCAR posters. Each owner left his own legacy behind. These included memorabilia that had lost their meaning to other store owners. Hayden came from Detroit after retiring from GM.

"Tell me all there is to know about Paris," said Hayden running his hand through his curly gray hair. "What's the story of that motel?"

"It's a halfway house and a motel," said Colin. "I know the owner Megan. She's a fine gal. Can't say the same about the customers. Most of them came from the locker."

Hayden leaned back in the chair still smiling.

"How did you end up in Paris all the way from the old country?" he asked.

Colin had stayed at the motel several times before he got his own dwelling. He also camped at the park near the Eiffel Tower enshrined in the surrounding forest. Colin took welding classes in the university town of Big Rapids.

The 20-foot tall Eiffel Tower welded by the Chippewa High School students hovered above the fowl pond near the river. The students used the metal from the bunkbed frames from the bunkhouses, that housed the Workers Progress Administration (WPA) workers in the area.

"I wish I had welded that tower," Colin sighed sipping on the hot coffee. "This is some good coffee you got."

"Yeah, man, I brew it fresh through the afternoon," he said. "Not too many takers nowadays. I wish we got some snow. It brings in people from the trails and the motel."

Colin stepped outside the back door to smoke. From the back porch behind the store, he could see the trail cutting through the sassafras shrubs. Some still had berries hanging onto the branches. He walked to the

trail made from a railroad bed. It stretched south to Big Rapids and north to Reed City and Cadillac. A nice wooden bridge traversed the brook, a tributary into the Muskegon River.
Colin imagined the trail some 100 years ago with puffing locomotives pulling train cars loaded with wood. He wouldn't have a problem getting to Reed City for his groceries if the GR&I was still operating. The Grand Rapids and Indiana Railroad (GR&I) ran from Rockford to Cadillac during the 1800s and 1900s. It transported supplies to the thriving logging industry in northern Michigan.
Even the old railroad trusses were gone now. New wooden structures replaced the old ones, not quite in the same glory. Puffing on his Tin Star Gold Tobacco, Colin could see and hear the approaching train.
"Hayden, I wish those trains came back, don't you," Colin asked lowering himself into the chair behind the last aisle. "You'd be busier, man."
"Wife said not to do this," said Hayden.
"Do what?" asked Colin.
"You know, buy the store in the middle of nowhere," Hayden sighed picking up the paper.
"How did you find out about the place?" asked Colin.
"We used to camp at the park," Hayden said. "I fished the Muskegon River and I fell in love here."
"How about you, man?" Hayden laughed.
In that moment the store bell rang announcing a customer. Colin got up too and walked to the window. Snowflakes were coming down from the sky onto the gravel parking around the store. He pulled down his hat tighter over the ears.

"I am going to head back home and hope for the best," he said as he slammed the door.
"Easy buddy," said Hayden with a large smile. "Come back soon. I'll have more fresh coffee."

Colin got up early the next morning ready to hit the trail and take off to the north. He noticed he was running out of his Tin Star Gold Tobacco. Without snow, he had no choice but to walk, hitch a ride or even worse yet; take the MODA bus. He walked the old railroad bed at least a hundred times, rain or shine. He put on his large boots and tied up the shoelaces, since on long treks he didn't trust himself not to stumble. He liked to listen to the sounds under his big boots. They changed depending on the weather from a dry hard thump to a soft touch in the quiet snow.
Colin stepped on the trail near the Paris Park Fish Hatchery built in 1881. It was a great shelter open from all the elements in season.
He tried opening the door behind the fish pond, but it was locked. The day like the trail stretched ahead of him with endless possibilities.
He liked the title of "The Trainman" that Colin bestowed upon himself due to the lack of other worldly titles. He veered off the track to the trout ponds on the east side. Colin walked further into the woods and stood at the foot of the knoll. He glanced 20 feet high to the top of the metal Eiffel Tower replica.
Peace and hope settled in his heart in the chill of the morning. A breeze was coming from the river. The

park was completely deserted with only a few cabins locked for the season.

"Aren't you afraid going into that park by yourself?" Hayden asked once. "You don't carry a gun. What if someone jumps you?"

Colin took off his right glove and touched the cold metal of the base frame. His finger almost stuck in the frost to the metal. He had to peel it off, but the top layer of his skin stuck to the metal.

"Ouch, that hurts," he whispered.

He could hear the fowl from the duck pond. Colin followed the winding path around the knoll and by the creek to the pond. He watched the swans and the ducks float gracefully on the water. The quacking of the ducks woke Colin up from his daydreaming.

On his way back to the trail, he passed the eight-foot-tall statue of an Indian Chippewa Chief chiseled from stone in two dimensions by an unknown Bulgarian in 1937 as a WPA project.

"Was your country part of Russia?" Hayden asked him once. "You know like that Bulgarian dude who carved the Indian in the park."

"What Indian in the park?" Colin asked. "I don't know what you're talking about. I don't know any Indians."

"It's a statue Colin, you told me about it," said Hayden. "You go out there and smoke."

It was chilly back on the trail too. The chill crawled down Colin's spine, and he shivered. He turned back only to try again tomorrow.

In the morning, Colin stepped outside for his first cigarette as he listened to the coyotes tearing their

prey. He wondered if it was a chicken or a weak bird. The cold without any snow had settled in.
The dry frost was biting into his nails and skin.
"Hayden, I really wish we got snow," said Colin easing himself into a chair behind the last aisle. "I really need to get my groceries in Reed City."
"Mine are not enough for you?" asked Hayden laughing.
"Yes, but I need to do my banking and check things out, you know," he said.
"Be careful on the trail," warned Hayden. "There had been some bear sightings, and I hear coyotes all the time."
Colin finished his coffee with Hayden and headed out on the trail. He noticed the trail markers. It seemed like a long walk under the cloudy skies to Reed City, a small community at the crossroads of several trails. He sought out his newest friend Buck at the second-hand store. Buck worked part-time at the store without any particular ambition. But they shared the same love for trains and layouts. They talked trains for hours.
"I'd be a conductor, if trains hadn't gone out," said Colin nostalgically.
"You'd be a lot of things, Colin," said Buck. "Just be Colin for today."
"Do you know when we're getting snow?" Colin asked.
Buck walked to the big store window and looked outside on the Main Street. He wished for snow for Colin's sake. Buck liked the dry winter without any

snow because he didn't have to shovel the sidewalk in front of the store.

"We should get a train show going man," said Colin.

"We will soon. You have to be patient," said Buck.

"I am going to head to the Depot to check out things," said Colin.

Colin walked into the deep freeze on Main Street. He looked at the old sign across the street from the yogurt factory. That was all that was left of the Osceola Hotel, an old rusty sign. Colin felt like most of his life was disappearing with the old landmarks and the railroad tracks. Everything he had loved was gone; and everything he was looking forward to, wasn't coming.

He could hear the hard thump of his own boots; the city was deserted. The Herald Newspaper office was vacant along with the pizza place. What was left of the city, moved toward the freeway.

"All we have left of the city are those 100 feet tall poles with the yellow arches," a deceased friend once said.

He was right; only later a hospital joined the yellow arches. The only grocery owner retired after a heist at the store. Now, the city was waiting for someone to purchase the grocery.

The good thing about the Depot at the Crossroads was that Colin could use the bathroom there without having to pay for coffee at the coffee shop. Colin liked hanging around the Depot even when there was no snow for the snowmobilers to gather by the campfire.

He decided to make his own fire today to warm up his freezing feet and hands. Colin knew how to make a fire fast in the round pit with plenty of wood available. Once the fire was going, he sat on a stump watching the orange flame in the daylight of the afternoon.

In the flame, he saw the bodies of his past girlfriends including the girls from JWs. He had high hopes for them and for himself. About five years ago, a couple of well-dressed young women knocked on his door. They wanted to educate him about the end of the world. Colin was looking forward to the beginning of a new one with these women. They had books and pamphlets and they talked well without any scruples. The pamphlets usually had flames and the devil dancing in them. The Trainman who was also an artist closely looked at the devil dancing in the flames.

"What do you think about this?" he looked up at the girls pointing to the devil dancing in the flames.

The young women looked at each other, and then at Colin.

"Well, it's the devil himself," said the blonde shrieking with excitement.

The brunette seconded with a nod and she quickly swiped from the coffee table Colin's cigarettes and grabbed the beer.

"These are temptations from the devil," she said. "I am taking these, confiscating them."

Colin turned red from anger and jumped up from his chair.

"Give that back to me," he snagged the pack of cigarettes and the beer from the brunette.

Next Sunday, the women were back. Colin was excited and quickly opened the door. The women walked in with pamphlets and books. He didn't care about the books; all he cared about were the women.
"We came to put you back on the right track," said the blonde seriously.
"How do you know I was on the wrong track?" asked Colin running his hand through his graying and thinning hair. He touched his round belly. No matter how many times he rode his bike, Colin couldn't get rid of the belly. It never bothered him before, until these two had shown up.
"You have to stop drinking and smoking," said the brunette handing Colin a pamphlet with the devil dancing in the flames.
Colin looked at the picture and then at the two young women.
"What do you know about the devil?" he asked.
The women straightened their backs in the couch moving into a stiff position holding their heads up high.
"He will steal your soul," said the blonde looking at the brunette.
"I would have to have one first," said Colin lighting up a cigarette. He had been rolling them all morning long instead of going to church. He let out the gray circles of smoke in the direction of the two women.
They leaned back into the sofa trying to escape the smoke. Colin laughed loud in his chair.
"You girls think I have a soul to sell?" Colin kept laughing.

They both stood up and packed up their books, leaving the pamphlets behind.
"You might want to come and see us next week," the blonde said. "Call it a date. We'll call you with a location next week."
Colin stood up.
"You mean both of you?" he asked with a smirk sizing them up in his beady eyes.
They left quickly, as Colin was puffing smoke behind them. He sat in his chair and picked up one of the brochures. Since, he had the Sunday afternoon ahead of him, Colin decided he would look at brochures after taking a nap. Colin dreamt of lust with both girls. First, he touched the blonde, then the brunette. Then both were on top of him; one from each side. The blonde was on the top of his head, the brunette was on the bottom and between his legs. He had never felt as much ecstasy. A sweet stream of love flowed through him from top to bottom. The women were in constant motion and in unison with him moving up and down in the rhythm of the Sunday afternoon.
Colin woke up sweating and his pants were wet. He grabbed a beer and lit up a cigarette letting the gray circles of smoke out of his mouth quickly. He never felt better in his life; even the sun came out from behind the checkered flag. Colin finally picked up a pamphlet with the dancing devil in the flames.
Now, he knew what it was like to dance with the devil, two of them, not just one. It was the beautiful dance of lust forged by fire. Colin touched the burgundy sofa fabric around him to make sure they were gone. He could still smell the cheap perfume on

the blonde with the pony tail, and the smell of lemon on the brunette's blouse. He should have just ripped the blouse open to see her big breasts that showed through the soft silk. They would have spilled on him. But he did touch them on the surface of the blouse. Colin could feel the flesh under the silk. They were nice and round, comforting.

Did the devil forbid the act of love or did he ignite the flame in Colin's heart?

"Are Demons real?" Colin read out loud the title on one brochure.

From the brochure, Colin found out that demons are angels who had gone bad.

Could he be one of the angels gone bad?

He felt good about the young women. After all they were going to call him with a date.

"Did you ask them for a phone number," Hayden seemed concerned.

Colin stopped at the general store for a cup of coffee still with no snow on the horizon.

"Tell me how you ended up in Paris all the way from the old country?" Hayden remembered the old question.

Colin leaned back into the chair and searched his memory.

"I've always liked Paris more than Big Rapids, and then I like Reed City more than Big Rapids," he said. "That's where my folks had settled down because of the university."

"I heard your dad was a professor at the school," Hayden said.

"Where did you hear that?" Colin started tying his shoelaces before heading back out on the trail.
"Read it in the Pioneer," Hayden said. "Come back again, tell me about the girls. Good luck."
Colin went out the back door and lit a rolled- up cigarette from Gold Tin tobacco puffing the smoke into the frosty air. The dry frozen leaves crunched under his boots helplessly. He felt his crouching stomach.
Back at the mobile home, he turned on the locomotive to watch it run its course. It was a yellow LGB. Now, he had to wait for that phone call. The call came in the afternoon.
"Meet us at that shrine by the wooden cross in an hour," one of them said.
"Come and pick me up, I can't get there in an hour," Colin said. "There is no snow."
"Ok, we'll pick you up," a voice said.
The women arrived in 20 minutes in an old beaten up van. It finally started to snow heavily. There was no one in the building. It didn't look like a church. The service was over, but it was still warm inside.
"We would like you to join our church," the blonde said.
"I can do that," Colin said. "It doesn't look like a church."
"But you have to give us money first," the brunette said.
"Why? Colin asked. "You're not prostitutes, are you?"
"No, we're angels who turned into demons," the blonde said.

"In that case, you don't need any money," Colin said. "You have all the money you need."
Colin got up to leave smelling a hoax.
"You know even if I had money, I wouldn't give them it? to you," he said.
"You would be giving it to the church," the brunette said.
"You are both liars and now I will have to walk back in that blizzard," he said, "or will you give me a ride home to Paris?"
The women looked at each other and laughed. Colin stumbled out the door and headed out for a cold walk home.

The next day Colin rode his snowmobile to have coffee with Hayden.
"All they wanted was money," he said sipping hot coffee.
"That's what they always want," Hayden said. "You have snow now, and I will have more customers. We're lucky men. One of these days we'll go to Cranker's and have a Professor IPA."

Six Palms by the Tiki

Amora was watching the bluish gray waves swell before they hit the shore with a thunder echoing yesterday's storm. The pier was all wet from the morning sea fog doubled by the fog coming from the land.

That morning walk on the beach to the fishing pier seemed endless even though it wasn't even a mile long. Her feet sinking in the wet sand, Amora could hardly see the jetting structure in the distance. The warm westerly wind combined with the cold Norte bent the tall palm trees and whipped a white foam on top of the waves. Slender beach pines along with palms served as markers on the beach walk between the dunes and the Gulf waters.

The tide had washed ashore treasures galore: large speckled cockles, coquinas, calico scallops, whelks, sturdy white jewel boxes, twisted conches, translucent jingle shells in shades of orange, olive and bubble shells.

The yellowish coquina and turkey shells were still attached holding on tight to each other. The mollusks have long jumped out of the shells digging themselves into the sand, only for the seagulls to find them later.

The perfect morning cup of jewels hiding inside a large cockle shell was still filled with water. A skilled paddle boarder navigated the wild waves falling only once, and climbing back up again. A sailboat rocked in the waves.

A dead seagull found its final resting place on the beach. A trio of pelicans delighted in the wind flying ten feet above the water then taking a sharp turn to the beach to glide on the warm wind columns.

The beach life had its own rhythm much like Amora's life that pulsed through the veins of her body. She planned on having a cup of Venetian coffee at the Papa's bait shop on the fishing pier.

After a while, she sat in the sand to collect the treasures from the sea. Having nothing but a small black purse on her with a few bucks, she would leave the shells higher by the sand dune to collect them later.

"You know Amora, you have plenty of those by now," a male voice said.

She collected them over the last two decades, not every morning, but whenever she walked any of the beaches; from North Jetty to the rocky Caspersen Beach closing off the Island of Venice.

Walking on the morning of the high tide, she threw back into the sea a large cockle and watched the waves throw it at her feet and engulf it back with them.

"What kind of secrets were hiding in those calcium skeletons built by slimy mollusks that have no spine?" Amora often wondered.

After all, the mollusks were long dead when washed ashore eaten by another sea creature. Most big shells had broken fringes and fragments of shells were more usual than whole intact shells. To find shells still attached to each other was out of the norm completely.

Amora paid $2 for a cup of Venetian coffee at Papa's. The hot dark liquid still steaming vaguely reminded her of mornings Up North. Seadog George was always available for a chat. He had a tan of a sailor and considered himself to be one, since he had spent the last 15 years on the pier's deck hovering 20 feet above water.

"Do you ever get seasick?" asked Amora naively searching George's tanned hardened by wind and sun.

"Sometimes, I do when the wind is high and the pier sways in the waves," he said. "But they built to withstand anything from Brazilian swamp wood that has already grown in water."

Tall seadog George wasn't a native of Florida, although he wished he was. Once he tried to pretend in front of tourists that he was a Floridian.

"Come on buddy, you sound like the Yankees, you can't lose that," laughed the New Yorker. "I am a fourth generation Yankee, I know."

From then on, George stopped pretending. With blonde hair matching the tan and the beard, Amora guessed he must have been Norwegian or Swedish. She hasn't found the guts yet to ask him; Amora didn't want to be either too friendly or too nosy, or worse yet: Seadog George could think she was hitting on him.

She only engaged enough in casual talk to finish the cup of Venetian coffee without having to walk with it.

By now, the sun was high up above the head and most of the serious fishermen were done casting lines; packing up their gear and heading home for lunch.

"Are the dolphins coming in today?" she asked naively.

"You gotta be here, when they're here," George said. "You just missed them. People tell me they saw four of them about half an hour ago."

Amora looked at the dregs at the bottom of the cup; there was not much. Lore from the old country had it, that you can tell one's future from the sediment. She never learned how to do that.

"Have you ever heard that you can tell one's future from the sediment left in the cup?" she asked George.

"I've heard a lot of things, not this one," George rubbed his beard. "I will ask."

The sun was pounding in her back on her stroll back to the "Cottage Nest" condos. She felt the heat on her biceps and other large muscles of the body. Amora stopped by to pick up the gathered shells from earlier in the morning. They were still there untouched.

Back at the cottage living, she laid down for her afternoon nap listening to the cheap clock bought from Goodwill tick away time. Once, she even took down the clock, but then she missed the ticking.

The ticking sound brought the "Cottage Nest" alive, since there wasn't much else allowed. That meant no loud music or TV from 9 p.m. to 8 a.m.

Who needs 11 hours of silence? Who needs any silence at all when insomnia has permanently settled inside the "Cottage Nest?" What did all those people do when they couldn't sleep?

Amora compared the cottage silence to the silence inside a grave. She could of course make noise somewhere else like on the pier or go out for a walk in the moonlight.

Widow Margot of Irish origin from Chicago who lived above her gave her a piece of advice, “Go for a walk at night and you might catch a glimpse of the Luna moth.”

“I don’t know what a Luna moth is, plus it sounds too creepy,” said Amora.

“Not, when you’re old,” Margot concluded. “When you’re old, nothing is creepy.”

Amora decided to further think about a night walk under the moon in pursuit of a glimpse of the giant silk moth.

In the meantime, she would do some research about the luminous winged wonder, and find a clock that wouldn’t be as noisy.

Worse even yet in the cottage living, you couldn’t release any stink either; like frying a fish on a Lenten Friday or on any Friday. Being a good Catholic, Amora made sure she never ate meat on Fridays. Unlike Margot, who both ate meat and drank on Lenten Fridays, Amora stuck to her acquired routine. Undisciplined Amora had to build up her routine from a wild flower to an orderly bee trapped in her own beehive.

“Are we going out on Friday, Amora?” Margot asked when they were gossiping on the balcony.

“We shouldn’t,” Amora said. “It’s Lent. You should know that, you’re Irish.”

They decided to go anyways to the old Irish Pub with dubious reputation in downtown. They settled at their favorite table in the corner.

“Will it be the usual two Killarney’s for the ladies?” asked the waiter.

"Just one," snapped Amora. "It's Lent."
"For you, mam?" the waiter looked surprised at Amora.
"No, for her," Amora pointed at Margot.
"Slainte," Margot smiled at the waiter. "That's cheers in Irish."
The waiter brought the reddish beer and a glass of water full of ice. Margot disciplined herself and ordered fish and chips like Amora.
"At least it's cheap," Margot said eating her chips. "Tell me all about him."
"Who?" Amora was shocked.
"People at the cottage talked about you hanging out with seadog George," Margot said watching Amora's every twitch. "You know at the monthly gathering that you don't go to. Somebody must have seen you or heard George talk about you. You know we're all friends around here, and we talk to each other."
Amora looked at Margot in disbelief; she quickly finished her fish got up from the table and wiped her mouth.
"You find a ride home because I am leaving," Amora said angrily. "Waiter, the bill please."

It was a beautiful morning on the Gulf as Amora hammered the sand in her thongs that kept slipping off her feet. The anger over yesterday's gossip was still filling her up like the proverbial cup. She had never left a friend behind anywhere in her entire life. What she did to Margot on the third Lenten Friday was totally against her beliefs and upbringing.

But, how dared she repeat somebody's lies.
"You should be going to those," Anthony told her on the regular Sunday phone call from permanent home up North by the big lake.
"All they do is gossip and complain," she said. "I'll never go there unless you come with me; that is if you ever decide to come."
"You know I can't come yet," Anthony repeated the old story. "I have too much to do up here."
All this was going through Amora's head as her feet kept sinking into the wet sand, occasionally washed over by a wave. Her anger did not match up with the beauty of the day just opening itself up to all possibilities. One of those possibilities was seadog George on the pier built from the Brazilian swamp lumber.
Why hasn't he asked her out yet? She wasn't that old; Amora was the youngest one at the "Cottage Nest," maybe not even eligible yet for the age requirement. That kept changing too, according to who was in charge of the association.
"I keep telling you that you should go to those meetings," Anthony's words were still ringing in her ears.
The last Sunday afternoon argument over the phone reared its nasty heads that kept multiplying like Medusa's. Amora nurtured her habit of hating Sundays to perfection. In spite of that, she wanted to communicate.
Everything was game on Sundays; from the stupid politicians to the family members.
"No one is exempt on a Sunday," she would say.

The Sunday wrath turned into obsession to share the anger with others, and lash out on them.
Now, with the sun high over her head, she had to sit down into the sand on the low beach dune. The anger will wash away into the turquoise-colored waves. She will let it melt in the sun, before she talks to George. Neither Anthony nor George deserved her Sunday wrath.
"I think I am not the only one who hates Sundays," Amora tried to justify the inexplainable. "There's plenty of other people who would rather jump into the lake on Sundays or kill themselves."
Amora watched the washed ashore "wrack" that served as a buffet for everything alive except for her. The seagulls flew to it for its sea-washed abundance of live or dead creatures. Wrack communities are native to Florida beaches; it is stuff cast ashore by the sea.
Watching the feast, Amora realized she forgot to eat because of her anger. Now, she was feeling and hearing the empty stomach growl and her ulcers acting up. Amora didn't even pack a sandwich or fruits; she will buy a candy bar at Papa's from seadog George.
From her vantage point on the low dune, other than watching the "wrack" community of plovers, sanderlings and grasshoppers, Amora also took in the happy couples strolling up and down the beach. She envied them their happiness, without knowing whether they were happy or not; off course everyone was happy except for her.

Amora reached the snack shop Papa's totally exhausted from anger and hunger. She was determined to let George have it, even though it wasn't a Sunday. She had exactly $4 to buy Venetian coffee with dregs and Almond Joy.

"A coffee and Almond Joy and by the way, George, I want to talk to you," she barked without looking up.

"George is not here today," said the strange young man.

"What do you mean he's not here today," Amora felt a tinge of anger rise in her again. "He's always here. I need to talk to him, now."

"That's too bad, lady, because like I said," the man paused, "He's not here. Did you still want your coffee and Almond Joy?"

"Forget it," Amora said turning away from the snack shop with bait. "I can't drink coffee walking and I have nothing to say to you."

She turned around and continues on the pier toward its far end jetting into the Gulf. She felt the heat in her and on her in a fusion of frustration with anxiety. That was a deadly cocktail that had been fueling her for years.

Amora leaned over the wooden boards staring into the waves that were rushing toward the pier. Why in the world did she leave Margot at that Irish dive in downtown? What if something had happened to her? How will she know?

She got out her cell phone and called Margot; there was just empty ringing on the other side. A young boy next to her reeled in a baby shark. Then he proudly

showed it off to everyone around. The little white shark was flapping around helplessly.
"Can't you just let it go," she snapped at the boy with the flapping baby shark.
"Don't worry, lady, I will," he said holding on lovingly to the dangerous fish. "I want everyone to see it first; what I had caught."
Amora waited around with the crowd marveling at the baby shark until the boy let it free back into the Gulf. The sun had moved in the meantime and the rays were less beating on the skin.
"Give me that coffee and the candy bar before I pass out," she said to the young man at the snack shop.
"I'll put a lid on that coffee for you, so you can walk with it," offered the young man.
Amora took the cup and ripped the wrapper from the coconut bar walking past the Tiki Bar and Sharky's to Brohard Park. She skipped having the "Miami Vice" cocktail at the Tiki, mainly because she didn't have enough money for it.
She sat on a bench without noticing the dedication plaque to Nora Owens, 1924-2010, a radiologist, beach walker and a bridge player.

Back up North, at the health center, everything had changed in the meantime as the winter passed by faster than it did down South in the monotony of the heat. The medical center owner was new with her staff as well. There were new pictures, plants and magazines in the otherwise impersonal waiting room with plastic plants. They were placed carefully not to litter the floor. She noticed Dali's reproduction of "The Persistence of Memory." Amora had always loved those perfect melting clocks. Amora was on a never-ending quest to find one of those melting clocks for up North. She had that noisy one down South. Anthony thought that both Dali and Picasso were idiots.

"You can come in now," a nurse motioned her into the examining room. "The doc will be with you soon. You still have that pain in the stomach?"

Amora was impatient; she missed her old doctor and she didn't like nurses.

"Yes, I have the pain in the stomach," she said.

They had the stomach pain discussion before with the nurse and the old doc, so everything must be recorded in the protocol of the past.

The new doctor was neither young or old, just mediocre with a stiff face. He was holding the manila folder, leafing through various papers and test results. He looked puzzled.

"I am doctor Mosa," he said in broken English. "That abdominal pain is persisting? Is it the same, worse or better?"

He touched Amora's stomach on the right side as she shrieked in pain.

"Than what?" she snapped at the doc sitting up.

"Than the last time you were in here," he said looking through the papers again.

"It's worse along with everything else," Amora said.

"Ok, we'll do another test, and you will come back," Dr. Mosa said.

"What am I supposed to do with the pain in the meantime?" Amora asked.
"Does it hurt all the time?" he asked looking at her through his thick eyeglasses.
"Not all the time," she said getting ready to leave.
"Well then, take whatever you take for pain," he said.
It was nice outside as she sat behind the wheel of her Buick; driving through the small town was relaxing. Amora stopped at Walgreens to buy Ibuprofen, 800mg in the large packaging. She was used to a lifetime of pain and she had learned to wallow in it.
In her persistence of memory, Amora couldn't get the picture of shock on Margot's face out of her head that Friday night at the old Irish Pub in downtown Venice. She tried calling her again several times with no response.
But here up North, Amora had Anthony's support in anything she did. Their relationship was forged in the crucible of politics of the late 1960s. The walnut wood wall clock in the living room wasn't as loud as the one down South, but she still would prefer a melting one. Anthony was the opposite of seadog George: intellectual, calm, pale and contemplative.
However, both were equally masculine and stubborn like the Midwest weather. As she caught herself, comparing the two men, Amora realized Margot's comment about George wasn't just gossip. That's why she got so angry beyond herself. Moreover, Amora was brought up strictly to believe any gossip was just as sinful as an outright lie. Margot wasn't lying to her, but she was spreading gossip and

inuendo. She remembered one of their conversations on the balcony of the "Cottage Nest."
"Margot, you're spreading words from the association gatherings without knowing if they're true," she challenged her once.
"You don't know if it is a lie either," Margot fought back.
Phew, Amora realized she was glad to escape from that looney woman and the looney "Cottage Nest." Everything felt normal up North, even the cold. Anthony was more than normal and above all, he was perfect unlike seadog George.
She shook those thoughts away of Margot and seadog George. The obnoxious pain in the stomach kept coming and going, but the painkillers were still working.
By the time her next doctor visit rolled around, Amora didn't go. The pain wasn't excruciating, just making its presence.

New and exciting things were happening; summer in her garden and her wedding anniversary. It wasn't until in the heat of a July night, when the pain came back: strong and relentless.
She waited two more days before going back to the health center with Dali's melting clocks.
"Well, you missed one appointment," said the nurse. "Dr. Mosa did want to talk to you. You have that pain in the stomach?"
"It's worse now," said Amora.

Dr. Mosa walked in the office with his manila folder going through the papers again puzzled.
"I think you have pancreatic cancer, even though some of the results appear to be inconclusive," Dr. Mosa kept staring into the folder without looking up at Amora.
Amora was confused. She requested the results before on the phone; and they ruled out several things while not confirming any particular diagnosis.
"The tests didn't show that," she argued. "Are you sure?"
"I can never be 100 percent sure, and we certainly will do more tests," he said. "You can seek a second opinion."

It was Sunday again after that terrifying Friday diagnosis. The pain was back, and the sun refused to stop shining into her bedroom with drawn blinds. She listened to the birds sing outside her window. Amora hasn't told anyone yet, not even to Anthony.
Heck yes, she knew the prognosis; at the best she had six months to live. At the least, two months. She could get a lot done or nothing in that span of eight to 24 weeks.
Did she have any plans? Well, the anniversary was coming up, and she wanted to travel. Travel was the cup of her life, filled with joy and exotic countries. In the later years, the desire to travel waned a little, like the phases of the moon.

Most people with a terminal diagnosis want to see at least one place where they never had been before. But she didn't believe Dr. Mosa.

Fighting the dubious diagnosis alone was creepy to use her own words. She told Anthony.

"We'll see when more tests come back negative," said Anthony.

The pain kept her awake at night and during the day.

"No matter what they say, I don't feel normal," she complained.

"You have to get some rest sometime," Anthony said. "Sunday is a good day to rest. We can go out for a drive. Sunshine will do you good."

They headed out for a Sunday drive to fight off depression and anxiety.

"He could have told me on Monday," she said angrily.

"He probably didn't know and we don't know if it's true," said Anthony.

"I should probably go to a confession or do a moral inventory of my life," Amora said.

"You've done hundreds of those," said Anthony. "We don't know if he is right."

The Sunday drive in the sunshine was alleviating the pain; both physical and mental. Amora had to be reasonable, how many times had she received an incorrect diagnosis in her life?

But she did feel weak and wondered if she should call Margot again? She refused to stop at the pizza depot by the lake resort.

She will call Margot tomorrow. What was confusing her was the fact that she wasn't losing weight, even

though she didn't feel hungry and lost part of her voracious appetite. Amora still loved sweets and desserts; mostly her own. Even a candy bar like that time she bought almond joy from that boy on the pier, when seadog George wasn't there.
She must call Margot and find out what had happened that Friday night and later with George. Since, Amora couldn't sleep at night, she decided to write a letter to Margot to her address at that looney "Cottage Nest." She sat down behind her new desk in the middle of the night and started writing to Margot.

Dear Margot,
You haunt me at night. I wanted to let you know that, even though we're friends. I am not going to apologize for leaving you at that old Irish Pub, because you were gossiping.
I hate gossip. Gossip is worse than lying. Gossip is immoral. Gossip is the sister of secrets and lies. You should have asked me first about seadog George. You know I still have Anthony.
We're both old, and we can die any day.
But you were the only friend I had at that looney "Cottage Nest." Friends are hard to come by. The older you get, the harder they are to find. You know you should be picking up your phone. I hate when you don't answer your phone.
I also know if I lose you, I won't find a new friend.

Amora paused and looked at her piece of writing to a dear friend. She did not even know what had happened to Margot after leaving her at the pub on that Lenten Friday.

She clearly remembered Margot's advice to go for a walk at night and try to find the elusive Luna moth. But she would have to put on some clothes. Amora ran to the closet to pick a light sweater. She put on slippers.

Amora hurried through the garage into the garden lit by the super moon. She could see everything bathed in silver: rocks buried in the dirt turned into diamonds and flowers into pearls.

She walked further back into the woodlands bordering the garden. Then she spotted the Luna moth perched on a leaf. Finding of the Luna took her by complete surprise. Amora stood flabbergasted in the middle of the wooded knoll. She touched her head and pinched her skin to make sure she wasn't dreaming. The pinch hurt and the lime green Luna with purple spots just sat there.

"What does this mean?" she asked herself out loud. "What did Margot say? I bet it means bad luck."

The illumination by the moon and now by the moth enhanced the feelings of the night. Margot was right; there's nothing creepy about the night or the moth. Amora breathed in the night air. It was fresh. She hesitated to return back into the house. She wanted the moment with the Luna to last forever.

When Amora returned into the house and looked at the unforgiving clock, she realized she spent more than an hour with the Luna moth.

The doctor's office was just as impersonal as the last time with the exception of Dali's "The Persistence of Memory."

"You have less than three months to live," said Dr. Mosa. "We will do all we can. Here is a good prescription to kill your pain."

Amora looked at the Rx script; all prescriptions were high dosage opioids.

When she got home from the doctor's office all sweaty, Anthony was working in the garden. He noticed the footsteps in the dirt.

"What were you doing in the garden last night?" he asked. "Those are your footsteps. How did the visit go?"

"It went normal," she said. "The test results are within parameters, still inconclusive. The pain comes and goes. I got some medication. I will be fine."

"I told you to just wait and see," said Anthony digging in the dirt. "You shouldn't be going out at night. You're going to catch a cold."

Amora was shaking although it was warm. She watched Anthony dig the dirt.

"I am not worried about the cold," she said. "I will be leaving to go down South early this year. I miss it."

"You've never missed it before," Anthony said.

"I'll be fine, I have friends down there, you know," she said. "I never said goodbye to Margot. I kind of feel bad about it."

"That's the Irish woman from Chicago?" Anthony asked still digging deep into the dirt, almost as if he was expecting to dig up something. He always spoke of wanting to go on an archaeology expedition.

"Yes, Margot from upstairs," she said. "You can go on your archeology expedition, finally while you still can. I know you have an opportunity to go now."
"You've been going through my papers?" Anthony asked amazed.
"You go through mine," she snapped. "Feel free to leave. I have stuff to do."
"You're feeling better, right?" he asked.
"Yes, I am," she said resolutely reaching for her pills in the pocket.

Amora went to treatments, and the team did what they could as promised within the boundaries of time. Amora knew enough about the disease to create the visions of her own end. She wanted to write her own obituary, while she could.
The opioids made the pain bearable, life lighter and more leveled. It didn't matter anymore if the neighbor's leaves flew over Anthony's yard. It didn't matter that Anthony was on an expedition while she was going through the pointless treatments.
There was one thing that did matter; at the most two that Amora wanted to take care of. She looked in the mirror at herself, at her smooth skin well-maintained for years with expensive lotions. Amora always wanted to die while she still looked good. That was her final wish; to die beautiful. She didn't want to die wrinkled and rickety. She wanted to look beautiful in the coffin, all gussied up. For that reason, she never even considered cremation to ashes. Ashes are not beautiful, they're just grey like bare tree trunks or like a wolf.

Oh, yes, she did lie to Anthony, but that was to protect him. Or was it to protect her?

She grabbed the phone and dialed Margot's number. The mail box was full and could not accept any more messages. That was it. Amora packed her suitcase with underwear, flip-flops, a swimming suit, a tanning lotion and a sack of pills with white labels. She had to sign a bunch of consensus papers before she got the useless medicaments with a fancier name, but these large white pills in the sack were good.

She realized it was a Sunday as she boarded the airbus. Amora didn't even hate Sundays anymore since the final diagnosis. Sundays were now acceptable, along with all the other days of the week such as Mondays.

The silver tinsel on the Gulf waters fused into a steel sheet from the altitude of 33,000 feet. Her heart of steel was warming up to the sun. The first thing she will do is to knock on Margot's door before opening her own door at the "Cottage Nest." But before that, she will buy Margot the oldest American beer known for its high quality. They will have a few glasses together and forget about what had happened on that Lenten Friday at the old Irish Pub.

"Have a nice stay," the pretty young flight attendant wished Amora on her way out of the airbus. "It's bright and sunny."

Panting while climbing the stairs to the second level, Amora knocked on Margot's door. Nothing has changed at the "Cottage Nest." She could hear the drying machines from the laundry room rotating in their eternal hum. No one answered the door.

Amora drove to the fishing pier leaving her suitcase in the hallway unpacked. She walked on the boards of the pier listening to the splashing waves against the timber construction. She saw George's tall figure immediately standing in the wind silhouetting in the sun.

"You never even said goodbye," seadog George looked at pale and sweaty Amora.

"You weren't here," Amora said.

"I wasn't," he said. "I am not hard to find."

"I would like to talk to you," she said.

"Well, you're talking to me right now," he said.

"In private," she insisted.

"No one hears us here," George said. "Only the waves are listening. They do not tattle. Is it important?"

Amora paused to catch her breath and to stabilize herself as sharp pain shot through her stomach. She shrieked in pain.

"We can meet tonight at that old watering hole in downtown," seadog George said reluctantly. "It's not Friday or anything. We should be fine."

They sat at the same table in the corner where Amora sat with Margot on that fourth Lenten Friday.

"Two Killarney's?" asked the same waiter from that ominous night.

"How did you know what we want?' asked Amora.

"I remember you," he said. "You left that other lady here without a ride."

The waiter was standing there and fidgeting with the menus in his hand staring at Amora.

"You're going to eat, right?" he asked.
Seadog George watched closely the exchange between Amora and the waiter. He was tickled and wanted to laugh really bad.
"How did she get home?" said Amora.
"The gentleman next to you should tell you that," the waiter smirked. "I'll get the Killarney's."
Amora turned to George as her face turned into a grimace. The waiter turned on the music box loud. It was blasting ACDCs "She shook me all night long."
Suddenly, Amora felt that same urge to get up and leave, except this time she wanted to enhance her departure by slapping that bastard George hard.
"She called me," he said. "I picked her up and gave her a ride home."
"You freaking bastard," Amora raised her voice. "Did you sleep with her?"
George rubbed his beard and looked around him to track where the music was coming from.
"I'll leave that up to your imagination," he said.
Amora turned red with anger as the waiter brought two tall glasses of ruby-hued Killarneys. She grabbed the glass and took a long gulp, then she looked through the glass at seadog George. He was looking straight back at her.
"You were gonna tell me something important," George reminded her. "You're kind of early this year."
Amora leaned back into the chair and placed the beer carefully on the square coaster. She searched George's face for any traces of guilt. She wasn't finding any.

"Oh, it's nothing," she said. "I just wanted to see you and chat somewhere else than on the pier. That's all."

George looked deep into Amora's green eyes. He thought he saw in them little yellow flames flickering like cat's eyes.

"How was it back at home up North?" he said.

Amora snubbed him with a mere shoulder raise.

"It was okay," she said. "How about you down here; you and Margot? Where is she now?"

"I was gonna tell you that on the pier, but you're the one who wanted to come down here," he said.

"Yes, I did," Amora said. "I wanted to know how she got back home when she didn't answer the door at the Nest. Where is she?"

"She returned back to Chicago," he said.

"For good?" Amora held her breath.

George paused and looked around the pub again as if he was searching for Margot. The waiter brought the burgers. George stalled with the answer biting into his juicy burger.

"These are delicious," he said.

"Did Margot return for good back to Chicago?" Amora insisted.

"Yes, she did," George said.

Amora took a deep breath and leaned back into the chair staring into the air in front of her.

"Was she upset with me for leaving her here at the pub at night?" she asked.

"If she was, I wouldn't know it," said George. "Come to the pier tomorrow at noon. The dolphins will be there."

Her feet sinking in the wet sand, Amora was slowly approaching the pier.

Amora knew she was a good catholic, while Margot was a bad one. More over Margot was too skinny; while not ugly, she was definitely not beautiful. After all she was the one who told her to search for the Luna moth. Spotting the gigantic silk moth in the back of her garden brought Amora bad luck. That much she knew. She still wanted to live.

"What if the doctor was wrong?" she asked herself. "He couldn't even speak English. Who knows if he read the tests correctly? The pain wasn't as bad anymore."

But then she recalled the office emailed her the test results with the values. Those could have been someone else's tests, too.

She could see seadog George from a distance staring into the waves. The pier was getting crowded again since people by now knew when the dolphins swim in. He was flanked by students with a teacher asking questions.

Amora sat on a pier bench to wait until the kids leave George alone. She always made sure that she checked the plaques on the benches in memory of loved ones. The one she was sitting on was dedicated to a young man, Jack. Amora wondered what he died of. She will never find out. He probably wanted to live too.

Next to the bench was a fisherman's bucket. She peaked in only to find shrimp for bait. Yeah, George sold those too by the dozen. Why waste a shrimp for bait?

"I want some shrimp for dinner," she said to George who was free now.

"Why not?" George wasn't surprised at Amora's request even though he sold shrimp only for bait. "You told me before you left that you can't even make any stink in that looney nest of yours, remember?"

"I don't care, I am going to have shrimp tonight by myself," she said. "We used to have dinner together with Margot."

"I could come you know," said George watching himself in Amora's large shades. He could see his broad shoulders and his beard.

A long pause followed as Amora leaned against the wall of the shop.

"Were the dolphins here?" she asked.

"No, not yet," George said. "You should wait for them."

"Why isn't Margot answering my calls, George?" Amora said.

"She's answering mine," he said.

"You call her?" Amora was surprised.

"Yes, I do," he said. "We're friends, like you were."

"Will she forgive me, George?" she asked.

"You're the catholic, you should know," he said. "Did you want me to come tonight?"

Amora was holding the plastic bag with the shrimp. She watched the pink crustaceans in locomotion. The waves were splashing against the pier structure.

"Is that egret here all the time?" Amora pointed at the white sleek bird sitting on the freezer next to the shop.
"Why? Do you want him for dinner too?" George looked at Amora as he placed his arm on her shoulder.
"I'll let you know who I want for dinner," Amora said.
George watched the woman walk away slowly with a youthful sway in her hips. He could clearly see the six palms by the tiki framing her departing figure in the background. The southwesterly wind picked back up again raising the waves higher.

Sitting at the glass top dinner table, Amora served up salmon with shrimp in dill sauce and asparagus. Seadog George was sitting across from her with his back to the mirrored wall. He noticed Amora watching herself in the mirror. She dressed up in her favorite admiral blue sequined dress. She got the dress at the second hand store "Fiona's" on Venice Avenue.
There were hundreds of dresses once used and loved by rich women from all over the world. In spite of their wealth, they still could not resist making a buck on a dress that had served its purpose.
But the cycle of dressing and redressing worked like a well-oiled machine. The poor felt richer, and the rich felt generous creating jobs for the local folks.
George pulled out of his closet the best shirt and dress pants he could find. When Amora opened the door, she could not recognize him. He didn't shave his beard, but he trimmed it and had an obvious haircut.

"I've never seen you like this, George," she said. "You do clean up, don't you?"

"I am honored that you decided to have me for dinner along with my shrimp bait," George laughed as he handed her a bouquet of pink and red roses.

They smelled beautiful embodying the glory of the evening. George could sniff the scent of "Forever Elizabeth" perfume on Amora. He once asked her on the pier what was the scent she was wearing.

"I love Elizabeth Taylor perfumes," she said.

"You don't need them on the beach," George laughed back then. "All you need is the smell of the water and the birds."

Amora and George enjoyed even though it was making a stink in the "Cottage Nest." Amora watched one of the candles, the flame flickering, burn out.

"George, I am going to die soon," she finally said.

"We all are," he said raising his eyebrows.

"I want to make peace with Margot, but she isn't answering my calls," Amora said.

"Let's just forget the whole thing between the two of you and enjoy the evening," George said.

The next morning with sunshine coming through the windows found the two in bed together, hugging tightly as if life was escaping them to the sound of the ticking clock.

"I've always thought that old people don't have sex," Amora said.

"Sometimes they do," he said, "when they're running short on time."

Seadog George found out about the death of a local woman from the Venice Gondolier newspaper. It said no foul play was involved. The waves washed ashore the drowned body on Sunday. They even printed her last note nailed to one of the pier pillars where water meets the sand. This was Amora's farewell to the world:

I cannot take the pain or numb myself with any more painkillers than I have been. I love life, and I hope that God will forgive me for this; Catholics are not allowed to kill themselves or others, according to the fifth commandment. I did not mean to hurt anyone else but myself. I remain forever grateful to George, Anthony and Margot. I especially wanted to say I am sorry for what I did to Margot on the fourth Lenten Friday. I left her at that old Irish Pub without a ride. My love for her will extend into my death and beyond. Forgive me, Margot.
Amora

Raspberry Rage

The mix of roasted almonds, cashews, raisins, cranberries and chocolate truffles with raspberry flavor offered peace to Klarette, who was nervously jamming on the gas pedal. It seemed like her small foot got stuck on the pedal, and wouldn't let go.

The trees along the road turned into a blur under the cloudy sky. She noticed the frozen corn on the fields waiting to be harvested in late November.
Klarette shivered from the November chill in her small automobile. She bought the "Raspberry Rage" mix after a good 20 minutes of helpless staring into the cave filled with everything from energy drinks, spiked Seltzer, twisted teas to regular beer. She quickly passed the shelf with over-the-counter drugs. Klarette had just gotten out of an intense session with Troy's Group at the Center between the pine trees. As she pulled into the Center, a drizzling rain was making its appearance on the worn-out asphalt of the parking lot. In vain, did she search for leaves, not to be found.
The pines and spruces were beautiful though. At that moment, she was grateful for the evergreen that she hadn't noticed before. She hadn't noticed the receptionist girl before either, or the empty walls of the center.
The first time she arrived here at the Center by an ambulance, Klarette woke up in the emergency room in the middle of the night. In vain did she search her memory for bits and pieces of what had happened before. There was no indication of anything in the blank expression of the nurse's face; no smile, no frown either.
"What am I doing here?" she asked into the whiteness of the impersonal white room.
Klarette stared into the white walls until little stars appeared in the corners of her eyes twinkling and jumping from the corners to the front. Now, they were

all over that impersonal nurse. Her navy-blue scrubs were sprinkled with goldens stars.
"Mam, you look like the night sky out there," Klarette breathed heavily as the nurse inserted the IV into her veins.
"What is that?" she asked. "Why are you poking me?"
"It's just a saline solution to flush your kidneys," said the nurse systematically doing her routine.
"But, why?" Klarette questioned. "What happened to me?"
"You overdosed," said the nurse without a hint of anything in her monotonous voice. "Get some rest."
"Am I going to die?" asked Klarette.
The impersonal nurse in the navy-blue scrubs looked at the pale woman lying on the bed in front of her. Her long dark hair was spread over her shoulders and a blouse that was too light for this time of the year.
"I am cold," said Klarette with her teeth clattering. "Can you turn up the heat, mam? Please?"
The nurse put Klarette's belongings in the closet.
"Why are you putting away my coat?" said Klarette. "I am going home."
The nurse examined closely the dirty jacket and returned it back to Klarette and bent over her to adjust the IV. It was then that Klarette noticed the name on the name tag.
"You are Victoria, that's a pretty name for a nurse," smirked Klarette, but immediately felt bad as her empty stomach growled.
The room with white walls had one painting right in front of Klarette and next to the "Goals" board.

"You're leaving me, Victoria?" begged Klarette. "What if I get sick again? Who's going to help me?" Klarette immediately felt her hand for the small white box with a switch on her pillow next to her head. She sunk deeper below the blanket and continued to stare helplessly into the painting on the wall as she heard the door close behind Victoria.

The painting had some scribbles on it in cursive, but Klarette couldn't read it from her bed. She tried to get up, but was all entangled with the IV, so Klarette sank back into her bed.

The small hand on the big white clock on the wall was crawling closer to 3 as the big hand inched toward 12. She quickly looked outside the window: the Orion constellation was shining brightly with its stars, Nebula and Rigel.

Klarette, sick to her empty stomach, tested her mind if it could bring back memories of the past few days. Sounds instead entered her head giving into vibrations. She realized that she was shaking and sweating in the cold room. The shakes, the sounds and the sweat refused to go away. Her head was a swirl of the last 24 hours prior to arriving in the ambulance.

The swirls began to take shape of dancing flames, as goose bumps covered her body. She was itching all over. Klarette wanted to crawl out of her own skin. The cold eyelids were safely covering her hot eyeballs, that might have jumped out if it wasn't for them. The eyelids still had smudges of make-up on them; the dark blue was smeared with the grey into a smokin' hot explosion.

Yes, now she recalled putting on all that heavy make-up prior to going out. That thin blue blouse had to match the grey shades on her eyes and in her eyes. Now, her eyes were burning from the excessive make-up.

Klarette looked up and away from her physical misery to the painting again. Her eyesight was clearing up now and she could make out the image coming out of the painting. It was the blue grey face of a wolf coming out of a forest.

The scribbles of the cursive became clear now. She noticed the small hand moving between 6 and 7. When it struck 7, Victoria walked into the room with a doctor. The doctor had dark hair and a dark mustache; he appeared too dark by Victoria's fair features. They both approached her bedside with no signs of any emotions.

"How are we doing?" asked the dark-haired doctor. "We did the blood tests and everything. You overdosed on your painkillers."

The dark-haired doctor held up her hand, that was getting more stable, but it was still cold.

"We're going to give you lighter meds to wean you off the painkillers," he said. "Don't abuse them. You'll come back for intensive outpatient treatment next week. The nurse will show you around the facilities, before you are discharged."

Klarette watched the doctor write on the "Goals" white board.

"Discharge: today. Intensive outpatient treatment for the next six weeks."

The doctor shut the door behind him turning around one more time.
"I don't want to see you in here again," he said touching his mustache. "Stay away from here, and you will be fine."
Klarette, still in her blouse, crawled out of bed and walked to the painting to read the cursive: "Today is all you have."
Together with Victoria, the two walked side by side, between the white walls of the hallways in the Center. They walked past different rooms with different names. Victoria stopped by the "Mosaic" room.
"You will be coming here, three times a week for the next six weeks," she pointed to the Mosaic room.
With that, Victoria handed Klarette her cell phone, jacket, purse and prescription.
"I don't want to see you back in the emergency either," Victoria said tucking her blonde hair back behind her ears. Klarette noticed the big earrings in her ears.
"You can leave now," said Victoria. "You are discharged."
"Wait a minute. Who called the ambulance for me?" she asked Victoria.
Victoria shrugged her shoulders.
"I have no idea," said Victoria. "Just, thank them, once you find out."
Klarette was standing in the lobby by herself watching the snow falling on the bare trunks and branches of the old oak trees. She called for Uber to take her home to the singles apartment complex in the nearby village of Tremontville. She was surprised to

find money in her wallet. She quickly paid the driver and stepped inside her apartment. Klarette was hoping for signs of what had happened prior to her wakening up at the emergency center.

The apartment was neutral as always; neutral to her feelings and neutral to her being. She opened to fridge to grab a soda as she realized she was really thirsty. Klarette downed the soda and opened another one. She recalled people at the emergency telling her to eat something. They gave her some crackers without any flavor.

She locked the apartment, and walked to the nearby shopping center still looking for clues of what had happened not that long ago.

“I need to see your driver’s license and sign this paper,” said the pharmacist. “It’s still a controlled drug.”

Klarette felt dizzy and sick inside, almost like she would faint if she didn’t lay down. Back in her apartment, she laid down in her bedroom with dark curtains that successfully diffused the daylight.

The dreams didn’t help either; now that they were combined with visions from the emergency room of fair Victoria and the doctor with dark mustache.

The “Mosaic” room was filled to the last seat with various individuals. They were assigned to the “Mosaic” for different reasons ranging from encounters with the law to dangerous encounters with loving partners.

Troy was standing up front by the blackboard as Klarette entered the plain room. She sat by the small windows, so she could look outside at the bare trees covering the large campus known as the “Center.”

The “Center” was converted from an old asylum dating back to the turn of the century. It definitely needed more renovations than just freshly painted white walls of the hallways and lobbies.

“Would you like some water?” Troy asked her to start a conversation. “We’re going to be in here for a while.”

“Yes, please,” she said. “I am thirsty.”

The class sank into the silence of meditation for the next five minutes.

“Why does everything have to be measured by time?” Klarette thought to herself. “Time means nothing. Today is everything I have.”

“Is today everything we have?” asked Klarette out loud in the middle of the sacred meditation period that started off with the bell.

No one responded. She was too scared to open her eyes. Klarette wondered if Troy was meditating as well, or what was he actually doing while the rest of them meditated.

Then, the bell rang softly wakening everybody up from the tranquility of time.

“Okay, everyone will check in, since most of us are new in the program,” said Troy. “We’re going to start on the left side of the room and go around the table.”

Klarette was relieved to be on the tail end of this psychoanalytic dragon. She closed her eyes and listened to different voices of those strangers seated around the same table with her. Klarette almost fell asleep. But then, someone started talking about missing her boyfriend.

"I just left him. He was too controlling," the voice said. "He was driving me to drink, even if I didn't want to. I knew I had to stop seeing him."

Klarette shrugged her shoulders while listening to the different voices who owned different stories. Then, Troy interrupted the flow of the stories with his bell. Somebody asked him where he got the whole "voodoo set-up."

Troy's voodoo consisted of a pin-shaped colorful glass bong and different bowls.

"Ok, we're going to take a break," Troy said. "You want to get acquainted. We'll be spending the next six weeks together. Make good use of your time and mine."

As if Troy was reading her thoughts. Klarette was already considering all this a major waste of her time. She needed to get back to work and pick up where she left off prior to that ambulance trip. Klarette still had no idea who called the ambulance for her.

Some individuals stepped outside to smoke or vape in front of the main "Center" building. For Klarette, who was still shivering like the first time she had arrived at the "Center's" emergency, it was too cold to smoke.

Klarette walked over to the girl who was missing the boyfriend she had left.

"Maybe you shouldn't have left him," Klarette said to the young girl.

"You're right, I shouldn't have," the girl said. "I miss him."
Klarette rubbed the hat on her head fixing its position slightly.
"You know what, I feel like we're being brainwashed," said Klarette.

"Okay, folks, we're ready to start," Troy invited the group back inside the "Center."
They filed back in the class. At times, Klarette noticed things she had noticed before: the empty coffee maker, the nuts brought in by the old lady, and Troy's tray with fidgeting toys.
"Does anyone need one of these?" Troy said holding up the tray.
"I will take one," said Klarette and reached out for the tray.
"Take anyone you want," he said.
The old lady in the corner of the room refused to fidget arguing she brought in snacks.
Klarette gave preference to the gecko sticking out of the box. But he was too nasty, so she exchanged him for the magnetic floating top. Unfortunately, Troy ran out of the popular fidget hand spinner high speed anxiety relief.
"I still say snacks are the best," said the old lady munching on nuts. "I gotta have something in my mouth. You can't stick that spinner in your mouth."
The class was getting out of control as they started to argue with the old lady over what is right or wrong for anxiety relief.

"You know what, Xanax is the best," said the overweight blonde in a green shirt.
"Yeah, but they won't prescribe that to you," the farmer boy joined in laughing. "Guess why not? Because it's too addictive."
Troy rang his meditation bell to bring the class to order. He stood up rubbing his hands and everyone could tell that he was a nervous wreck himself.
"I used to do drugs and drink," Troy said at the beginning of the intensive class, that Klarette had missed. "Watch for your triggers. Mine was a certain time of the day. My friend always called me at 5 p.m. after work how depressed he was."
Klarette could relate to the link between time and getting high.
"Always watch your memories," encouraged Troy.
This was almost too much for Klarette and the rest of the folks. How do you watch your own memory?
"Put it in a heart-shaped box, and don't let it out," Troy suggested. "And create another box for your emergencies."
Klarette drove home to her apartment thinking about the emergency box:
"What is she going to put in it?"
Now, Klarette had to create two boxes: a memories box, sort of like Pandora's box, and an emergency kit that will appeal to all the senses.
She considered stopping at a store open 24 hours a day. However, listening to Troy's voice in her head, Klarette changed her mind.
"We're heading into the trigger season for everything," Troy said, "and those are the holidays."

Oh, yes. It was the seven weeks of temptation, not the 12 days of Christmas. The seven weeks of temptation started one week prior to Thanksgiving and ended on the first day of the new year being sick. But, for the "Mosaic" group, it was more like 52 weeks of daily temptation.

To trap 52 weeks of temptation into one emergency box was a major challenge for the "Mosaic." Klarette walked into her apartment, still oblivious, to who had called the ambulance for her to get her help.

"Will I ever know?" she asked out loud. "I could have been dead."

Her loud self -talk was streaked with wishful thinking.

Klarette worked on her emergency box. The old lady talked about using incense to calm her senses earlier that week in the class. The theme was self-soothing.

"Describe, what you feel like, when you want to get high," Troy said.

The old lady was first to speak with others anxiously jumping into the conversation.

"It's easier to define in sex, you just get horny," she laughed a harsh deep laugh.

"You can soothe yourself with sex," said the smart ass in the corner.

"We're talking about self-soothing," Troy stirred the group. "How do you soothe yourself without getting high?"

Klarette dug out of her closet a black shoe-box from the Massini brand of her new hip ankle-high boots that everybody else was running around in.

It was the right size of box to hide all the things that would soothe your vices. The old lady said she would use incense and food. But, what type of incense or smell do you use?
Klarette went for the rainforest scent, since she's never been to the jungle before. The sense of touch was hard too, and easier again with sex. She added a velvety covered wire that could be bent into anything. She felt like she had lost all her taste buds. However, the persistence of memory kept nagging at her with the exception of that night when she ended up in the emergency room.

The group was back at it at the "Mosaic" room at the Center.
"How are we doing folks?" asked Troy. "We're heading into Thanksgiving. Some of you need to check in this week. Some of you will be travelling."
The girl who kicked out her old boyfriend only to exchange him for a new one was ready to talk. The talk was dedicated to the new guy on the block.
"I can't hide from him, he lives across the street," she said.
"What's wrong with meeting him outside by the mailbox?" somebody questioned. "Does he know you kicked the first guy out?" a voice questioned.
The girl didn't look innocent at all. On the contrary, she was wearing a very low-cut sweater, and the black tights were too tight showing off her perfect buns.
"He knows everything," she said. "I can't hide from him."

Klarette knew the story; it was always the same thing. "Resist temptation, resist temptation," Klarette spoke out of order. "Learn to resist temptation."

The clean-shaved guy in the green shirt with short sleeves was getting ready to talk after taking a break from the "Mosaic" for two months. The guy was overly confident, chatty, obviously cold and loved to display the tattoo on his right wrist. He looked familiar. He acted and sounded like a car dealer.

"Go ahead, Stan," said Troy. "Tell us what you have been up to since the last time we've seen you."

Stan wiggled in his chair looking around the room for familiar faces. He stopped at Klarette seated by the window.

"I thought, I had this, but Paul offered me some," said Stan. "I thought I'd have just one. You know I love the ritual."

Troy stretched in his chair and put his arms behind his head.

"This group remembers you saying that you had this," said Troy. "What happened Stan?"

"You know it was all Paul's fault," Stand defended himself. "Like I've said; I thought I would have just one."

Troy fidgeted.

"Stan, you know there are no firsts, only lasts," he said. "And the last one can take you to your grave. Haven't you learned that? Go ahead, enlighten us."

Klarette looked up to her right and rested her eyesight on this somewhat familiar guy, perhaps in his late thirties. He seemed outdated to her, since his black hair was greased with pomade. He had a twitch in his face and his eyelids fluttered.

"Wow, that guy is screwed up," Klarette thought.

As Stan continued to share about his newest escape to the cocaine haven, he stopped and looked directly at Klarette.

"What are you smiling about?" he attacked. "You haven't been there."

"Yes, no kidding," said Klarette. "I've only been to hell and back, and back to hell again. But you wouldn't know, you're too screwed up."

Stan's story confirmed Klarette's suspicions about dealers of all sorts. They don't just deal in the brand names they advertise; more importantly they deal in what they don't advertise.

"Paul got me a batch of coke for $500," he said. "I wouldn't let that go to waste."

Stan went to work high and he was obnoxious with customers, according to his own account. That's when the employer decided to suspend Stan until he straightened out.

"That's why I am back, I couldn't stop again," said Stan. "I was demoted at work, and almost lost my demoted position."

"That makes you what?" Klarette was sarcastic. "A used car salesman or you just move the cars on the lot?"

"Tell us your plan, Stan," Troy said stretching in his chair.

Stan explained to the "Mosaic" group the truth he believed in.

"I need to be pushed to the wall with nowhere to go, and then I won't do it," he concluded. "My girlfriend won't talk to me until I quit for good. I promised her, I would."

All those promises that went into thin air.

"What if Paul shows up with the stash this evening, Stan?" Troy asked not allowing for any wiggle room.

"I swear I won't open the door," Stan turned red as he swore in front of the group.

Yes, swearing always came after the empty promises magnified by the desire to get high one more time. Was it one more time or one last time?

"I have a lot to lose; my job and my girlfriend," Stan was backing off now.

Troy nodded his head now as if he understood every problem in this world, including his own struggle with substances.

"People like Paul will always be out there waiting for you," said Troy. "But even if Paul is gone, you will remain by yourself with your own temptation."

Troy left that wide open, as the group began packing up to head out into the real world of temptations. They got plenty of handouts; the old lady was doodling on them. She smelled of nicotine and caffeine.

To top it all off, the old lady and the group were concerned about the recent legalization of weed.

"Another temptation to fend off," the old lady said. "How many more temptations will I have to fight?"

Troy had one more thing to say to the group anxious to leave the white walls of the Center.

"Before you go to a party determine its focus," he said. "Then decide if you need to go. Always say no to all those Pauls out there."

That was a good one, Troy. Klarette tried to remember the focus of the party she had gone to before she blacked out, and someone apparently called the ambulance to resuscitate her at the "Center."

She saw it clearly, now. It was a surprise birthday party for a friend's friend. They were all waiting locked up in the pole barn before the friend would come to fetch his daily beer and a stash of cocaine.

"Surprise," they yelled at the dude with greased up black hair.

Klarette tried to shake off that old feeling of not knowing what had exactly happened at a party.

Stan stopped her at the doorway and gave Klarette a hard look.

"You were at my surprise birthday party," he breathed into her face. "Now, I recognize you."

Klarette backed away against the white wall.

"Did we have sex?" Stan asked her. "I don't know I blacked out. Do you know?"

Klarette was relieved that Stan didn't remember anything either.

"I am not sure," she said. "I prefer to think we didn't."

Oceans Away

Norma Livingston was a Slavic girl with a Slavic accent from the hilly village of Vesovia. She changed her name to Norma Livingston to forget her haunting past.

At first, she worked hard manually in vain to escape her own destiny. Later, Norma moved to Pittsburg to work in the Warhol Museum.

She led an impersonal and anonymous life amidst the city lights and streets. Without any friends or family to lose, Norma navigated big cities easier than small neighborhoods from the old country.

Moving between the old and the new, Norma never made any real friends. In her studio apartment above the boutique, she nurtured old dreams and disappointments.

She could no longer draw a distinct line between the real world and her fantasies. Norma's fantasies encompassed her real world with a big cold hug. Even though, she could no longer lie to herself about her age, Norma still lied to herself about men.

Norma found that handsome guy from the faraway lands of New Caledonia just by trying out a new dating app on the market.

"Try us out, and you'll see," screamed the ads.

Even though she was suspicious at first, Norma went for the app and diligently filled out all the fields about herself.

Paul was good looking as she requested, blonde and tall; while she tallied up to his expectations as well, brunette and medium height and weight. Their first rendezvous was in Budapest, Hungary on a boat.

Norma insisted on neutral grounds such as Europe. It was Paul who picked the capital of Hungary for their first meeting. The app set their date on a boat

"Princess" floating on the Danube to explore the river towns.

They had separate cabins on the boat. The first night, the boat was just anchoring in Budapest and they took a taxi into the city.

Paul told Norma everything about himself. He was a doctor of Slavic origin, who wanted to get away from the nationalistic France. Norma wasn't ashamed of her new job of the Warhol Museum executive director, either. She worked hard to get the job studying online for her master's degree.

Budapest at night was like a star waiting to shine on the night sky. They sat long into the night on the deck bar on the boat eating shrimp and drinking red Hungarian wine.

"Will you come and see me in Noumea?" Paul asked on the boat looking at Norma.

"That's quite a way, Paul," Norma said. "I won't have that much time off. It will be better if you come to see me in Pittsburg. Come for Christmas."

Paul accompanied her to the boat cabin and he retreated to his own without attempting further contact.

The next morning, they enjoyed breakfast together as the boat departed Budapest for Vienna.

Paul was surprised by Norma's knowledge of history of the Austro-Hungarian Empire even its architecture. She explained that the old country was part of the Austro-Hungarian Empire until its demise after World War I in 1918.

"I used to like history too, but both my grandparents died in Nazi concentration camps," he said. "I don't like it anymore or the French history for that matter. They are revolutionaries. Look at the mess that's happening now."

"I do have two passports and dual citizenship," she smiled. "Just in case if everything goes to hell."

"You mean like all over the world, then where will you go?" he asked carefully. "Your two passports might not save you. That's why I have thrown one of mine out."

"What kind of a doctor are you, Paul?" Norma asked with true interest in this man who seemed to have no past.

Paul hesitated with his answer looking around the breakfast room on the boat.

"I am a plastic surgeon," he answered humbly. "At the Noumea plastic clinic. We have a lot of foreigners there."

Norma was literally burning in her seat with another question. She watched Paul eat his omelet.

"Have you ever been married?" she had to ask him.

Paul kept eating his omelet pausing before he answered.

"Yes, I was married once," he said. "She left me for another guy, who was cuter and had more money. I wasn't a surgeon back then."

Norma wasn't sure if she could trust this man.

"We didn't have any kids, luckily," he said. "I got over it, and so did she."

Norma was nervous waiting for Paul to ask about her past.

"What about you?" Paul finally asked.

Norma shook her head.

"I've never been married, but I've been hurt a million times," she said. "I don't want that to happen again." Paul was courteous as he offered Norma strawberries with whipped cream.

"You don't have to answer me," he said. "It doesn't matter what happened in the past. All that matters is today. As long as you are not married now or that you have a guy somewhere in Pittsburg waiting for you."

When the boat docked in Vienna, they walked through its streets not wanting to leave the beautiful city ever.

"You know that I am flying back to Pittsburg out of Vienna in two days," she said quickly.

Paul was well aware of Norma's departure, as well as his own.

"What can I do to make you stay in this city of love?" he asked genuinely. "I will stay longer too. I can call the clinic, and we can stay at a hotel."

Norma was afraid to say anything that would spoil the moment.

"We still have two nights on the boat," she said.

Vienna at night was a shining city of palaces, parks and unspoiled romance. The mist rising from the Danube filled the autumn air.

The last night was the captain's gala dinner in the fancy "King's Room". Norma wore her blue mermaid's gown with a long slit up to the top of her thigh. They danced the waltz "The Blue Danube," by Johann Strauss II.

"Where did you learn how to dance?" Paul asked.

"We had mandatory dance classes in school," Norma said. "That is classical ballroom dance. You are a very good dancer, Paul."

It occurred to her, that Paul could be an experienced dancer because of his surgeon high-class job in New Caledonia.

"I practice a lot," he admitted reluctantly. "Mostly with myself. I don't have a lot of friends."

Norma never had many friends either. She left her Slavic homeland and traveled the world never finding what she was looking for. Once she returned home to Vesovia only to leave again. Her family never contacted her and she forgot all about them as well.

Paul became everybody and everything for her. But she was careful not to show it. She nurtured past disappointments in her with a passion.

"I would like to sleep with you," Paul said shockingly blunt.

Norma wasn't ready for a big move.

"We've known each other for hardly a week," she said dancing in his arms.

"I want to be with you forever," he said drawing her closer.

"Forever, Paul, is a long time," she said. "I am not ready for a serious relationship."

Later at night, Norma did give into Paul's warm arms. They made love in the small cabin on the boat called "Princess."

After making love, they watched the stars and the moon.

"I don't want to lose you, Paul," she said wiping tears. "I don't speak French. I cannot join you in Noumea. Can you come to Pittsburg?"

There was the barrier of distance separating them from each other. Paul was so many oceans away that she couldn't name them all.

Paul caressed her brown hair and cheeks.

"My love we knew about the distance from the app and it didn't stop us from meeting," he said. "It shouldn't' stop us now that we are together."

Norma loved her new job at the Warhol Museum.

"You can move to Pittsburg, right?" she questioned lovingly and Paul was touched.

Paul was in a partnership at the clinic. He invested a lot of money into it.

"I don't want us to break up because of the distance," he said kissing Norma on her neck. "We can find a solution."

A quiet desperation was settling in between the two lovers.

"You can easily learn French and join me," he said.

She was watching the Atlantic Ocean from the airplane window. It looked like grey blue steel. They wished each other a soft goodbye at the airport. It was true, they both knew about the distance from the app, yet they flew out to Budapest to seal their destiny. Was that foolish? Norma was asking herself.

The night with Paul on the "Princess "boat was a night she would never forget.

Back at work, she asked assistant Connie what would she do in her situation. Connie led a simple life with an American husband.

"Well, Norma I don't think you're asking the right person," Connie said. "I have never even left Pittsburg. Let alone would I leave America for a French-speaking country in the middle of oceans."

They were sitting in the office overlooking the Delaware River with beautiful bridges and the riverfront.

"Your guy wouldn't come live here?" Connie asked. "Let's take a walk through the museum. Andy might give us a clue in his work."

The two women took a walk through the exhibition halls with Warhol's silk screen paintings of Marilyn Monroe and portrait of Mao Zedong.

Norma was expecting a phone call from Paul at the end of the week. She was feeling lonely all over again. Paul finally called when she got home to her apartment in downtown Pittsburg.

"I miss you," she said.

"I miss you too, and we're like 20,000 miles apart," he said.

"Will you be able to come for Christmas?" she asked quickly walking to the window and watching the busy street.

They both could feel the distance between them; the distance of endless oceans.

"You never told me how you ended up in New Caledonia?" she asked.

"It was the job and I wanted to get away from France," he said. "You could get used to living here."

Norma wondered to herself what would she do in New Caledonia with her life and her new friend.
"You know we could open a business here," Paul said.
"With what?" she was curious. "You're a plastic surgeon and I am a museum director."
"Just come for a visit, and you will see," Paul said to reluctant Norma.
Norma already regretted answering the darn dating app.
"You don't want to stay by yourself your entire life," Paul said. "We do have good things going on between us."
"You are oceans away from me, Paul," Norma wiped off a tear.
Paul was in his office looking outside the window. He felt lonely too.
"We have to find a compromise where we want to live," he said.

Finally, Norma gave in to Paul and flew to Noumea. It was very hot and humid with trade winds coming from the ocean.
"You will get used to the weather," Paul was very encouraging. He was determined not to let Norma go back.
"I want you to definitely stay here with me, forever," he said drawing her closer to his body. "I will find you a job."
She would be even farther from her Slavic origins than in Pittsburg, plus she didn't speak French.

"How long did it take you to get used to living here in the middle of nowhere?" she was scared of another major change.

"Let's go sailing," Paul said.

They boarded Paul's sailboat "Queen."

"We can sleep on the sailboat," he said hugging her gently.

They made love again on the sailboat just like near Vienna. They docked at the harbor.

"I have something for you," he said.

Paul knelt and gave her the engagement diamond ring.

"Now, you are mine forever," he said.

Paul did everything to make Norma feel at home in this distant land east of Australia. Norma worked in his office as a receptionist, but missed her museum job.

"We will look for a different job for you," Paul said.

It was too late for them to have kids. They were both almost 50. Paul genuinely loved Norma and hated to see her suffer from loneliness.

"You know you have me forever," he said lovingly.

But Norma suffered from increased depression and loneliness, combined with the job she didn't like.

"You know you don't have anyone in Pittsburg either," he said watching her closely.

"You're a smart girl, you will learn the language fast," he said tenderly. "I enrolled you in an evening class."

Norma went to evening classes without much interest. Paul suffered with her. She happily showed

him the certificate when she was done with her French. Paul could tell that she wasn't happy.
"What can I do to make you happy again?" he asked.
"Let's go to Europe for that boat trip where we met," she begged. "It is our anniversary. We'll pretend like we're doing it all over again."
Paul looked at Norma not quite understanding.
"We won't even fly together?" he asked.
"No, I want to meet on the boat in Budapest like the first time," she insisted on reliving their romance.
Paul was waiting on the deck of "Princess" looking at the beautiful shining night in Budapest. He looked at his watch. It wasn't like Norma to be late. They will be serving dinner soon. He went to get them seated in the fancy dining room. The waiter asked him for his name.
"Are you Paul, sir?" he asked.
"Yes, I am," Paul said.
The waiter handed Paul a letter. It was Norma's handwriting. Paul had trouble reading it, but then he deciphered it.
"My dearest, Paul. I have to leave you because I cannot live in New Caledonia. I thought I could, but I can't. I don't want you to suffer through another departure. Don't look for me. I have applied for a divorce. Love always, Norma."

Devil's Elixir

On the day of the second highest box office opening in North America of Star Wars, Tom and Bella drove to a hospital on the west outskirts of town. The locals lovingly called the joint sitting on the connector freeway "Hotel."

The building sprung up amidst farm fields gone bankrupt and sprawling urban development.

To get to the hospital, they had to pass the huge billboard on the ground warning of dangers of socialism: "Marxism equals poverty." Cows were grazing around the billboard.

The farm with cows and the billboard was surrounded by a development called "Whispering Farms" with three-story houses towering to the sky.

It was noon when they checked in at the registration of the hospital and proceeded to the busy hospital café. The doctors and nurses flocked to the café sharing their daily stories and gossip about patients.

Bella was holding onto her new computer bought on Black Friday as she ate the hospital healthy salad grown in the hospital organic garden. Tom had to fast due to the upcoming surgical procedure. The hallways were decorated for Christmas with an enormous tree in the middle of the main lobby.

If it weren't for the ambulances, the white coats and patients in wheelchairs, the place felt more like a luxury hotel than a hospital. A boutique peddled everything from books, stuffed animals, mugs to t-shirts with "Live, laugh and love" decals.

In the main eatery, there was even a piano idling before the pianist arrives.

A nurse ushered them through the spidering hallways into the Cardiovascular Lab.

Inside Bay 9, the nurse hooked Tom up with all the vital-reading equipment. Bella did not notice the sign warning: No jewelry. It was cold and dry in the bay. After an hour, Bella felt her cold feet and touched her briefcase to find out the only heat was radiating from the new computer.

Tom dozed off for an hour. The nurse checked into the bay from time to time giving updates about the doctor's delay.

When he finally entered Bay 9, the short doctor with dark hair was out of breath himself. He was wearing a biker's cap in yellow, blue and red Colombian national colors and a matching magnetic floral apron. At first, he looked like the chef from the hospital café on the main floor. It was cold because of the overheated equipment and personnel. Moreover, on a Friday night, everyone hurried to get out of the feared hospital hotel. Many neighbors or friends have died at this hospital.

"If you don't have chest pains, why are you here?" the doc snapped at the scared blonde guy laying on the bed with wires attached to him.

"I had shortness of breath," the scared guy answered, eying the doctor. "You suggested this procedure."

The doctor looked surprised. In the sea of patients with varied diagnosis that he made every day, there was no way he could remember this blonde scared dude.

Yes, the blonde dude was a bit overweight, and over 50. But still that wouldn't be the major reason for catheterization on a Friday evening unless the blonde dude came from the emergency room.

"Did they send you in from trauma?" the doc asked, while the blonde dude detected a slight accent, worse than his own.

Well, this heart doctor was from Colombia in South America. He came to the North American Midwest with solid credentials from the University of Antioquia in Medellin.

Dr. Joseph Kuraz liked his Friday nights off, except when he was doing the emergency room shift.

"Do I look like I am in trauma?" snapped the blonde guy back.

Dr. Kuraz barked at the nurse standing in the corner of the bay. She was holding a folder.

"Give it to me," he said. Dr. Kuraz was getting increasingly angry as he was running two hours behind schedule because of the emergency room. He was scratching his head to pull out a memory.

Then, he started explaining the procedure that he had done so many times. As he heard himself talking, he went back to that distant memory, when he performed the heart catheterization for the first time.

"We may do heart repair and insert balloons or stents if necessary," said Dr. Kuraz. "If we do that, you will have to stay overnight."

His first heart repair was in a small hospital still back in Columbia, where he got his training. The elderly patient never made it through the procedure. Dr. Kuraz was trying to remember the guy's name. He didn't even know this guy's name; how could he remember the other guy's name. Later he visited his grave near Medellin to search for clues of what he had done wrong in the procedure.

The headstone only read: He died like he lived, in good spirits. Dr. Kuraz tried to recall the old gentleman's anamnesis.

The doctor looked at the magnetic white board on the white wall that designated who the patient was, his driver, nurses' names, pager number, procedure and his own name.

"Well at least they put in those white boards for something, huh?" Dr. Kuraz looked at the nurse. "Okay, let's do this, Tom. There are all sorts of outcomes including death, but the benefits outweigh the risks."

Tom looked relieved as the tranquilizer was beginning to take over his fear. He feared this procedure for weeks. Fear permeated his body and life for the last 10 years of struggles with jobs, aging and economy.

"We gave him a light sedative," said the nurse to Tom's wife, who also appeared to be scared. "Our goal is to keep him pain free and anxiety free."

The sedative was Fentanyl, an opioid used for anesthesia and as a recreational drug. At 3:21 p.m., another nurse wheeled Tom off into the surgical room. Bella was losing track of the nurses' names looking from time to time at the white board.

A nurse handed her a pager #614 with kind words:

"You can leave now," she said.

Bella left the cath lab for the reflection seating area next to the coffee bar, that was just about to close. The anxious barista was ready to go home, as she started cleaning up the coffee bar with no wi-fi.

"What's a coffee bar without a wi-fi?" Bella asked the clerk.

The clerk shrugged her shoulders as she continued to sweep the floor.

"I just work here, I don't rule the place," she said looking up from her broom.

Bella eased herself into an armchair of the reflection seating area and stared outside through the large window panels lining the lobby. It was getting dark outside; just to think that they had arrived at Hotel 6 at noon in time for lunch at the crowded hospital café with whitecoats and nurses.

The seating area overlooked the Healing Garden that was covered by early snow. The snow caps served as cushions. The ghastly garden was in the enclosed atrium formed by two wings of the hospital. The coffee tables were covered with caps of snow. The bare tree trunks and branches took on the form of winter monsters with Christmas lights. The walls were covered with artwork.

Out of the white stood the yellows and reds of the painted walls. The reds reminded Bella of the blood that flew out of Tom's broken skin, as the nurse was searching for the port for the catheter that Dr. Kuraz will insert into the left artery leading to the heart.

"We might have to use the groin to enter," she said.

The waiting was exasperated by another unknown; if a repair to the heart is necessary, they will have to stay overnight at the real hotel in the hospital village. Bella was thinking about the people who were present at the hospital cafe before the procedure. At that moment, they all shared a common bond of fear of the unknown. Fear gripped her tight in its arms.

"Dance with the unknown," a teacher told her once.

She was tired of staring into the ghastly garden, so Bella walked back into the café. She passed the big waterfall sign with rolling water over donor plaques with philanthropists' names. That reminded her of another rolling waterfall sign with water rolling over little plaster sharks and shells in a resort on the Gulf. All the donors had deep ties to the hospital from birth to death. The hospital timeline boasted a lifetime span; for some shorter, for others longer.

This time the café was deserted except for a few patrons: a young intern, a student and the cleaning crew. She noticed trash bins marked "compost." A chain link wall closed off the check-out registers from the other side of the café. Bella carefully touched her pager #614. A small section of the café with healthy drinks, snacks and irritated clerks remained open. Bella bought Peace Tea with Georgia peach flavor in an orange can. There were hand sanitizers per foot of space everywhere. The piano was still waiting for the pianist to come and play dinner music.

The term "elective percutaneous coronary intervention" kept ringing in Bella's ears as she looked around. She felt like screaming:

"Does anyone know what an elective percutaneous coronary intervention is?"
The doctors in scrubs from lunchtime were long gone; they could have explained it to her.
"Yes, the doc did say something about balloons and stents," she recalled.
Bella thought about the woman in the neighboring bay enjoying her time waiting for a procedure that would repair her heart. She didn't realize that some hearts couldn't be repaired.
"Grace, did you take the four aspirins this morning?" asked a nurse.
"No, I took Tylenol," the old woman said smirking.
"You should know better by now," said the nurse. "You've been around."
Unlike Bella, the woman knew everything there was to know about coronary interventions. She had been travelling among the regional hospitals for the last 10 years searching for the best experience in heart repair. Grace travelled from small to large hospitals.
"You know in Greenville they have worse food than here," Grace said to friends. "I like it here better. In Greenville, patients die from eating the hospital food. That's a joke."
Bella forced herself back into the evening reality of the deserted café. The student with a backpack next to her was studying for exams.
Yeah, there was a time when Bella wanted to be a doctor; a cardiologist. The dreams- for the better- dissipated in someone else's dreams.
The reality of a Friday before Christmas spent at the hospital was settling in. Bella should have been

baking, cooking, shopping and wrapping gifts. Instead, she was sitting in a deserted café, behind the glass wall of the Healing Garden with a student and a cleaning crew. Her stomach was crouching. Bella was looking at the garden from a different angle of another hospital wing. The moon over the garden was peeking out from the dark cloud cover. Bella answered the phone ringing into the silence.

"I know you won't be able to concentrate, but I am in pain," mom said.

Mom described exactly where her pain meds were 110 miles from Hotel 6.

"In the bedroom on the night stand to the left, you will find a small box with pink gel capsules," the voice said. "It's Dilthiazen. How is it going?"

"I am still waiting," Bella said. "We've been here since noon. I've got to go see if they're done."

Right then, the pager started vibrating and flashing red like crazy. Bella ran through the silent hallways past the hospital staff's art. It was a huge painting with purple, blue, orange and green bold streaks.

It was 5:06 p.m. when Tom got out of the surgery room. He was awake. His arm was all bloody and bandaged up like it was broken. They did not have to use the groin port; the veins at the right wrist were good enough.

"He's good to go," said Dr. Kuraz. "The arteries that feed the heart are clear. There was nothing to fix. He can shovel snow now."

Bella gave the doc a big hug; there will be a Christmas holiday.

Dr. Kuraz headed home from the hospital to his luxurious mansion in "Whispering Farms." The brisk December wind whispered to him:
"That old guy could have lived if you had studied his anamnesis more. You would have found out that he was born with a heart defect."
"But the technology wasn't as good back then. They had no records when the guy was born. It wasn't in the anamnesis- his heart defect.
Bella tried to keep up with the fast pace of the assistant who wheeled drowsy Tom down the hallways to the exit. Another ambulance had just arrived.
As Bella drove the car through the suburbia decorated for Christmas, Tom said he could see stars in his eyes.
"That must be from the Fentanyl," said Bella. "But there are stars tonight, look at the sky."
Large inflated Santas in red and white with LED lights and fans inside them bowed to the stars in the December sky.
Many years later, Bella traced back Tom's usage of opioids to that moment in Bay 9 when he got Fentanyl.
"That was Devil's Elixir they had given you at the hospital," she said. "Now, you can't stop."

Cupcake Wine

Gladys Orion was sitting at the round table inside the huge room with a stage. There were colorful posters decorating the green walls. A white headband was pushing her dark blonde hair away from her tall forehead.

She always introduced herself as Mrs. O. while staring into the posters rather than at the other people around the table. Whenever it was her turn to speak, she nervously fidgeted. Gladys had a pretty figure with lots of curves to show off. Like most mornings, she really didn't want to be in that big room with the stage.

"Why is the stage there?" she asked once pointing to it rather than talking about her feelings and thoughts.

"Mrs. O, do you realize there is a difference between thoughts and feelings?" asked the smart-ass chairman Rupert. "Plus, the stage doesn't really matter."

"It is distracting me," she said.

Mrs. O tried to remember what got her to the round table. Was it the Camelot of her fancy upscale life?

Gladys had a beautiful life lined with rose petals, exotic fragrances, colorful yarns and silver dollars. Her only struggle was with her father, who tried to make her go to college.

"I've always done only what I wanted to," she bragged proudly on regular basis at the round table discussions.

"Look where it got you," snapped the stubby chairman with thinning hair. Aging was taking over this man. Rupert was always resentful and jabbing.

Mrs. O really didn't need this coming from a guy who meant less than a yesterday's minute.

They fought often about the things that got them to the bare round table without a tablecloth or proper silverware.
"You're out of order Rupert," Mrs. O. screamed. "You're abrasive and raw."
She looked around the enormous room again with just that one round table in the middle in front of the stage. The air from the ventilators was blowing on her head and fluffing her thoughts even more; tangling and twisting them into a skein of Alpaca yarn.
She had a farm with Alpacas and sheep where she worked hard to chase away her thoughts of arrogance. Those she shared with Rupert. They were basically made of the same raw fabric with the exception of wealth.
Gladys was born wealthy and married a wealthy man who owned a distillery business. Rupert had none of the above, except for the drive to succeed again after he had turned his life upside down.
In that aspect, he wasn't a lot different from the other people around the table.
Gladys was an atheist, who had trouble believing in anything but herself. She never thought of herself as being insane, just empowered in a wrong way, following a wrong path at the wrong time.
The family's wealth gave her a position in the high society. She didn't need the struggle of the rest of the folks around the round table.
She never quite understood why they called themselves "Happy Joes & Jills" on top of the hill. It wasn't even allowed to be happy, as one could be considered intoxicated or high if happy. And many

did fly in with yesterday's dreams of happiness on floats of vodka or Margaritas.

"We're all equal in here," once Rupert snapped in response to Gladys' sassiness. "Once you walk in through that door, you become one of us. And you are lucky to walk through that door. You're lucky that you found that door. You could have ended up outside in the gutter like I did."

Rupert pointed at the door and looked Gladys in the eyes. She straightened her headband and looked away at the stage and the posters. One of them had orange leaves falling down from a bizarre black tree. She examined the tree and the leaves closely to avoid Rupert's gaze.

Gladys steadily refused to admit she was insane.

"Give me a proof that I am insane," she challenged the group often.

Indeed, sometimes it was hard to believe that this elegant woman who stepped out of her burgundy Audi twice a week was an insane nut. She was always well- groomed sporting the latest haircut and tight jeans. Gladys had a valid driver's license without any record. Although, she did come in sometimes wearing a checkered flannel shirt straight off the Alpaca farm.

Being late was not allowed, so Gladys made sure she was on time. Everything always started with the acceptance of others and her own denial.

"If you don't want to say it that way, you can rephrase it," someone suggested.

"Like what do I say?" she snapped. "I am a wicked witch of Eastwick? Is that good enough for you? I haven't done anything wrong."

Gladys folded her arms across her chest and leaned back into the uncomfortable chair.

"Could you all just leave me alone?" she lashed out often at the "Happy Joes & Jills."

After all, she had the support of the knitting club that had convinced her she was fine and dandy. Every week the knitting ladies got together to knit and chat.

"You don't belong up there with those losers," said a long-time friend. "You're one of us."

She was making the collar on a sweater that could be really tricky, since you had to use round knitting needles.

"Why did you start going up there, anyways?" the friend persisted. "Most people are ordered to go there, but not you. You haven't done anything."

She was looking forward to the holiday travel to the upscale condo on the ocean in the Pelican Resort. She wanted to escape both groups. Gladys wondered how many times she reknitted that purple sweater. It wasn't that she didn't have money for more yarn or enough ideas. She needed the calming action of the knitting. She loved to listen to the click of the needles against each other, and watch the rows grow.

"You're right, I haven't done anything bad," she said. The escape to the ocean convinced her that she was totally sane. She diligently packed her suitcase with light airy clothes and tropical fragrances. Gladys was determined to forgive herself whatever she was going to do on the oceanside.

She must erase the images of both groups from her mind with a stroke of unforgiveness for them for disturbing her consciousness.

Gladys planned well her escapes to the last detail never leaving anything to a chance. The private jet was always ready in the hangars. However, there was one more meeting left before her escape. She put on that purple sweater and jumped in her Audi.

The drive to the meeting up on top of the hill was a challenge. Many times, Gladys felt like turning around and driving back to the safety of her home. The contrast of the pretty drive on the banks of the river and through the hills with the somber mood of the meeting inspired her poetic nature. The trees were bare and looked like the ones on the poster inside the huge room with the stage.

During winter time, Gladys had trouble making the drive up the hill in the snow tracks. The pick- up truck drivers with their snow plows and blades never got all the snow of the road. Sometimes, she used the road conditions as an excuse not to go at all.

But this time she had to go. It was a must before her escape to the Pelican Resort. She must seek forgiveness before she does anything bad. Gladys was the only one who knew that nothing has happened, yet.

But that was the old adage of the club, “Things that haven’t happened, yet.”

The keyword was yet. How many times will she have to listen to that bullshit, “Not yet.”

The last time she heard it was from an astute business person with a new house, a new wife and a new car. It was a variation on her own denial of insanity.

“I haven’t had any trouble with the law or love,” he bragged. “I am loved.”

The jargon of the "Happy Joes & Jills" club was maddening.

It was a while before she learned it; things like the "wiring of the brain" and Einstein's definition of insanity.

"The definition of insanity is doing the same thing over and over and expecting different results," Rup said. "Are you expecting different results, Mrs. O?"

"I do know what I am doing," she said. "I have a degree, you know."

Most of her knitting friends had no education at all. Gladys was an exception thanks to her father. She never used the education, but she had a piece of paper that said "bachelor's degree in fine arts." Gladys displayed that in a frame on the wall, so did her father in a golden frame.

She considered her brain to be "wired" well for what she did in her life. She took care of the Alpacas and the sheep, and she knitted with their wool.

But then came that bothersome dreadful night when she found a dead body on the property back in the woods.

"Anyone has a theme today?" Rupert looked around the table setting his eyes on Gladys.

She fidgeted nervously and shuffled her feet in her boots looking at the heels.

"I can talk. I do not believe we are insane," she said. "We're troubled like other people. We just deal with it in a different way by using whatever makes us feel better."

Gladys looked at the poster, at the stage, and around the table.

"There is nothing above us," she said. "We render our power from the inside and we surrender it to the outside folks. We surrender, and we either win or lose."
Yes, and surrendering was the key word, unlike the other clichés used. Gladys had to surrender long time ago to the power of money, in spite of her diplomas and awards.
"The only power I know is money," she finished. "Thanks for listening to me."
Gladys got up and left to the astonished audience. This has never happened before, that someone would just get up and leave without excusing themselves.
"Hey, we're not done yet," Rupert ran after her.
He grabbed her arm and tried to pull her back into the room, but she pushed him away.
Gladys didn't even turn around as she slammed the door of her Audi.

The view from the Pelican Resort of the ocean waves was like a balsam on Gladys' nerves. She finally didn't need any posters of bare trees and leaves falling, just the clashing of the waves in their constant motion.
Rupert's chastising was refusing to leave her. She felt attracted to men like Rupert. She liked the way he stood up in front of the boards in that room with the stage.

"I want to explain to you," he always started, "How I messed up my life."

"Yeah, like who cares?" Gladys snapped back.

In his own words, he screwed up a big part of his life. In his own words, he regretted screwing up his own life and blaming it on others. Then, he thought he would never do it again, but kept repeating the same mistake over and over again with the same results. Now, that was Einstein's definition of craziness modified; repeating the same mistakes with the same results.

That is insanity. That much Gladys knew that Rupert was insane. She walked in the sand watching the night set in, breathing in the salty air. At the Pelican, she wanted to be alone, but Rupert was intruding into her thoughts. He was riding on the waves of her "wired" brain, as the club jargon had it.

One day, he broke into tears at the table. Now, that was allowed. Everyone did that; tears were encouraged for all purposes. Gladys couldn't remember if she ever cried at the "Happy Joes & Jills" meetings on the hill. Not, that she didn't have a reason. She broke into tears that night she stumbled over the dead body in the woods.

That new girl with shaved head cried too over her own misery, and that she ended up on the hill inside the big room with the stage. She cried on several occasions along with others. It wasn't a chorus of tears; those were individual tears shed over personal destinies screwed up.

The rest of the club members listened to the tears and the gulps of misery showing its face. A crying face turns into a strange grimace full of pain of what once was pleasure.

All of a sudden Gladys felt like calling Rupert against the club policy.

"Yes, this is Rup," Gladys heard him swallow hard.

"I forgot to say goodbye," she said quickly.

There was a long silence on the other end. Gladys did not expect the silence to be that long. What does a "wired" brain think about this long?"

"Do you realize it's night?" Rup said slowly. "What if I was sleeping?"

"But you weren't," she said.

Gladys was standing by the window watching the ocean change at night. She didn't want to be alone anymore.

"Do you want to come down and join me?" she breathed the question into the phone.

She heard the silence on the other end again. It was more like the sound of sheer disbelief. There was another "wired" brain processing.

"How do you think I am going to get out of the house in the middle of the night?" Rup was practical, never for a moment thinking he wouldn't do it.

"I can lie about a conference tomorrow. Wait for me at the airport," he said.

And that was all it took, one phone call from a "wired" brain to another "wired" brain.

It wasn't the first time they got secretly together during the 31 months they've known each other from the meetings on the hill. They were masters at hiding. The double secrecy of these clandestine encounters fueled their passion for one another.

"Do you think we're going to burn in hell for doing this?" asked Rup as they lay together on the white couch positioned in the window for the ocean view. Rup set the glass on Gladys' bare chest, and then poured some wine between her breasts.

"Yes, I do," said Gladys raising her own glass of wine. "I'd rather burn in hell than suffer in purgatory."

Then the glasses clinked, and Rup licked the wine from Gladys' body.

"It's worth burning," he said and drank more.

Usually these were only one-night stands, just long enough not to break the secrecy.

For the rest of her stay, Gladys enjoyed the ocean and the sweet memory of Rup's touch.

"Who wants to start today?" Rup looked around the table.

There were no takers, but even if there had been any, Rup wanted to talk today.

"I want to talk about guilt," he said. "I want to talk about guilt in all its dimensions. I want to talk about complete guilt and I want to talk about partial guilt."

The members of "Happy Joes & Jills" stared at Rup as he walked dauntlessly to the stage like the master of his own destiny.

"Have you ever felt guilty of anything?" he asked intrepidly. "Name your list. I will name mine first."

He tore down the poster with the bare tree and the leaves, crumpled it up and threw it at the trash bin. Rup missed the target.

"This is how I feel about guilt," he said. "I rip it down. I don't want it. I get rid of it."

He glanced at Gladys' empty spot around the table. He hadn't seen her since their secret oceanside rendezvous at the Pelican Resort.

Many months later in the dead of the winter, Rup was seated at the helm of the round table to satisfy his egoism. There were only two other people because of the freezing rain and the roads were bad.

He felt scared driving up the hill, but not scared enough to keep him away from confessing his own conscious guilt.

"I am going to throw my hat in the ring," he said willingly turning to the guy who took Gladys' empty spot.

He remained seated with dry eyes.

"You know, I really miss Mrs. O," Rup said. "I miss my old life, too. I don't know if I will ever go back, but I would like to. I know I can't handle myself."

"Do you know what happened to Mrs. O?" the new guy asked.

"They left town and moved their business by the lake," Rup said. "I don't know exactly where they went. She was a good resource for us. She always shared her misery."

The Orions moved out of town because of the corpse found on the property. The autopsy report stated that the person died of overdose. They were listed among the "persons of interest."

Booksafe Code

Legends circled past the Covered Bridge into the pioneer village boasting a one-room schoolhouse with a belfry, a dilapidated farm with blue siding and the main artifact museum in the center.

The buildings dated to the 1840s. At its peak, the village had a grist mill, a saw mill, a grocery store and a hotel. It sat on the stagecoach line from Ionia to Grand Rapids.

The main road framed by large oak trees winded through the village up the hill and past the old cemetery with graves of the founding fathers.

The museum housed treasures like the WWI women's cards, the Footprints property book, old attendance ledgers from the school and the "booksafe."

The villagers retold stories from generation to generation. Old timer Lena went to the one-room schoolhouse, much like her mother and grandmother did. Her grandmother Mrs. Charles enlisted in the World War I (WWI) second line of defense effort offering her housewife's skills.

"Did you know that Mrs. Richmond comes back to haunt the school?" Lena said at a meeting of the historical society.

The sentence landed from mid-air on the 10 members of the historical society seated at the big oak table inside the farmhouse with creaking floors and broken window panes.

The society president was standing at the head of the table in the dark room.

"Look Lena we already have stories of this farmhouse being haunted," said President Barry. "Are you trying to tell us there is more haunting going on?"

"More than you dare to think of," said Lena smirking. "Remember those ghost hunters found ghost activity at the schoolhouse and at the cemetery. They heard Mrs. Richmond walking between the desks."

The fall ghost buster hunt in the village uncovered ghost activity at all the village buildings. People saw shadows of Mrs. Richmond walking in the schoolhouse and heard her footsteps.

"So, what, we have ghosts here. If we get stuck again on this haunting business, we'll never get anything done," Barry said. "If we don't get anything done, we'll go belly up like the societies before us. If we go belly up, we have nothing left from our past. Have you forgotten the last time this has happened?"

How could Lena ever forget the day the post office was sold to save the historical society from bankruptcy?

For years, her dad was the post master at the village post office. And now because of Barry, all this was gone except for the artifacts saved at the main museum. Moreover, Barry was the only one with a coded access to the artifacts including the booksafe.

"Let's get down to business," said Barry. "We have to find the secret letter from Phoebe."

"Why?" asked Lena. "What do we need the letter for and who knows if it even exists? You make up a lot of stuff Barry."

"We all do, Lena," Barry said. "It's history that plays tricks on us. It's Miss History and Mr. Orlin, the builder."

"We should have kept the post office," Lena said, "Dad is turning in his grave at the cemetery. The post office was his only love."

Back then, the society was in the red and they had no choice but to sell some of the buildings in the village to preserve the existing ones.

Nostalgia, melancholy and Miss History worked well together on the members. Each member had a different memory tied to almost any tree or rock in the village.

"I was here long before you came along Barry," Lena attacked the president often.

Barry slammed his fist on the oak table.

"Will you just shut up," Barry screamed. "The sale of the post office saved us. Ava explain that to her, please."

Ava was the president's assistant.

"Barry is right, the sale of the post office saved us," she said. "But not completely. We're still in the red. We need to sell off more buildings like this creepy farm."

Ava turned to Barry steaming with anger.

"What do you want to get done in this cold and creepy, dirty building?" Ava didn't give up easily. "We owe money on some of the buildings. Why don't we sell this piece of junk, ha? We don't know what to do with it, why not get rid of it now before our events."

Barry wasn't ready to give up on the society's treasures like the dilapidated Orlin Farm. William used to grow melons on the farm.

"I've always wanted a successful watermelon business," laughed Barry??. "We can start growing watermelons here."

Ava didn't give up.

"We don't know what to do with the building," she said. "Why the hell do we have to keep it?"

Barry grew up in the forgotten village basking in its bygone glory of a thriving community with a stagecoach route from Ionia to Grand Rapids. Destiny had it that the town was bypassed by the almighty railroad three miles south, and thus rerouted its economic growth.

"We can't continue to sell off buildings, or we will have nothing left to sell," he said. "We can't sell our past. That's all we have left."

Ava nurtured her own sentiments about the past, that were more comfortable than the future or the present. No one knew the details of her past that originated somewhere across the ocean in the old country. She guarded her past with a passion of a warrior.

"If we raise memberships and ticket prices, we won't have people coming in," she said.

Finally, the members agreed that the discussion was going nowhere.

"We'll meet again in two weeks, right here in this old building," said Barry.

Barry had just crossed the Covered Bridge's white pine trusses all shaking under the weight of his pick-up truck. There was a camera placed on the bridge. He was hoping it wouldn't get his license plate number.

Barry had the keys and codes to all the buildings, including the booksafe code, and he was determined to look in the basement of the Orlin Farm. He wanted to find the secret letter from Phoebe that could have willed them some money because of her love for the village.

In his eyes, Phoebe was a beautiful woman deeply devoted to the pioneer village cause. He wanted to prove her devotion to the rest of the group, if he could only find the letter signed by Phoebe.

He was running out of time, if Ava has her way and gets the members to agree on the sale of the dilapidated farm.

Barry arrived in the middle of the night at the Orlin Farm equipped with tools to dig under the house. It was Wednesday night, and most of the villagers were fast asleep. The full moon was shining bright over the village and the Covered Bridge over the Flat River.

He dug up a lot of wet and heavy dirt. Still, Barry didn't come across anything. Finally, he came across an old chest with leather straps. Barry couldn't open the lid. The chest was locked. Barry checked his tools; he probably could cut it open without causing a lot of damage. He took the hand saw and started to cut the chest open, but he found out the chest had been opened. Moreover, he heard footsteps coming from the hallway. It was 2 a.m. in the morning; there was no way anyone could have seen him or entered the old farm. The footsteps were clear and coming closer above him.

Barry was thinking who else had keys to the building. Now, the footsteps were coming down into the basement. Should he hide from the intruder? He himself was an intruder inside the dark building.

“What are you doing down there?” said a woman’s voice.

Ava was standing above him with a huge grimace.

“I knew you were going to come down here,” she laughed. “I’ve been waiting for you.”

Barry stood up and straightened his hurting back staring blankly into the dark where he could only sense Ava. She stepped out of the dark shining the flashlight into his face. She was holding a paper in her hand.

“First of all, if you’re looking for Phoebe’s letter,” she smiled. “I have it. Secondly, if you’re looking for something else in here, you better watch out or you might find it.”

Barry looked at Ava holding the letter he had wanted all along.

“Give me that god damn letter,” he said. “Where did you find it? How the hell did you get in here?”

Barry snatched the letter from her pushing Ava to the wall behind the hole with the chest as she shrieked in pain. She dropped the flashlight and knocked his light off; they were completely in the dark in the basement under the Orlin Farm. Ava tried to free herself as Barry picked up the flashlight. He found a rope in his tool box. Ava was kicking but he tied her to the stud in the back of the basement. He tied a cloth around her mouth to prevent her from screaming. When she finally shut up, Barry crawled back into the hole with the chest and finished cutting it open.

He froze at what he had found out. Under a few old rags and boards torn and stinking from the rotten air in the basement, there was a skeleton. Barry backed away from the large chest. There was a musty smell in the basement that made him sick to his stomach, and he could hear Ava struggling to free herself. He noticed closely that the chest had been cut before.

"Where did you get the letter with Phoebe's handwriting," he barked at Ava. "We've been looking for it for years."

"I found it," she said slyly. "In the booksafe."

"What were you doing down here?" asked Barry. "How did you get in?"

"You would have to read the letter, first," Ava said. "I have the secret code, remember?"

Barry recalled giving Ava once a code to the lock box and the booksafe.

"How come the code didn't disintegrate?" he asked. "It should have disintegrated within a day."

There wasn't enough light to read the letter. Ava again tried to free herself, sticking a foot out. Barry tripped on her foot falling into the hole with the chest, and Ava managed to run out to the car taking his flashlight with her. Barry felt sharp pain as he hurt himself when he fell into the hole with the chest.

He had trouble climbing out and knocked the chest back closed and covered up the hole with rotted boards and rags. Barry ran out of the Orlin Farm to his car shocked. It was 15 minutes past 3 a.m. He realized he struggled in that basement for more than an hour with Ava. He left his tool box in the basement.

The next day, Barry sent out letters inviting everyone for a special meeting at the Orlin Farm on Monday night at 7 p.m.

Everyone came except for Ava. There were only 10 members sitting around the table.

“I have the secret letter from Phoebe,” Barry said angrily. “I am not going to point any fingers. Someone tried to steal it.”

“We’ve been after this letter for years,” said Lena. “Why is it so important that we have to get together here in this freaking cold because of a stupid old letter.”

Barry turned to the group.

“We’re going inside the basement,” he said. “I want to show you something.”

The group reluctantly went down the stairs into the musty and dark basement.

“The floor could cave in on us at any time,” warned the treasurer. “We will be buried alive and no one will ever know we were in here. Ava won’t tell.”

Barry uncovered the rags and threw away the boards. He climbed inside the hole and with a squeaking noise opened the trunk while the society’s members moved closer to the hole to look inside.

Barry threw away more rags and turned the flashlight on the bones. Lena first shrieked and then cried out, starting to run away.

"No, everyone stays here," said Barry who locked the door behind them. "No one leaves the basement, until I know, whose body is in that chest."

The members looked at each other in sheer disbelief and back into the hole with the bones.

"No one has been down here for years," argued the treasurer. "How could we possibly know whose bones are those?"

"Someone must have been down here because when I went down looking for the letter, the chest had already been cut open," said Barry.

"That's crap, let us out," said Lena. "Why did you lock us in here?"

Barry stood up to the group hovering over the hole.

"I have the letter from Phoebe," said Barry. "I found it down in that hole near the bones."

"What's in the letter," asked Lena.

In the meantime, Barry unlocked the door and led the group back upstairs ~~to~~ the meeting room.

"I wanted you all to see the bones in the basement," he said. "Now, to the letter."

A winter storm was moving into the village without any cell phone signals, and the only light bulb was flickering.

"The letter is actually a bequest to us, the historical society," Barry said looking closely at the members.

After years of struggling without money, the members were in total disbelief as Barry read the bequest.

"It is my will to leave all our monies to all the societies that will preserve our founding heritage of the village."

"So, the people before us didn't spend it all?" the treasurer asked bewildered.

"No, they didn't find Phoebe's letter," said Barry.

"How much is it?" asked the treasurer.

"It's everything they had from the combined sales of the grist and saw mills, and other properties in the village," said Barry. "The founders bought a lot of land here. Someone tried to steal our money."

The group sat petrified to the old rickety chairs in the living room of the Orlin Farm.

"We can't call the police," said the treasurer. "We'll just cover everything back up again. No one will ever know."

Barry looked around the room at the members.

"There's one other person who knows about the letter and the bones," he said looking around the table. "And that person is not here."

The storm was moving in and the branches, the limbs and the window panes were creaking and squeaking in the wind.

"It's Ava. She tried to get the money for herself," said Lena. "She should have destroyed the letter."

"What about the bones?" asked the treasurer puzzled. "Do you think they could be Orlin's? He died of natural causes."

The group sat quiet around the table looking at Barry.

"We'll bury the bones in the woods behind the house," Barry said. "No one ever goes there. It abuts to the cemetery, and some graves are in the woods, since there is no fencing."

The society secretly swore that no one will ever tell what they did that late November night. They buried

the unidentified bones into the woods near the cemetery under the old oak trees.
Barry and the treasurer took the letter with attorney's seals to the society's attorney in town.
"I see you're getting some money in," he said. "I've already seen this letter. A woman brought it in. She said she was a member of your society. I don't trust just anyone. I told her to come in with the two of you."
And there was Ava standing in the doorway.
"You thought you would get away with this, Barry?" she laughed. "I have the original; you only have a copy. How's that for you?"
The attorney looked at all three members of the society.
"I can call the police or I can deposit this into the society's account," he said. "I don't know how many of you really want to go to jail for embezzlement of the society's funds."
The threesome looked at each other thinking about the bones found in the basement of the Orlin Farm.
"Could it really be Orlin's bones?" they asked themselves.
The attorney looked through the files, as he pulled out another letter.
"It looks like somebody also deposited here another letter to support Phoebe's bequest to the society," he said. "It's also saying something about bones buried somewhere. Hard to say. I can't read that part. The main thing is Phoebe's bequest, and now we have the original and the copy. Shall we go ahead?"

Ava protested stating that the Orlin Farm should be searched for the bones.
A later police search in the basement of the farm found no bones, to Ava's disappointment. This time she wasn't allowed to go inside.
"Lady, there's nothing inside. It was your imagination playing tricks on you all along, go home."
It was Miss History who played tricks on the society; maybe Mr. Orlin had something to do with it. The second letter was found in the booksafe, a red leather-bound book.
Placed on a shelf, no one would know that the booksafe was not actually a book, but a hollowed-out storage container. Inside the "booksafe" were found various poems, letters, and essays written by the founding family.
That's where Phoebe's original will to the society was stored, along with the supporting letter.

Author Emma Palova biography

Emma Palova (Konecna) born in former Czechoslovakia is a Lowell-based short story writer, novelist screenwriter, journalist and a photographer.
Palova wrote for Czechoslovak Newsweek and Prague Reporter in the 1990s. She has a bachelor's degree from the University of Brno. Most recently, she worked as a reporter for The Lowell Ledger, and

as a freelance writer for regional newspapers and magazines.

Palova started an election collection of short stories during her studies of creative writing at the International Correspondence Schools in Montreal, and at the Grand Rapids Community College.

Palova's passion for writing dates back to the middle school in Stipa, near Zlin.

"I've always had knack for languages and adventure," she said. "Our family immigration saga has been a tremendous inspiration for all my writings."

She completed "Shifting Sands: Short Stories" in the summer of 2017. Her first novel "Fire on Water" has yet to be published.

In 2009, she wrote the screenplay "Riddleyville Clowns" ©Emma Palova inspired by a hometown clown parade. It is registered with the Writers Guild of America, West, Inc.

"Shifting Sands: Short Stories- Secrets" book 2 was created as an overflow from the first book of short stories, and as part of the National Novel Writing Month in November of 2018.

"Life provide endless inspiration for all my writings and photography," she said.

Palova worked for print media from 1990 to 2012. From 2012, she has written for digital media mainly on the WordPress platform.

She is working on the Konecny family immigration saga from former communist Czechoslovakia "Greenwich Meridian: Where East meets West." She became an American citizen on Aug. 19, 1999.

"I am deeply humbled by the opportunities this country has given to me," she said.

Awards

Palova has received several awards for community reporting:
2000 Ionia Area Chamber of Commerce, Ionia Sentinel-Standard
2003 Jim Neubacher Award for outstanding reporting in reducing the stigma of mental illness, Ionia Sentinel-Standard
2011 Department of Michigan and the Veterans it serves for coverage of American Legion, The Lowell Ledger
2018 Winner of the National Novel Writing Month

Palova has developed her own literary style, which is a fusion of the real and the fictitious, aka magic realism. He writing has been influenced by Paulo Coelho, Ernest Hemingway, Gabriel Garcia Marquez, Tennessee Williams, poet Stanley Kunitz and playwright, former Czech president, late Vaclav Havel.

I also would like to thank everyone in advance for writing reviews.

For posting a review go to Amazon Author Central customer reviews:

https://authorcentral.amazon.com/gp/community

Join Emma's mailing list for special offers at www.emmapalova.com

Connect with Emma Palova on Facebook

https://www.facebook.com/emma.palova.9

Emma on Twitter

https://twitter.com/EmmaPalova

Made in the USA
Columbia, SC
20 June 2021